T0354288

THE TEN THOUSAND THINGS

Adventures and Misadventures on China's Silk Road

By Brooks Tenney

Order this book online at www.trafford.com
or email orders@trafford.com

Most Trafford titles are also available at major online book retailers.

© Copyright 2009 Brooks Tenney.
All rights reserved. No part of this publication may be reproduced, stored in a retrieval system, or
transmitted, in any form or by any means, electronic, mechanical, photocopying, recording, or
otherwise, without the written prior permission of the author.

Note for Librarians: A cataloguing record for this book is available from Library
and Archives Canada at www.collectionscanada.ca/amicus/index-e.html

Printed in Victoria, BC, Canada.

ISBN: 978-1-4269-1679-3 (sc)
ISBN: 978-1-4269-1680-9 (dj)

Library of Congress Control Number: 2009935519

*Our mission is to efficiently provide the world's finest, most comprehensive book publishing
service, enabling every author to experience success. To find out how to publish your book,
your way, and have it available worldwide, visit us online at www.trafford.com*

Trafford rev. 10/07/2009

www.trafford.com

North America & international
toll-free: 1 888 232 4444 (USA & Canada)
phone: 250 383 6864 ♦ fax: 812 355 4082

THE TEN THOUSAND THINGS

*"The great Tao flows everywhere, both to the left
and to the right.
The ten thousand things depend upon it; it holds
nothing back.
It fulfills its purposes silently and makes no claim."*

Lines from "Tao Te Ching"
Lao Tsu
Translated by Gia-fu Feng and Jane English

Heaven and Earth are impartial.
They see the ten thousand things as straw dogs.

Tao Te Ching
Lao Tsu
(translated by Gia-Fu Feng and Jane English)

NOTE TO READERS; AND ACKNOWLEDGEMENTS

In writing a book that involves travel in China, some collisions with Chinese place names are unavoidable. This is particularly true in the case of *The Ten Thousand Things* because the reference material—history books, fiction, philosophy, maps, etc.—that I consulted was created over wide intervals of time. Consequently, variant spellings were often encountered for the same places. Additionally, many cities, provinces and other locales underwent complete name changes during China's turbulent recent history. Or in the past. See my problem?

For example: the city known today as Xian was once Changan. And even within recent decades Xian has been spelled as Sian or Xi'an.

The Chinese realize that their language taxes western pronunciation skills. They attempted to simplify things with the establishment of Pinyin, a universal system of pronunciation. Additionally, today's Communist regime has determined to make Mandarin Chinese—known as Putonghua or common tongue —a universal standard language for all China.

Older readers may recall bygone days when the capital of China was known in the west as Peking. Today, thanks to Pinyin, it is Beijing. Apply this transformation to all the names on China's vast map and you will have, at the very least, the makings of a severe headache. Thankfully no one needs Pinyin (or anything else) to read this book.

I have made no attempt at consistency with names in this tale, since it is not encountered in daily life. Names should not present a problem to attentive readers.

It might be marginally helpful to note than in the Pinyin system of pronunciation, X is pronounced as SH. Thus, *xie xie* meaning "thank you" in Chinese is pronounced *shee-eh shee-eh*. Or, if you prefer, *shay shay*.

Similarly Q in pinyin is pronounced as CHEE, as in CHEESE. Thus QU? meaning "Are you going," is pronounced CHWEE. To which the answer is either Qu, Pronounced CHWEE! meaning Yes, I'm going, or *Bu qu*, meaning, No, I'm not going.

There's lots more to say about the pronunciation of Chinese words and names but it has little relevance to this story. And who cares? Press on. Don't look back, unless it's to consult a map of China. None of this stuff is important to the story, but—hopefully—it adds a bit of color.

Scores of books, magazine articles, and newspaper clippings provided reference material for this book, and, for the most part, they are credited where used.

I am indebted to many people, not named here who have written knowledgeably and interestingly about China in the past, and whose materials I have drawn on shamelessly. Ten thousand lifetimes could never mine out this lode.

Several individuals read the manuscript for this tale and offered helpful comments. My thanks go to Bob Fischer for helpful comments and suggestions. I'm grateful to librarian-English teacher Cheryl Gravelle for a careful reading of every detail and invaluable suggestions. Thanks also to my history professor (also a former naval aviator and U.S. Congressman from Virginia), Dr. William Whitehurst of Old Dominion University, who read the manuscript and corrected several details about military aircraft. Most of all, I thank my wife Hope, always a critical reader, who put up with me while continuing to supply—among other things—coffee and useful advice.

Hopefully, this yarn contains some hints that are worth consideration.

Brooks Tenney

"We have tried since the birth of our nation to promote our love of peace by a display of weakness. This course has failed us utterly."

George Catlett Marshall

CONTENTS

"Combat pilots say they miss the feel of flying but say remote-control aircraft are here to stay.

'This is the future,' said Chad Miner, chief of weapons and tactics at Creech, a Predator trainer and an F-16 pilot. 'I would love to...jump in an F-16 and go. But I'm a more valuable asset to the military doing this. It's not the sexiest answer, but it's true.'"

"Faster, deadlier pilotless plane bound for Afghanistan"
Tom Vanden Brook
USA Today, August 28, 2007

PROLOGUE

Console pilots had the wind up. Something was in the air, but no one knew anything concrete. The team of engineers, pilots and project managers at Nevada's Creech Air Force Base are a close-mouthed bunch when it comes to talking about development work on the replacement for the Predator. Security is tight concerning the Reaper.

The Predator is the pilotless plane that first gained attention during fighting in Afghanistan. With its 27-foot wing-span and a top speed of 135 mph, the Predator carries a payload of 450 pounds. A bomb this size can inflict a lot of damage when it is delivered with pinpoint accuracy, but on-board cameras and GPS tracking devices are also convenient for directing strikes by other weapons systems.

No sooner was the Predator proving its worth on the battlefield than commanders and planners were seeking an improved capabilities version. The men at Creech were responsible for much of the field-testing connected with developing the Predator's replacement.

The Reaper is a substantially bigger drone than the Predator. A 66-foot wingspan enables it to deliver a payload of 3,750 pounds. This is equivalent to the bomb-carrying capacity of an F-16. Reaper's top speed is 300 mph, more than twice the speed of Predator, and its maximum altitude, 50,000 feet, is also twice that of the drone it is replacing.

One of its best features is its ability to remain in the air much longer than the F-16 whose pilots must refuel every two hours. Reaper can stay aloft for eight times as long as the F-16, which carries a comparable payload.

Most of the newly formed Reaper squadrons are based at Creech AFB, north of Las Vegas. Thanks to current technology, these deadly weapons can be flown anywhere in the world—by controllers located anywhere else. Right now that "else" is Creech AFB. This will change; is changing.

The jet pilots who fly these drones from sophisticated user consoles in air-conditioned trailer modules are, like most fighter pilots, a cocky bunch. Senior commanders recognize that this self-confidence is essential, but they occasionally worry about the thin divide separating self-confidence from hubris.

Some aviators think about this close relationship. Some. Not all.

On a sunny afternoon in late May, two jet pilots—assigned to duty as console pilots with newly formed Reaper squadrons—are enjoying a beer on the terrace of the Officers Club at Creech.

"Are you involved in these tests being set up by the honcho from ACC?" says the senior guy.

"I just heard about 'em yesterday. Why? Are you?

"I think I'm slated to be part of the test." Warren Kirkhofer, Major, USAF took a long swig of his Heinekens and belched. "Actually, I may be *most* of the test. Do you know anything about the guy in charge, Colonel Richardson?"

"Not personally. No. But he was at Nellis for a year when I was there and he had a reputation for a guy who goes out of the box. What are these tests trying to uncover?" Bobby Fritz, Captain, USAF, was another jet pilot assigned to the same Reaper squadron with Kirkhofer.

"The way it's been explained to me, it's gonna be a regular dogfight. Richardson is apparently bringing in a hotshot pilot from back east and he wants his top gun to go toe-to-toe with me. A real western shootout. Hell, I'm really up for it."

"Live ammo?" Fritz snickered.

"Don't I wish. But no such luck. Everything will be electronic. Either way, I can't get too worried. I've been spending a lot of time at the console."

"You're planning to kick some ass."

"However it turns out, Bobby." This is about as modest as Warren Kirkhofer ever gets. "However it plays. Ha! He's bringing this pilot in as a mystery guest. That's supposed to be part of the challenge. Kinda like those old wrestling matches. The Masked Marvel. The visiting team is on the base now. Since this morning. But they're lying low. For some reason they don't seem to want us to meet in advance."

"So when is this confrontation supposed to begin?"

"Tomorrow morning. Ten thirty. We'll be in separate trailers. We'll take off ten minutes apart. I'm supposed to fly west to Hawthorne and then fly back to Quartzite Mountain. The other guy has to head north and circle Ely first. Then back to Quartzite where we're supposed to duke it out. They want our birds coming from different directions."

"So how do they determine who wins?" Bobby asked. "You want another beer?"

"Nah. I'm nursing this one. Then I'm going home and sharpen my superb reflexes with some video games, and turn in early. Light breakfast, skip lunch and I should scare the shit out of these guys from ACC. Actually, it pisses me off to think that they can come out here and think they know more about these birds than we do. I'm gonna enjoy seeing them get egg on their face. But go ahead. You have one. By the way, are you and Sally up for a ride into Vegas this weekend?" I think Cirque Soleil is performing somewhere. Peg would really like to see them. Who wins? They didn't tell us yet how they'll score us."

The next morning Major Warren Kirkhofer, uniformed, clean shaven and well-fed, was in the briefing room where eight senior officers were gathered to go over the rules for the contests to be held over the next three days. Two flights on each of the first two days and a single flight on the last day. On the last day, the aerial combat was to be held to the north, on the test range at Wendover in the northwestern corner of Utah.

Colonel Roger "Slick" Richardson, from the Air Combat Command at Langley AFB in Virginia had proposed these trials and had pushed to have them approved, despite the fact that they were totally unorthodox, and well beyond the scope of the Squadron's mission. Richardson, a former fighter pilot from the post Vietnam era, still carried a bit of clout from the past. After a few introductory remarks by the base commander who introduced Slick after recounting some of their shared experiences overseas, Richardson's aide, a Lt. Col. from ACC, explained the rules of engagement.

Kirkhofer had read the briefing memo several times and he had no questions. The pilot who had challenged him was not at the briefing, but Richardson's aide informed the group that the challenger had seen the same briefing memo.

Members of the Reaper squadron had inspected both control stations inside the trailers and they confirmed that the planes and their support systems were identical.

At ten thirty-five, Major Kirkhofer had steered his drone out of its hanger and guided it into a perfect takeoff, westbound for Hawthorne. There, a prohibited air space over the Hawthorne Army Ammunition Plant required him to make a wide swing that took his plane over the south end of Walker Lake.

On the return flight, he switched on the radar that should detect his UAV opponent southbound from Ely. He was looking forward to seeing what stunts this pilot would attempt. But his displays showed nothing. What was happening? Had the other pilot gotten lost? Confused? Crashed?

As his Reaper crossed the boundary into Nellis he was within 20 miles of Quartzite Mountain and he knew that he should have been picking up the opponent. His Reaper was cruising at 15,000 feet, but there was still no sign of the challenger. Over the target mountain he went into a wide turn to the south, still looking and listening.

Suddenly, his attack alarm went off. Enemy plane approaching. The mystery guest was climbing up from almost directly below. It had apparently been flying at very low levels, using terrain features to defeat his radar. *Shit! This is not good. OK, now let's see what this guy can do.*

He put his drone into a nearly vertical climb and laid on max power. There were some occasions when he was happy to be flying without any physical feedback. Then he began a loop, with the expectation that he would come out on the tail of his pursuer. But somehow, during the brief inverted portion of the flight, his incoming fire alarm sounded, followed by red lights and the warning voice. *Incoming fire. Incoming fire.* Then to his dismay, the continuous klaxon sounded, signifying a hit, continuing until he threw the switch. Game over.

Shit! Shit! Shit! How had he let this happen? OK, if this bastard wanted to hug the ground then he could play that way too. Just wait 'til this afternoon. The rules called for best three out of five to be the winner.

The afternoon engagement, begun at three-thirty, had the same outcome. The following two days were more of the same, much to the chagrin and dismay of Major Kirkhofer—who was actually a very accomplished combat aviator. Despite his profound embarrassment, he was forced to acknowledge that he had met his match with an aerialist who could out-think, outperform and out-anticipate him. At the dinner meeting which was held in a private dining room of the Officers Club, he was actually looking forward to meeting this son-of-a-bitch who had whipped him in the air. *Could he be some kind of civilian pilot? Or maybe a computer engineer? The fucking Red Baron?*

His reaction was bitter when he learned that the pretty little boy he thought might be Colonel Richardson's grandson had been his opponent in the other trailer. It didn't get easier to take when he found out that the kid had just turned thirteen.

PART 1.
GROUND WORK

"The Chinese believe that never again should there emerge an educated class that is remote and isolated from the people, and they believe that this can be avoided only by concentrating on the practical education of the masses in fields of benefit to all. However, the lack of advanced specialization and the degree of politics injected into most subjects mean that education at all levels does not make the best use of individual talents nor does it lead to the production of highly trained specialists, who remain in short supply in China's developing economy."

The Chinese Way (Life in the People's Republic of China)
Gil Loescher and Ann Dull Loescher

CHAPTER 1

The Professor's Study

Fully awake, newly-appointed full professor Walt Roberts of James Buchanan University sat up on the edge of the bed and reached for his prosthetic leg. On the other side of the bed, Tara, his former grad student, made a little movement that he interpreted to mean *Fix your own breakfast.*

His clothing was on the floor beside the bed, within arm's reach and he pulled on his dockers; then pulled up one pants leg to wrap the elastic bandage covering his stump.

Saturday. He would grab some OJ and an English muffin and then try to get in three or four miles before Tara got up and started moving. They had been up late last night, working on their travel schedule and she had seemed tired by the time they got to bed. This trip was likely to be more difficult than any of the ones they made so far, and he was trying to plan for a lot of contingencies. Not that it was likely that the trip could be scripted. But a solid plan gave him a point of departure, and also a point to which they might return when the inevitable contingencies arose.

It was ironic that his professional life seemed to be going smoothly even as the details of his personal life were unraveling. No! That wasn't right. In the ways that were most important, he was living a wonderful dream and most of it was probably due to Tara's involvement in his life.

Until his divorce was final, however, he was uncomfortable; and after discussion with Tara, he had decided to put the house he had bought with Flo on the market and move into the girl's apartment on a temporary basis. Then, after the split was final, the two of them would wipe the blackboard clean and make some decisions about the rest of their lives.

The full professorship had come earlier than he had expected. It had, he knew, come about in large measure because of some interactions between the university president and some person or persons unknown from the agency that had used him for covert activities in the Central Asian States.

JBU's president had served four terms in Congress before resigning to head up the university that was the pride of his district.

James Buchanan University, where Walt was responsible for Central Asian Studies, provided much of the glue that held Mercersburg together. Walking up the main street at a steady pace, Walt paused to take in the storefronts that dated from an earlier century. Some of the cast iron columns had been manufactured locally back in the days when coal and iron in the ground spawned uncounted foundries that slowly yielded to efficiencies of scale in manufacturing.

Ninety minutes after he left his front door, Walt was back, sweaty and sticky, and ready for something a bit more substantial than OJ. Tara was up, and moving around in the kitchen, making something that appeared to be waffles.

"You're up."

"Thanks for letting me sleep. I don't know why I was so tired."

"Because we were up until after two. My god, Tara. You don't have on any pants."

She was wearing a shorty gown, and she had just bent to put something in the cabinet.

"Oh! Yeah! You noticed. I was hoping."

"My god, Tara. You are an anim..."

"I missed it last night. Besides, it's Saturday and you don't have any classes. And the real estate lady isn't coming until two this afternoon. We've got all morning."

"How many of those things are you gonna make? I probably can't eat more than two."

"You think you can just change the subject that easy? Who do you think you're dealing with?"

"OK. Waffles. Then a quick shower. Then it's Tara time."

"No shower, sweat boy. Hold out your plate."

It was nearly noon when Walt and Tara, fully clad, sat down at the big work table that dominated his study. The table was piled high with books, maps and papers relating to their planned trip to China and Central Asia. In his job as a professor of Central Asian studies, Walt had made himself into an authority on the Silk Road. One of his signature accomplishments at JBU was the establishment of at least one annual visit to important stations on this historic route. To date, most of his trips had been to the western portion of the Silk Road; usually focusing on the cities and oases between Tashkent in Uzbekistan and Istanbul or Antalya in Turkey. The trips had proven to be extremely popular with students and with JBU's power structure. Now, he was eager to extend the trip so that it included the eastern portion of this complex web of trading arteries.

Before he could take students, however, he would have to make pilot runs—maybe two or more—to work out most of the kinks. He would need to line up—or confirm—local drivers, guides and contacts at hotels and suitable stopping places for a group of unpredictable young students. He was hoping to make contacts at several of the Chinese universities along his planned route.

Tara had once accompanied him on more than one of these trips. The most noteworthy of these excursions had been the one in which he was employed by a government agency to herd a group of selected analysts posing as faculty and alumni on a junket. Their purpose had been to investigate the flow of illicit drugs along the ancient trade route; and it had resulted in information leading to the takedown of a major international drug-running cartel.

Despite the fact that most of the work had been done by others, Walt had been the nominal leader of the bogus "tour" and he had reaped considerable benefit, both monetarily and in prestige at the university. Nevertheless, despite his good fortune regarding this unique trip, Walt felt that much of the recognition he had received was undeserved.

His study of Central Asia had provided him with a reputation, a comfortable income and lifestyle, and interests to last a lifetime. But it had wrecked his marriage to Flo, and now it was a factor in his decision to sell this comfortable house, the first he had ever tried to own. On the other hand there was Tara. That tilted the whole equation.

"Sit down for a minute, Tara. You know, I've been thinking about you."

"Me too. Thinking about you. That was very thorough."

"No, little girl. Not that way. I've been thinking about you. As a person. About you and me."

"Sure, why not? Me, too. All the time."

"No, my heart. You're still not listening. I may not know who you are. You don't seem like a real human girl to me. Like a real woman. You are more like a male fantasy. A dream girl." She laughed.

"I can live with that, you moron. Lean over and kiss me. Then we can go to work."

"Tara, do you remember that first night in Turkmenistan? When you told me that you had put a spell on me? I think, sometimes, you actually did it."

"That was the plan." Big smile.

"I see you're not gonna be serious."

"This is what you call serious? And you, the professor? Maybe your credentials should be revoked. You sound like one of your sophomores."

"Tara, Tara..."

"C'mon, professor. You didn't get a long enough nap. C'mon. Let's work until the real estate lady comes. Then we'll go get a burger or something and you can come back and catch up on your sleep."

She placed a folder in front of him. "C'mon. Let's do Xinjiang."

The real estate lady was late. For the next two hours the couple immersed themselves in travel books.

"The Tao that can be told is not the eternal Tao.
The name that can be named is not the eternal name.
The nameless is the beginning of heaven and earth.
The named is the mother of ten thousand things."

Tao Te Ching
Lao Tsu
(translated by Gia-Fu Feng and Jane English)

CHAPTER 2
Silk Road-The Eastern Terminus

Walt's vision for his program for the eastern portion of the Silk Road extended from Xi'an in central China to Almaty in Kazakhstan. In his preliminary plans for the initial trip he envisioned a flight into Beijing followed by a train ride to Xi'an. From Xi'an to the western reaches of China it should be easy to make train connections, but he pictured the trip in hired vehicles, or possibly a single bus. This would provide his group with flexibility to make excursions in any desired direction, subject to local conditions and limitations.

In his preliminary planning he had put together an itinerary that would begin the Silk Road portion of his program at Xi'an. From there, traveling westward, he envisioned stops in Lanzhou, Xining, Jiayuguan, Dunhuang, Turpan and Urumqi. After Urumqi, his group would cross China's border with Kazakhstan. From there it was only a few hundred miles to the capital at Almaty, a city where he had contacts and knew his way around. The problems to be solved had to do with travel in the western half of China, a locale where he had no experience and where his language skills would be of no use.

There were a lot of kinks to be ironed out and, in the beginning stages, he didn't even feel confident that he could ask all the right questions. The only solution would be to plunge in directly and see what difficulties would be encountered. As soon as he had gotten this far in his thinking, he laid out his views to Tara.

"Why am I not surprised?" she said. "This sounds like the way you tackle a lot of things."

"You wouldn't mind taking the plunge with me?"

"Are you kidding? Don't hurt my feelings. I can be packed before you."

"There are still a lot of loose ends. I'd like to start the teaching part of the trip at Xi'an. I'm looking at this as four-credit hours, and it ought to be popular with the kids whose folks can afford it. Xi'an was once the capital of the early empire. But it's easier and cheaper to fly into Beijing, and the train connections to Xi'an are good. It would give students a chance to get accustomed to the size and complexity of China. What do you think?"

"It would probably be worth an extra day or two to stay in Beijing. For a lot of these kids it could be their only visit to China and an exposure to Beijing's attractions would be worth the time."

"Yeah. You got there faster than I did. I was focused too much on the Silk Road and not enough on the mysterious east. So what would you prefer? Should we look for an agency that specializes in trips to Xi'an, or should we just plunge in. Make all the arrangements ourselves?"

"I'm with you, professor. Anyway you want to slice it, I'm in. You'll be the first to notice if I ever get unhappy." He thought about Florence, still, to his chagrin, his wife. By this point she would already be complaining about imagined deficiencies in Chinese toilet paper.

The flight to Beijing was uneventful. The pair departed from Chicago's O'Hare in a rainstorm but the weather was clear from Alaska. Unfortunately they had to endure a crying baby a few seats away. The infant cried for a full thirty minutes before it exhausted itself and a harassed mother was able to get it to sleep.

In Beijing they visited the standard tourist destinations; Tiananmen Square. The Forbidden City. Walt wanted to see the Chinese Military History Museum. They visited the Summer Palace and took a cruise on Kunming Lake.

On the evening of their second full day in Beijing, they boarded the westbound steam-powered train for Xi'an. Their sleeping compartment accommodated four people and their interpreter was in another compartment. The two occupants were young Chinese women in their late 20's or early thirties, two friends, apparently on an outing, also bound for Xi'an. That was about all the information they could exchange. After an hour or so communication was just too much trouble and, after their interpreter turned in, everyone prepared for sleep. Walt took the bottom bunk, but he was reluctant to unfasten his leg. Tara climbed into the top bunk, then dangled her bare legs down on either side of his head as he sat at the edge of the hard bunk.

After the two young women appeared to be settled down, she pulled her legs up and hung her head down. "Can I umcay ownday?" she whispered. He recognized her quick morph into her now-familiar little bad girl persona.

"My god, Tara."

"I'll be good."

"Oh, yeah. I know how that works. We've been to that movie."

"Honest. Cross my heart."

"You are such a liar."

"Pleeeeeeze!"

"Good grief. OK! Come on! But try not to make a lot of noise."

The girl slipped over the side and quickly nestled in beside him. He raised the sheet and she snuggled up tight. He put his arm around her.

"I don't want you to compromise your principles," she said in the little pouty voice she occasionally used to drive him crazy. He couldn't help what was happening to him, but the leg was uncomfortable when he was lying on his side and he wished he had taken it off.

She turned her face to meet his and when he moved to put his mouth on hers, she bit him, very gently, on his top lip.

"You know we could, if you really wanted to," she whispered playfully. "Don't you want to do me on a moving train? In China? It would be a first for us. "

"But not good enough for the Guinness Book of Records," he answered.

"Just a little bit. Don't you want to? I wouldn't make any noise. I can be real quiet...if you want me to."

Oh god, yes, you little witch. Right in the middle of this floor. Til you squeal. He was reasonably certain that the two Chinese women were not asleep; that they could hear their whispered conversation. Possibly—he couldn't rule it out—even guess at what they might be saying.

"You didn't get enough exercise today, did you? We should have walked more."

"That's what does it. All that walking. Come on, professor. You want to. I can tell."

"What am I going to do with you, Silkybritches?"

"And what's with this Silkybritches stuff? This is the second time you've called me that today. That's not a very dignified name for a professor to call his partner. What ever happened to 'kitten?'"

"Yeah, well, JBU ain't exactly Princeton, and I ain't exactly Woodrow Wilson. Although right about now I can empathize with some of his problems in Geneva. OK. You win. Slip 'em down."

This time when she turned her head she did not bite his lip but she held her lips against his until that first key task was completed with minimal squirming.

After that, it was more or less conventional stuff that many aficionados of train travel will understand.

Tara is a very determined young woman, clever and resourceful. Walt marveled at the good fortune that had allowed their paths to cross. As he was drifting off into dreamland it came to him that many of the members of the camel caravans that crossed the desert were probably women masquerading as men, in order accompany their chosen companions.

Xi'an looked almost exactly like the photographs they had studied.

"This year, Predator flight hours are expected to exceed 70,000 hours, more than triple the total in 2003. Combat pilots say they miss the feel of flying but say remote-control aircraft are here to stay. 'This is the future,' said Chad Miner, chief of weapons and tactics at Creech (Air Force Base, Nevada) a Predator trainer and an F-16 pilot."

Faster, deadlier pilotless plane bound for Afghanistan
Tom Vanden Brook
USA Today, August 28, 2007

CHAPTER 3
General Zheng's Vision

Zheng Ju-baio had summoned a meeting of several experts on unmanned aerial vehicles for a thorough briefing; to be followed by discussions and a question-and-answer session. The old general was interested in understanding the full range of potential missions and applications for aircraft that did not require a pilot in the cockpit. The idea had intrigued him for a long time, and he had been paying attention to developments around the world, notably in the US, Israel, Italy, France and England.

The old general was one of the few senior officers within the PLAAF's General Logistics Department who had spent time in the U.S. While there, he had been given a tour of one of the western air bases where the USAF had developed the Predator drone. He was not briefed on the Predator itself, but he knew that the base where he was given a tour was the site where the pilotless plane had been put through its paces. He was reluctant to come right out and ask his hosts about work on this plane, or on its next generation replacement.

The general, who had flown fighter jets against U.S. airmen in Vietnam, considered himself something of an expert on aerial warfare. And, in fact, he had been a good fighter pilot. But the thing that made him valuable was not his intelligence, which wasn't bad. It was his attitude toward information. He was a natural born learner, an avid reader, and he made it a point to try to think about things systematically. Despite his age, he was a true visionary.

Years ago Zheng had been in London as part of a mission from his government, and while there he had been given an opportunity to visit the Pinewood Studios of Britain's largest film producer. The company, he learned, had been founded by a Hungarian immigrant who had immigrated to London with no money and no contacts, and had risen to become a multimillionaire, knighted for his service to his adopted nation. At a dinner, where most of the attendees were drunk, Sir Alexander Korda's grandson was describing one of the processes used by his ancestor to rise to wealth and fame. The young author of Korda's biography laughed as he told the story. It was simple, he said. *Grandfather put his head down on his desk for an hour every day. Was he taking a nap? someone asked. No. He was thinking.*

The story got a brief laugh from listeners and was quickly forgotten; but not by Zheng, who was an avid Taoist. He was fascinated by the notion of a penniless immigrant thinking his way to wealth, fame and knighthood by the simple expedient of putting his head down and using his brain.

Back in China he began to approach every situation in this way, and there was no lack of problems which required careful thinking. The general began to utilize this approach in a systematic manner. Each day he would prioritize the problems and select the three that were most pressing—or of greatest strategic significance. Then he would close his door and tell his staff he was not to be disturbed for an hour. This mannerism was considered to be eccentric, but it soon began to pay dividends. Zheng would dissect a problem, consider all reasonable solutions within his ken, and make an estimate concerning probable success of each alternative. Soon, his participation was being solicited for a wide range of problems facing the PLAAF, People's Liberation Army Air Force.

Word got around. Zheng Ju-Baio was some kind of military genius. With recognition came promotion, and he rose steadily within his organization. But, he noted with a degree of philosophical amusement, there was a paradox in his climb.

The skills that facilitated his rise were inimical to political success. Politicians do not succeed by selecting the best solution—they get ahead by finding out what it will take to protect their position. The old warrior was not a perfect man, but as human beings go, he was considerably more honest than most and he consistently sought the best answers to problems within the environment in which he was operating. In fairness, his primary motivation was not self-promotion. But his success as a problem-solver made him valuable to his colleagues with better political skills, and he rose as they rose—because he was valuable.

Zheng had access to key intelligence reports coming back from operatives inside the United States. The network of Chinese intelligence agents operating within the US defense establishment was one of long standing. Even before the crash of a U.S. stealth bomber during fighting in Bosnia, Zheng had received reports on stealth technology. Technical details of plasma formation were still unclear, and China's aircraft manufacturers were a long way from direct competition in this arena, but the broad outlines were clear.

In his Taoist mind, China had nothing to fear from the U.S. in the absence of any totally outrageous provocation. The only arenas in which this was a likelihood appeared to be Taiwan or Tibet. Tibet, situated deep within the heart of central Asia was not very likely to be a region where the U.S would throw down the gauntlet. Taiwan, on the other hand, was a potential trouble spot. It could be defended from the sea.

As he aged and his days as an active flyer had ended, he made a point of tracking developments in the U.S. aviation industry. A considerable amount of interesting information was available in the open. Between the Internet and legitimate publications of the American press, it was possible to see the broad trends in aviation. This was reinforced by periodic reports from engineers and technicians within the American aviation industry. He was receiving information from inside secret development workshops—typically called Skunk Works—operating within seven major U.S. manufacturers; including Boeing, Lockheed-Martin, North American, Grumman, McDonnell-Douglas and General Atomics.

Zheng's position in the Logistics Department permitted him to have access—and to serve in an advisory capacity—to China's space program. He had actually been a party to the decision made to use sophisticated ballistic weapons to bring down a Chinese weather satellite. Actually, his arguments had played a key role in the decision to make a demonstration of China's capability to take down a satellite. In any future war the US would rely heavily on satellite systems. If they knew that China possessed a knockout capability, the US would be compelled to spend considerable energy, and money, in their attempts to offset China's capability.

In his mind, it would serve as a warning to the United States, and others in the west, that China possessed the capability to select and destroy a specific satellite target. This would compel them to immediately expend resources on protective countermeasures. But what most of his colleagues—even those senior officers in the PLAAF—did not know, was that he had a secondary reason for approving the demonstration.

He was certain that attention to China's space activities would distract the world's attention from emerging development work with unmanned aircraft. In the near term, he was convinced that this was where the most significant advances could be achieved.

Take Taiwan, for instance. If America wanted to defend Taiwan against an invasion from the mainland, would they be more likely to depend upon the use of satellites or drone aircraft? Ships were navigating the world's oceans with precision long before navigation and weather satellites made things more convenient. But to have drone aircraft capable of assaulting beaches or defending against counterattacks—without risking the lives of military pilots—this would be a real advance. To Zheng, who had taken off on several occasions when he was not certain of returning to his base, this would be a true accomplishment worth the effort and expenditure.

The feisty general argued in favor of the satellite demonstration with supreme confidence that it would provoke an over-reaction from the Americans. At the same time, he was convinced that the activities over which he had more direct control would be more likely to succeed if he could distract America's political and technical communities. In this regard, this gray-haired ex-pilot, a man only slightly above average intelligence, proved to be substantially more shrewd than his counterparts in the U.S.

At age seventy-six, he was a widower, remarried, who looked and felt considerably younger. His age might be guessed as old as mid-sixties, but his step was still vigorous and his eyesight was still keen. Despite his age, Zheng did not require glasses or hearing aids. His heart, bowels and liver were in good shape. Nor did he suffer from the plague that had attacked western men of his age, erectile dysfunction. *Oh no! Not me!* A health food fanatic in China, he ate dog meat monthly and still got it up regularly.

Anyone with the least doubt of these facts had only to touch bases with his current lady, Hu Ting Ling.   This year, Ting Ling was exactly half the age of her paramour. She was thirty-eight, a slightly graying beauty whose regal good looks would easily have been discernable in any nation on planet Earth.

Zheng Ju-Baio and Ting Ling had a spacious home on the outskirts of Beijing, and they also had a comfortable apartment in the center of the city. When his duties called for the general to be in the city, their apartment was made ready. But whenever possible, they were at their home overlooking a small lake where everything, indoors and out, had been arranged in strict accordance with the principles of *feng shui*.

Ting Ling had been trained as a musician and, for a time she had pursued a professional career. She had attended the China Conservatory of Music where she polished her already formidable skills on the *pipa* and the *zhong ruan*, a large, lute-like instrument. But despite her natural gifts, Ting Ling had something of an indolent personality and she enjoyed being cosseted. In American jargon, Ting Ling was **high maintenance**. After she met the general and became his companion for a year, she decided to devote herself to becoming his wife and enjoying a comfortable life listening to others play the music she enjoyed. Once she had seduced the old widower into a new marriage, it was pleasant for her to become a patron of the conservatory she had once attended as a struggling young artist.

The marriage between the general and Ting Ling was a good bargain for both of them. Both got what they were seeking—at what seemed to each of them, very reasonable rates.

General Zheng, despite his connections and service to the party and the PLAAF, had enemies. These enemies did not hate the old man, but they believed that he was too old for the responsible positions he refused to relinquish. They sought ways to diminish his power and authority and, while there were no crimes of which he could be convicted, a lot of attention had been spent scouring his past activities for traces of wrongdoing.

The general's detractors had not hesitated to examine Ting Ling's background for behavior that could be used against her husband. But her past had been uneventful. Even the boyfriends she had seen during her conservatory days proved to be clean-living and not worth pursuing.

As one of the major instigators in China's use of a laser weapon to destroy one of its own satellites, Zheng had been certain that it would create consternation among his American counterparts, without provoking a crisis. Americans would—and of this he was positive—tie themselves in knots trying to understand the meaning of this demonstration, and they would expend a considerable amount of time and treasure trying to develop countermeasures against...what exactly? Thinking about the conversations that he was certain were taking place, the old general laughed with glee. Actually, anything that prompted development work in America's aerospace industry was going to be good for China's economy. Already their industries were lobbying Congress to relax immigration barriers to admit more Chinese engineers and scientists.

Now, past the age when his colleagues had retired, the general had reached a stage where he could see the future. In his mind, the future for military aviation lay with unmanned aircraft. There would be a slow, painful transition in the west, not unlike the switch from sail to steam or from horses to steam and then to gasoline. But gradually, fighting in the air that began like the combat between armored knights, would make a transition to a confrontation between robot machines—controlled from miles away by combatants who might never see one another. In his active, imaginative mind, this was inevitable. What was most interesting to him, however, was the notion that this transition could be substantially easier for China than for many nations in the west. China had less infrastructure to destroy. A nation moving from oxcarts to automobiles does not have to tear up any electric trolley lines. A nation moving from town criers to cell phones doesn't have to take down any telephone poles. China's coming future was clear to him, but sadly, there were not many people with whom he could share his vision.

The aging general realized that he had only a few years in which to translate his visions into action. Two, three, maybe four years, and the system would squeeze him into a comfortable anonymity. This was clear. He realized that he was fortunate to have remained in uniform this long. His marriage to a handsome younger woman was a reward for which he was grateful and he realized, perhaps as only a philosopher can, that he was a fortunate man.

The Tao had been his secret guide for much of his life, which, looking back, seemed almost like a miracle.

Fame or self: Which matters more?
Self or wealth: Which is more precious?
Gain or loss: Which is more painful?
He who is attached to things will suffer much.
He who saves will suffer heavy loss.
A contented man is never disappointed.

The Tao had been a guide and a comfort to him for most of his life; and for that he could thank his grandfather, a man who could scarcely have imagined the life his grandson had led.

Now, facing into his last days of power and influence, he had reached the conclusion that he should leave someone behind who could share his vision, and who would continue to move in the directions he considered were essential.

His real objective, one that he did not even discuss with his closest colleagues, was the desire to create a smoke screen that might divert his American opposites from paying close attention to China's activities in the arena of pilotless aircraft. Space might be, as the American television series proclaimed, "the final frontier," but in the general's pragmatic mind, drones would be more useful in the short term.

He knew the problems that the Japanese had been able to create for the U.S. Navy with their kamikaze program. But this program was wasteful of trained and dedicated pilots. It also required the continued expenditure of first-line aircraft.

Imagine how that chapter might have played out if substantially cheaper drone aircraft, controlled from remote locations, could have been flown against American warships. In his mind, the defense of Taiwan's straits under these circumstances would become untenable, even for the powerful American fleet. And if they attempted to take the offensive against targets on the Chinese mainland...well, that was simply opening what the west called Pandora's box.

"One widespread view is that the anti-satellite (ASAT) test was a shot across the bow of U.S. military power. Beijing's strategists have argued for years that it needs to develop asymmetric capabilities in order to close the widening gap between the United States' military might and China's own and prepare for a possible conflict in the Taiwan Strait. With the United States now depending so heavily on assets in space for real-time communications, battlefield awareness, weapons targeting, intelligence gathering, and reconnaissance, the Chinese rocket launch many have been an attempt to show Washington how Beijing can overcome its handicap in a relatively simple way."

China's Space Odyssey
Foreign Affairs, May-June 2007
Bates Gill and Martin Kleiber

CHAPTER 4
PLAAF Headquarters-Beijing

Major Ju Wentao of the PLA Air Force took steps at the entrance two at a time. The sprawling complex housed many of the administrative functions of China's PLA Air Force. Ju was slated to testify before a committee today, and his uniform was starched and freshly pressed. At the top, he looked at his watch. *Forty minutes from now to be exact.*

Li had kissed him shyly before he left home and whispered a few private words of encouragement for which he was grateful. He was nervous. That was a fact. The thought of standing before this committee of old men and talking about what was wrong with his branch of the service was enough to make anyone nervous. Given the choice, Ju would have preferred to jump into the cockpit of his Su-27 fighter and take off on a combat mission.

The major had first heard tales of aerial combat with American pilots over Vietnam from his uncle, who had two confirmed kills flying Russian-built planes. Ju, himself, was known as a competent pilot and a good squadron commander, but truth to tell, since Li had borne him a son two years ago, his philosophy concerning fighting in the air had begun to change.

His headquarters staff job required him to monitor and track information on America's unmanned aircraft programs with particular emphasis on the actual results of applications in the field. While information was sketchy at best, what he had learned convinced him that much of the future of fighting in the air would involve a wide variety of drones piloted from remote stations. American successes with pilotless planes in Afghanistan and Iraq had made it clear that continued developments were inevitable.

Information from military units in the field was often vague and misleading, but Chinese intelligence agents had succeeded in placing reliable informants in virtually every major American aircraft manufacturing firm. These individuals were usually either engineers or scientists trained to observe carefully and report accurately. When the information they provided was assembled into a composite picture, it was possible to envision, however indistinctly, the outlines of the future.

There is, the major had concluded, a promising future for a wide range of unmanned aircraft. Already America's military commanders had seen the potential of their first operational drone, the Predator, and had replaced it with a significant second-generation upgrade, the Reaper. This new model had been employed successfully in Bosnia, Iraq and Afghanistan. But the surface had only been scratched.

Ju had collected information concerning all the possible missions where unmanned drones could be used successfully. Some of the most interesting ideas came to him from examining the books and magazines published by hobbyists who specialized in remote control scale aircraft. These individuals, whose age range was substantially broader than those for conventional military pilots, spent countless hours at computer screens learning how to control virtual aircraft in complex maneuvers before they attempted to practice with real hardware.

One of the facts that Ju found extremely interesting was that the planes, ancillary hardware, electronic equipment and supporting software came predominantly from China. Even in the actual drone aircraft used by the U.S. Air Force, a significant amount of the componentry was manufactured in China. From Ju's perspective, the PLAAF might attain parity with the USAF in the field of unmanned aerial war-making potential without enormous expenditure. If only—and this was the big if—if only the wrinkled graybeards could be convinced of the inevitability of the future for drones.

Could he help to make the sale? He was, he knew, only one of many who would be testifying, but he hoped that the presentation material on the computer disk in his briefcase would be convincing. And memorable.

In the anteroom outside the committee hearing room, he tried to remember the exact words Li had whispered in his ear. "When the superior man has no Fortune, he waits for Fortune."

"And do you know the story of this, my peony blossom?" he asked. Li was small and pretty, with a mouth like a bow, and he was as fond of her after their years together as he had been when they were first married.

"You will hear it when you return, my husband," she answered.

Major Ju Wentao's presentation before the committee came off without a hitch. The questions from the group surprised him. They asked about the role for drone helicopters. They queried him about reasonable expectations for swing-wing drones, STOL and for tilt-rotor drones. As best he could determine, they had already formed opinions concerning jet-powered or rocket-powered drones. Basically, as he explained briefly with a series of charts he was proud of, a rocket drone would be like a World War II buzz bomb that was guided remotely from a terminal where an array of cameras and screens would have allowed a remote operator to fly the missile right into the door of London's Parliament Building. If Germany had possessed today's drone technology in World War II, Londoners might still be clearing rubble, he had told colleagues back in his office. Some of those in his audience were old enough for this example to have meaning, even though the technicians who had helped him put the presentation together had to have everything explained to them.

His time allocation before the committee had been scheduled to take no more than twenty minutes; but with questions, he was at the podium for just over an hour.

Back home, he set his cap in the hall closet and carried his briefcase into the bedroom and slid it under the bed. Li welcomed him from the kitchen where he found their little boy playing with several aluminum pots on the floor. Li was stirring a steaming pot of noodles.

He picked up the boy who promptly began to tug at the insignia on his collar. Placing the toddler back on the floor among his pots he approached his wife at the wood fired stove and placed both his hands on her shoulders. She leaned back to rest her head on his chest.

"And what have you prepared for my supper, my lotus blossom?"

"Take a look under the cover," she said. "I shopped for an hour."

"It looks like scorpion kebabs. Am I correct? It has been a long time since you prepared them."

"But you liked them very much, I recall."

"Yes, but I have done nothing special to deserve such a treat."

"You had such a big success today, I got them for myself..."

"You didn't like them before. You didn't eat any as I remember well."

Li blushed to the roots of her black hair. Her voice dropped to a shy whisper and she was looking at the floor.

"You remember only part. But not all. I got them for you—selfishly. Hoping you will sting me. Afterwards. For a long time."

"A woman who acts the falcon, does it in furthering a plot in which two persons are involved."

Proverbs and Common Sayings from the Chinese
Arthur H. Smith
American Presbyterian Mission Press, 1914.

CHAPTER 5
The Professor's Assistant

Tara Kuchenko had made a major move on Walt at a time when his marriage to Florence was falling apart. Tara came from Cleveland, where her Ukrainian-born father was employed as a janitor by the city. She grew up speaking Ukrainian at home, and in college she studied Russian, in which she was moderately competent.

At JBU she pursued a double major, in Middle Eastern Studies and in Fine Arts. She made several trips to Central Asia with Walt and, because of her language skills coupled with considerable maturity, she was a valuable addition to his meager roll of helpers. But, as often happens in programs like Walt's, the attraction between student and teacher become unmanageably intense. Tara developed a world-class crush on her favorite teacher.

Walt Roberts obtained his Ph.D. from Princeton before coming to JBU. Before Princeton, he served for several years in the Army's Special Forces during which service he lost part of his right leg in Afghanistan. His wife, Florence, had difficulties in dealing with her husband's injuries and, bluntly put, she was repelled by his stump.

Florence was the pampered only daughter of a wealthy corporate lawyer, and physical appearance loomed large in her criteria for a suitable husband. After Walter Reed, Flo's ardor for her husband cooled rapidly and it was exacerbated when he accepted a teaching position at the university in Mercersburg, Pennsylvania.

Despite his efforts, Walt's marriage was already foundering when he began conducting his student tours of the Silk Road. Early in marriage they had spoken of children but, in their first Mercersburg winter, Flo changed her mind and continued to stay on the pill. Ever cautious, she combined contraceptive techniques. Her friends had told her too many stories of failures.

Tara—intelligent, perceptive, pretty, and in the grip of a passionate desire for a possibly inaccessible man—had several opportunities to see man and wife together and she correctly read the signs—which were all too visible.

When events transpired that enabled her to offer herself to Walt, she did so. The circumstances under which she placed herself on the sacrificial altar were so vividly burned into Walt's memory that they would last a lifetime. Needless to say, she succeeded by entangling herself in Walt's life.

He and Flo would have separated even without Tara, but she made it astonishingly easy. Not pain free exactly, but certainly less painful than otherwise. But although Flo had actually initiated their breakup by leaving him for another man, her paramour delayed his stated plans for leaving wife and family. Flo moved in with her widowed father.

Walt wanted a divorce but he was not anxious to embarrass Flo or her doting father by pursuing his freedom on grounds of adultery. After Tara came on the scene, that option was, for all practical purposes, closed. He expected, and was led to believe, that Flo would grant him the divorce based on mutual incompatibility. Then, it was his intent to marry Tara. After living with her for a year, he felt ten years younger, and he realized that the gods had favored him far beyond most men. In truth he was, bluntly put, a lucky bastard. Tara was as undemanding and hard working as she was pretty, and she adored him. It was incomprehensible. *She really doesn't care at all about my leg. She doesn't even see it as a defect.* For almost the whole first year he could hardly believe it could be true, but gradually he came to accept the wonder of it.

In the middle of plans for a second trip to China's Silk Road, Tara learned that her father, living alone in Cleveland, need a brief hospital stay for observation. Walt offered to accompany her back to her home but she declined on the grounds that her father, a traditional Ukrainian Orthodox churchgoer, might not be overly welcoming to a man who was living with his daughter outside marriage.

"After we're married," she countered. "I want you two to get along. He's kinda old-fashioned. I'll be OK. But I am grateful to know that you'd go if I asked." And she kissed him hard. Tara's way of kissing was to equate enthusiastic affection with pressure. Sometimes, making love, she made his lips bleed from cuts against his teeth. Also, she was a biter. This was new to him. But she was always exciting.

In Cleveland, Tara's father was groggy for much of the time that she was with him. On the day before she drove home she called her closest girl friend from high school days, Larisa. She and Larisa had been inseparable pals for the last two years of high school. Snow White and Rose Red.

Larisa was fair-skinned and dark-haired, with hazel eyes and eyelashes that looked almost fake. Tara's blond looks were more conventional, but both girls had nice bodies and together they always attracted male attention. *Tara and Lara, T and L. Double Trouble.*

Larisa's parents had been unable to send her to college, and, she was eager to marry her high school boyfriend who was now driving a truck for UPS. She had recently given birth to her second child, but she was elated to hear from Tara and invited her to the couple's modest home for lunch. The two young women hugged each other ardently. Tara was surprised that her lovely friend now looked tired and her skin had lost its radiant glow. Her eyes were as great as ever but she looked like she needed a vacation.

"Look at you," Larisa said. "Oh, gee, you look wonderful!"

"You, too," Tara lied. "You look as if you're thriving. And I'm dying to see your children."

"I want you to see them, too. But let's let 'em sleep a while. I just got the baby down, and Bobby, the oldest, has been on a tear all morning. So let's talk a bit, and have coffee. Some lunch. And by then they'll be awake and not so grouchy. Little Elisabeth has been a dream. She sleeps through the night. Nothing like Bobby who had colic all the time. Come on in. Give me your coat."

At the dinette table, Larisa wanted to know about Tara's life. "I'm living with a professor of Central Asian Studies. I'm crazy about him, and we're getting married as soon as his divorce is final. His wife is being a bitch."

"That's so exciting. So what to you do?"

"I help him with his programs. He takes groups of students to locations on the Silk Road in Central Asia. Occasionally he makes two trips a year. Usually between six and twelve students."

"So what do you do with him?"

"I help him. Travel bookings, visas, visa applications, legal agreements— hold harmless, etc. Plus there are hotel bookings, restaurant engagements, tour buses, in-country guides...."

"I mean...what things do you actually, *do*?"

Tara resisted the urge to say something cross. *Damn, girl, are you listening? What part was hard to understand?*

"Well, Lara, when you start out for a day's ride with twelve students, two American guides, a foreign guide and driver, you better have at least ten gallons of potable water in some form or another—preferably small plastic bottles."

"Don't you get bored with getting water?"

Tara was beginning to wonder if Greg had been feeding Larisa stupid pills. Or if something happens after two pregnancies.

"Sweetie, it is so wonderful. So far I have had a chance to visit all of the "stans" except Afghanistan. Plus China and Russia. Walt and I spent a long weekend in Istanbul. He speaks Turkish. It was heavenly. I feel like I'm living in a dream with him."

Larisa had her elbows on the table supporting her face above her coffee cup and Tara could see the envy in her eyes.

"So tell me. What are the 'stans?' Is this a place? Or what?"

"Countries, Lara. Formerly members of the Union of Soviet Socialist Republics, SSRs. The ones we travel to include Kazakhstan, Tajikstan, Kyrghizstan, Uzbekistan and Turkmenistan. It's like a magic carpet ride. We go to Turkey, too. He can speak Turkish. Like I said."

"Geez," said Larisa. "I've never even heard of some of these places. You've been to places I've never even heard of. I hope this guy is a nice guy."

Tara opened the brown paper bag she had brought. "Come on. Let's open this carton of shrimp salad I got at the deli. It won't keep. We can either eat it while we're talking, or put it in your fridge and you and Greg can have it tonight."

When Tara left three hours later she had held both children. Elizabeth wet herself and had to be handed back, and Bobby was already a little tyrant. The shrimp salad was in the fridge for Greg's supper. She had learned that Greg was bad in bed, that Larisa was unhappy, and that they were looking for a bigger place they could afford. They thought it would be easy to get a loan.

Larisa learned that Walt was older than Tara, that he was still married to a wife reluctant to release him, that he was in the process of selling the house he owned with his wife so he could move into Tara's apartment. This part, to Larisa, was incomprehensible. She knew that Tara had visited several countries whose names were unpronounceable and that she was ecstatically happy. She believed most everything Tara had told her. But the sublimely happy part? *No way! She's gotta be lying!*

The two young women were genuinely happy to see one another. Their past friendship had been mutually satisfying and they had never competed with one another—for attention, boys, recognition, awards. Through high school, they had been real pals. But the last question Larisa asked before

Tara left continued to ring in her ears all the way home. "What are you going to do when something happens to your old guy?"

Tara's father was discharged after angioplasty and three days later, back at home, he resumed all of his old habits. His daughter left after telling him that if he continued smoking, she might not come back next time. She was glad to get back to Mercersburg. She felt sorrier for Larisa than for her father.

"Each window sells tickets only for certain precise and limited circumstances—such as non-express trains leaving on Monday for Xinning. Another window will handle tickets for Tuesday. Another entire series of windows exists for express trains. None of these are marked or arranged in order. To discover the designated purpose of each window, one waits in line. And waits and waits."

Night Train to Turkistan
(Modern Adventures along China's Ancient Silk Road)
Stuart Stevens

CHAPTER 6
Planning a Train Ride?

With Tara in his life, every day was a dream. While they were planning their first China trip, his real estate broker found a buyer for the house he had bought with Flo. He put all his remaining furniture and books in storage. For several months—one whole summer—he moved into Tara's small apartment, and they lived like a couple of students. It was fun; showering together, candlelight suppers seated on the floor, eating outdoors on the small balcony where her place had a good view of the campus and the football stadium. But he missed the space he had enjoyed when he had a roomy study, with a big work table and shelf space for his growing library on Central Asia and the Silk Road.

After several months it was apparent that they needed more room. The divorce from Flo had still not come through. For reasons he found it difficult to understand, Flo had been dragging her feet and throwing up obstacles. She had not made a go of it with her paramour who had gone back to his wife; probably because he missed his children. But Walt suspected that the poor bastard had simply figured out that Flo was a controller, and he had decided not to sign up for the duration.

He offered Flo her choice of anything in the house they had shared. "Except for the stuff in my study, books and papers and my school stuff, you can have anything. Or everything. It's just stuff. Take what you like."

"What about the things we bought together," she pouted.

"Anything. Everything. Whatever. Just roll up with a van and get it all."

She took most of the good furniture and moved in with her father. Her furniture and personal things naturally wouldn't fit in the home that her father had shared with his wife for three decades, so she parked most of it in storage. Walt was happy that she had taken so much. It made things much easier for him.

One night after Tara had served him a big meal of fried oysters washed down with a pretty decent bottle of champagne, they sat entwined on her comfortable sofa and talked about their future together.

"I don't know how I could be any happier," he said. Then he belched.

"That sounded pretty happy," she laughed.

"Maybe, though, I could be just a little happier."

"Tell me. Shall I get naked?"

"In a bit. After I digest these oysters."

"A lap dance?"

"Boring."

"What would make you happier?"

"Well...it would be nice if we had a bigger place. I could use..."

"Why haven't you said something before?" Feigned pique. "I thought you liked our snug little love nest." It was in the pouty voice she used to tease him.

"The love part I do like. Yep! Adore. Really and truly. But the nest part is too small."

"I'm not enamored of this dump, you know. And the lease is up in sixty days. We could go live somewhere else."

"OK. And then there's the part about getting you pregnant. I think you are gonna be even more beautiful with a big belly."

"I've been wondering about that, myself," she said, snuggling up and kissing his chin. "I know you want to have children, and I want you to have them with me. But when I think about it, honestly and selfishly, I wouldn't mind waiting a couple of years. It's wonderful to have you to myself. Like we do now. I love the things we do together. I love it that we travel and make plans and do stuff together, and that I'm involved in your teaching. Even though it's just a small bit of you, I want a few more years before I have to share you with a son. Can I get you to wait a couple of years? 'Til I get tired of you?"

"Or a daughter," he said.

"Do you even know how this baby stuff works, professor? No. I don't think so. I don't think so. Although I'm willing to try daughter stuff. I just don't think you can pull it off."

"Don't tell me any more. You're getting me all excited. Let's go back to the part about this apartment and a bigger place. Did you already tell me that your lease was almost up?"

"I thought I did. But, I dunno. Maybe not. Anyway. Point is we could probably find someplace bigger within sixty days." She jabbed him in the ribs with her elbow. "How are you coming along with your oysters?"

Four weeks later they had found and rented a comfortable old farmhouse that had just come on the market after the old couple that owned it decided to relocate in New Mexico to be near their children. The couple didn't want to sell their place in case any of their children wanted to move back to Pennsylvania at some later date, but they made it clear that it might come on the market after they had a better understanding of the property expectations held by their large family. It turned out that none of their large family coveted the old place.

The house was big and roomy. Old. It needed painting, but Walt told them to cut the price slightly and he'd take care of it. When the broker wanted to write something into the existing lease agreement, the old man bristled. "I heard him, and his word is OK with me. This man is a professor at JBU." The place came with creaky floors and rust stains in the bathroom fixtures, but it was well insulated and the furnace was only five years old.

A few weeks into their lease, negotiations began and the sale deal closed quickly. The couple—enthusiastic new owners—moved Walt's remaining furniture out of storage and they bought themselves a large screen, hi-def TV as a house present. The new place was definitely not cluttered but it suited them both. For a house warming, Walt invited half a dozen colleagues and their spouses—and they all showed up. It was a pretty good party, and it was nearly two in the morning before everyone went home. They were settled in their new place before Tara's lease expired.
"What did I ever do before you came into my life?"
"I don't even want to think about that," she said. "We're leaving for China in a week. Let's go to bed."

The final route across China was easy to select because they were not interested in breaking new ground. They simply decided to take the train for part of their western journey. Their planned route began with a flight to Beijing where they stayed for two days to adjust their clocks. From there they would fly to Xi'an, ancient Chang'an, once the world's largest and wealthiest city. Today it is visited by tourists from around the world, not for its Silk Road heritage, but as the site of the Terracotta Army.
From Xi'an their planned track ran westward to Jiayuguan—the fortress at the western end of the Great Wall—skirting the northern fringes of the Taklamakan Shamo, the desert whose name means "You can go in, but you can't come out." Continuing toward the setting sun, they would stop briefly

at Turfan, one of the lowest spots on the planet with an elevation of 505 feet—below sea level.

Next major destination beyond Turfan was Urumqi, a city little known in the west but one with a population over a million people. Against a background of the magnificent Tien Shan range, the capital of Xinjiang province was a blend of Hui, Han and Uighur, descendents of traders from Central Asia, Arabs, Persians and other Asiatics.

From Urumqi, Walt would have liked to continue west through Uighur country to reach the key city of Kashgar, but this would have required him to retrace his steps and would have added several days to a trip that was already jam packed to fit within fifteen days. He opted to continue westward toward the border with Kazakhstan and exit China before continuing on to Almaty. From there it would be relatively easy to make air connections to a major hub in Europe—Istanbul, Frankfurt, or even London.

The train ride they made from Xi'an to Urumqi was enough to make up Walt's mind. When they brought students, they would need to make arrangements to hire a bus.

"After meeting China's president, Hu Jintao, last month, America's Defense Secretary, Robert Gates, left Beijing with promises of greater co-operation between the two armies, including the installation of a hotline. But China's top brass is not making it easy to fulfil Mr. Hu's hopes of a growing friendship. A fortnight later it unexpectedly cancelled a Thanksgiving Day port call in Hong Kong by *Kitty Hawk*, an American aircraft carrier, and several other vessels."

Goodbye Kitty
The Economist, December 8, 2007

CHAPTER 7
Chinese Hot Dogs

The team of PLAAF personnel operating out of a secret base on the southern fringes of the Taklamakan desert had been in place for over two months and the results of their testing had shown substantial promise.

Major Ju's headquarters, located in a cluster of six specially configured *gers*—portable yurt-like structures designed to be inconspicuous in the landscape—actually stuck out like a sore thumb because of the collection of command trailers, military vehicles, trucks and hangars used for assembling the drones. There were also several prefabricated barracks buildings used for the detachment that was on duty at any particular moment.

Usually, one third of Ju's group were back at leased quarters in Dunhuang and they were rotated on a regular basis. Conditions at the gritty field location were not particularly pleasant. The major had developed a duty cycle consisting of two weeks on and one week off. The system was working reasonably well, and so far, there had been no problems in Dunhuang where off-duty personnel were housed.

For the first two months of the program Major Ju did not include himself in the rotation. Everyone else had time off but he remained at the campsite continuously. He wanted to be certain of every detail of the program, including arrangements in the feeding tent and kitchen, the toilets, and the primitive shower facilities that were as important as the control trailers and the planes. The control trailers proved to be extremely reliable.

Six large power generators were located in a special shed designed to minimize the impact of sand and grit. Only three were used at any one time and the generators were switched in two-week cycles.

Prefabricated hangars for the planes were covered with corrugated metal. A single building could accommodate four drones at a time. When a plane had completed the desired number of flights, its wings were removed and it was returned to its coffin-like container. Only four drones were ready for the flight line on any given day.

At the end of two months, Major Ju was exhausted and he felt the need for time off. He was missing his wife badly; her letters only intensified his longing. She was a very pleasing woman; pretty, and he harbored a wish to bring her for a visit to Dunhuang at some time in the future. From the stories his men brought back, the oasis city was pleasant enough with many interesting places to visit. Ju's plan was to use his first scheduled time away from the site to find appropriate accommodations—comfortable and affordable—where he might place Li and their child, during some future visit. He also wished to have an itinerary of attractions that his wife might find entertaining.

The controllers flying the Chinese drones were split evenly between experienced jet fighter pilots from the PLAAF and youngsters with recommendations from the manufacturers of hobby equipment. The former pilot-operators had actual cockpit experience in high performance aircraft. The latter group had no previous military flight experience and their backgrounds were limited to computer games, flight simulators and competitions between companies making radio-controlled planes for hobbyists. A few of these youngsters had participated in international competitions, but for most of them, except for military camp training usually conducted in their own military district, this was their first time away from home.

At the beginning it was thought that the actual drones would be launched and landed by fighter pilots, and then handed off to amateur flyers while they were aloft. It was believed that the youngsters would be unable to take off and land the actual aircraft, heavier, more complex—and certainly more costly—than anything they had handled in the past. In a very few days it became apparent that the youthful operators learned very quickly. During the second week all of the civilian flyers were capable of taking off and landing without assistance. Everyone seemed to be surprised, but Ju had harbored strong suspicions that this would be the case. The major was pleased to be confirmed in his opinions. This reinforced his beliefs concerning the future for unmanned flight. Nevertheless, he suppressed his elation because he wished the results from their experiment to be clear, unequivocal, and without the least indication of bias, or prejudgment.

After two months, Ju's staff appeared to be capable of running the remote base in his absence. He threw his meager belongings, underwear, civilian clothing, and a few toilet articles into a bag and climbed into the military bus used to rotate his team members. He was looking forward to a few days in Dunhuang. He had already made up his mind to return a day early to see if anyone had let down the standards in his absence.

On the first full day following Ju's departure two of the young controllers got into an argument at breakfast. They had been playing cards the night before and their tiff was mostly youthful hubris, but they had known each other prior to being tagged for the desert tests, and they had been competitors. They still viewed themselves as competitors.

"It would be gratifying, Ling Quan, if we could arm these planes and meet each other in the air."

"And I would be like Baron von Richtofen in his Fokker triplane. You would perish in the flames."

"Your fondest hopes, Ling, but I, on the other hand, would be like Billy Bishop, the famous ace from Canada. You would find it difficult to stay aloft after I shot off your wings."

"White flower snake!" Ling hissed. In Chinese lore, the white flower snake has two heads and is a symbol for talkativeness. With its two heads, no one can answer this creature.

"I challenge you to a private test, Wang Xia. We will decide in the air."

The two friends decided on a test that would involve a timed flight over known landmarks; each flight to include several predefined maneuvers and a return flight with a safe landing. No mishaps were to be tolerated, and both flights to be video-recorded for inspection by the other operator. Then, all records were to be expunged. Up until now, the amount of fuel expended had not been precisely monitored and both flyers felt confident that their competition would escape without detection by the absent major, or his assistant, who seemed to be stuck in the *ger*.

Their course would include a straight run to two remote but well-known landmarks located to the west of Dunhuang. These landmarks were two ancient gates surviving from an earlier era when the city was an important destination on the Silk Road. Four passes would be performed within sight of the gates—including one inverted pass. Then a straight run toward to the nearest point of elevation, Bai Shan, located to the northeast from their base. They would make one full circle around the mountain and then return to the base.

They would choose a time when Major Ju would be away from the base. They had to wait for over a week before the Major took another day off to visit Dunhuang. He was thinking about making plans to bring Li and his son for a visit. Within an hour of the major's departure, the two youngsters had enticed their female judges, with much giggling and blushing, into their command trailer.

By mutual agreement the young men had agreed that the winner would be determined by two PLAAF females. The young women were uniformed members of the mess staff, and had been the recipients of mild flirting from Ling Quan and Wang Xia. The females, sworn to reluctant confidence, had finally agreed to review and judge, but Ling and Wang had realized almost immediately that they really needed a third judge. The youthful fighters and their female collaborators enticed a third female into participating in an event that seemed harmless enough.

The event came off without a hitch, except that on the second flight by challenger Ling Quan, there was a vehicle at one of the ancient gates and they probably got a brief look at the drone during several of its passes over that landmark. But the vehicle on the ground was clearly recognizable as a carrier for tourists. How could a random Chinese tourist recognize an unmarked aircraft as a military drone?

Ling Quan realized that he had acted a bit like what American slang described as a *hot dog*. But no more than his boastful White Flower Snake opponent. The young ladies unanimously agreed that he won the contest, and later that afternoon all five participants met in the mess hall for a handshake and five large glasses of lemonade.

The major found accommodations that he thought would be appropriate for his wife and he returned pleased with his day. The flying contest had gone unnoticed except by hangar mechanics who had made several wagers on the outcome.

"America is still the world's greatest superpower, and the U.S. military's capacity to take out a moving vehicle using a drone piloted from half the world away should still provoke a little shock and awe. But the IED—cheap, easy to make and adapt, and deadly—has in its own way proved equally powerful. The bombs have bled the U.S. military in Iraq."

A New Way of War
Evan Thomas and John Barry
(Newsweek, August 27, 2007)

CHAPTER 8
West From Dunhuang

Captain Jeffrey Anderson, USAF, was a graduate of the Air Force Academy and a skilled jet pilot. He grew up in Helena, Montana where much of his boyhood was spent outdoors with his Presbyterian minister father who was an avid naturalist with a keen interest in birds.

Jeffrey Anderson was a natural born explorer who enjoyed poking around in places that were new to him. A few years after graduating from the Academy, while on leave, he went solo hiking in California's Los Padres National Forest. At a remote campsite up the Beaver River, he encountered a woman camping alone. They talked a while and, by mutual consent, he ended up pitching his one-man tent beside hers.

Claudine, a stunning redhead, was eighteen months older, divorced, a nullipara, and highly intelligent. She had grown up in Summerland, south of Santa Barbara and was Californian to the core. She knew how to camp in the woods and she was a good judge of men. She was also, if anything, a Buddhist. Jeffrey was bowled over by her. A year later they were wed.

When Jeffrey married Claudine, he had never even heard the words Bodhisattva, Sakyamuni or Amitabha. But two years later his education in Buddhism was well underway, and when he was stationed for two years in Korea, he took Claudine to Kamakura in Japan to visit the Great Buddha and the statue of Kwannon. His wife was a compelling teacher, but she was not a proselytizer. So, while Jeffrey learned a great deal about Buddhism, he never became a practitioner of the philosophy. Neither, for that matter, did Claudine. It was an affectation, an effective *schtick*;—part of her considerable charm—but it was based on genuine knowledge, understanding and respect for Buddhism. She was a walking encyclopedia of Buddhist lore. If it hadn't been Buddhism, it might have been Tarot.

A few years into their marriage, when it had become relatively easy to travel in China, Jeffrey and Claudine managed to get thirty-day visas to visit some of the many dramatic Buddhist monuments in China.

Their ramble in China was not an ordinary tourist adventure. They traveled like a couple of college kids on the bum, shunning big hotels and western style restaurants—almost like a couple of hippies. They rode trains, buses and, in a few cases for longer hauls, they flew local airlines. Language was a big problem for them in some places, but they were tolerant and good natured when they encountered delays, misunderstandings and the inevitable official obstinacy.

It cost more than they had planned, but together they visited the enormous Buddha at Dafo in Sichuan. Heading north, they made for Qinghai where they spent three days at Maiji Shan, Corn Rick Mountain, overwhelmed by contemplating the haystack dome riddled with more than 200 caves decorated with Buddhist images.

Finally, inevitably, they headed toward Dunhuang and the Mogao Caves where they paid the exorbitant fees to obtain a permit to take photographs. Both adults were astonished by the variety and complexity of Buddhist art, surviving after centuries of inattention, looting by western nations and defacement by Islamic fanatics opposed to depictions of human faces. By the evening of the third day of their stay in Dunhuang, Jeffrey was saturated with Buddhist art.

They were side by side in the hard bed of their guest house after a supper of noodles, pork and onions.

"Did you finish shooting everything you wanted from Mogao?" Jeffrey asked, belching from onions and grease.

"I still have film left. Four rolls."

"Sweetie, I may be Buddha'ed out after today. That was a lot of climbing."

"Yeah, but there's more to see."

"There's always more to see. It's a huge planet. We could never see it all. Why am I telling this to you?"

"You've got something else in mind for tomorrow? We're not booked to leave 'til the day after."

"Yeah, I have a request. But y'know what got me today? That picture of Buddha letting himself be eaten by the tigress, so she could feed her cubs. I can't buy into that. That's just too weird."

"And nobody's asking you to buy into the story. But as an allegory for compassion..."

"Don't explain. I know what you'll say. But I also know you don't really buy it either. I will say this. The art is mind-blowing."

She leaned over and kissed him on the ear. Easy at first; then with her tongue.

"Yeah, OK. OK. But tomorrow. Let me pick. OK?"

The next morning, after breakfast of fried eggs, rice and some kind of soft, sweet bun that went well with the green tea, Jeffrey disappeared for an hour and hired a four-wheel drive vehicle with a driver. The couple, armed with the driver and a good map, headed west, out of Dunhuang, into the ocean of sand shimmering in the distance. Sand whipping off the tops of dunes reminded Jeffrey of the wind-blown snow sheeting from the rugged peaks surrounding Helena.

Fifty miles out of town they were in dune country, with the trackless Taklamakan stretching into infinity. Then, unexpectedly, some large man-made object appeared in the distance. As they approached the strange, cube-like objects, Jeffrey leaned forward and touched the driver.

"Yu Men Guan?" he asked.

"Shi. Nali. Yu Men Guan."

"What is it?" Claudine said.

"It's the Jade Gate Pass. Probably the westernmost part of the old Great Wall. This was the last outpost of civilization before they stepped off into the great unknown. Somewhere around here there's a second one. The Yang Guan. South Pass."

"Thank you for bringing me on this trip, lover."

"You are welcome, sweetie. I would never have done this without you."

"I'm glad I found you in the woods that time. You looked like you were lost."

"'Til I found you. Maybe I was. But now I'm found. Look. Over there. That may be the other one. These places were abandoned over a thousand years ago. This is amazing." She moved in close and snuggled against him. "How long can we stay and look around? When do we have to get back?"

Jeffrey laughed. "This is a picnic. There's food in the back. We don't have to be back before it gets too dark to see any more."

They had driven to the end of the line. The road heading west had ended. From here on...camel caravans had to decide on routes to the north or to the south of the desert.

It was a magical afternoon. They drove to both of the ancient gates, worn and abraded by a millennia of sand blasting but still standing, mute testimony to man's energy. They walked, they climbed and they contemplated. The driver smoked, snoozed and shared the packed lunch that Jeffrey had purchased in advance.

Sometime in mid afternoon they had climbed to the top of dune to get a shot from an angle Claudine thought might be interesting. They flopped down in the sand and lay back, enjoying the heat from the sand.

"We may have picked the best possible time of year to come here," she said.

"So it would seem."   He had just closed his eyes when the noise hit.

"Holy cow! What's that?" The plane was passing overhead about 200 yards to the west of the ancient Yang Guan Gate, now a brick pile, and it was no more than a thousand feet in the air.

Jeffrey watched the plane as it headed in the general direction of north, and then did an abrupt Immelmann turn to head back in the direction from which it had been coming. This time it appeared to be sighting on the ancient gate. It was much closer, and Jeffrey got a better look.

"That friggin' pilot must be deranged. What's he got in mind?" he said.

On the end of the second pass at the gate, there was another Immelmann, followed by series of snap rolls before resuming the original flight path. After the third pass, another Immelmann, without the snap roll, this time ending in an inverted pass over the gate. This time, Jeffrey had a close look. There was no pilot in the cockpit of this curious swept-wing aircraft that was flying without markings of any kind.

The Air Force captain realized, like a thunderclap of recognition, that he knew what model plane he was seeing. In watching the maneuvers, his brain had not consciously tried to match up the configuration with known aircraft. But the profile was too distinctive for there to be any question. The plane that had been performing maneuvers like those seen on many US amateur flying fields was a MiG-21. The configuration was known to American pilots by its NATO designation, "Fishbed." Exact model? Unknown. Obviously the ship had been modified substantially to accommodate pilotless flight, but there could be no question about the configuration of the Mikoyan-Gurevich—21, a model that he had actually seen flying on a visit to the test range at Tonopah.

It hit him like a thunderbolt. This MiG fighter was being flown as a drone. As an F-16 pilot he had been trained in specific tactics proven to be effective against specific configurations. But when the plane was being piloted from the ground?

Shit! He had watched the drone go through its maneuvers with shock and amazement. *I don't believe I could do that*, he thought. *Not without a lot of practice.* He snapped out of his reverie. Claudine was a few paces away, watching him, wide-eyed, waiting for his reaction.

"No pilot!" he said. "Did you see that? There was no pilot! If it comes back, try to get a photo! I can't quit watching."

"In Central Asia's back of beyond, where China tests her nuclear weapons and keeps a wary eye on her Russian neighbours, lies a vast ocean of sand in which entire caravans have been known to vanish without trace. For well over a thousand years the Taklamakan desert has, with good reason enjoyed an evil reputation among travelers. Apart from the handful of men who have crossed its treacherous dunes, some of which reach a height of three hundred feet, caravans throughout history have always skirted it, following the line of isolated oases along its perimeter."

Foreign Devils on the Silk Road
Peter Hopkirk

CHAPTER 9
A SECRET Report

When Captain Jeffrey Anderson and his pretty wife Claudine returned to the states from their two week vacation wandering around China, he still had five days of vacation remaining. But he was eager and anxious to get back to his station at Minot AFB in North Dakota.

"Explain to me why you feel like we have to go back early," she had complained. "We could spend the rest of the time hiking in California." She pronounced it *Kal-ee-forn-nee-yah*.

"I need to talk to someone at the base. To my squadron commander. You're not listening when I explain. But this could be important."

"Sometimes I think you've forgotten how we met."

"No."

"Then maybe it didn't seem all that important to you."

"No. C'mon Claudine. Don't be difficult. I'll find a way to make it up to you. But I gotta do this."

Even at the time, the full implications of what he was looking at back on the border of the Taklamakan hadn't sunk in. It happened too quickly, too unexpectedly. But as the days passed and he reflected, he realized that he was looking a drone with swept wings, which was flying at a high rate of speed. Exactly how fast was difficult to estimate, but it he were to ever see it again he would be better prepared to make some estimate of speed.

As he thought about the experience and revisited the circumstances in his mind, it dawned on him that the drone's operator must have been looking at him, in much the same way that he was looking at the drone.

This whole topic of pilotless aircraft, and the implication of weapons-carrying drones filling the air was one which he did not want to get into with Claudine. His wife, fascinated by Buddhism, was into compassion, into concern for all living things, into respect for life. She abhorred violence. Strangely enough, she was able to reconcile her personal beliefs with her husband's career choice, mostly because he encouraged her somewhat unconventional system of beliefs. Certainly she did not fit the mold for a conventional life in Minot, North Dakota.

Another important reason he didn't want to discuss his concerns with Claudine was because he had a strong suspicion that what he had seen in China might not be known within the U.S. intelligence community. Maybe it was; maybe it wasn't. He couldn't be sure. As far as he knew, the USAF Reaper was at the leading edge of pilotless military aviation. That is, unless China had skipped a generation and they were already working on something that could best Reaper.

He needed to get back home. And that's just what they did. Two days later they were back in their small, on-base apartment. He signed back in two days early and set up an appointment with his CO, Lt. Colonel Joseph "Harpoon" Harmoukian.

The colonel, who was also on leave, had been fishing for walleyes in Lake Sakakawea and, unlike Anderson, nothing was itching him to return early. So after giving up a couple of leave days, thereby incurring a slight measure of displeasure from his wife, the captain didn't get the immediate face time that he wanted, and he had no incentive to go over the Harpoon's head to confide his concerns to anyone else at Minot.

In order to make good use of his time, and to get out from under the feet of his somewhat puzzled wife, he spent time at the base library writing down his concerns in a spiral notebook, and searching the internet for latest information on the Reaper. He hoped against hope to learn that the next generation would have swept wings, increased speed, and other performance enhancements. But, if such work was underway it was classified and he could find not the slightest hint on the internet.

He would search for two hours, then write notes for an hour, trying to clarify what he thought he had seen. In this way, he spent the two days waiting for Harmoukian to return from his fishing vacation.

When the Colonel returned, there were a lot of tasks that had piled up in his absence, and it was after noon before Captain Anderson got to sit down with him.

"What's up, Jeffrey? Sergeant McKelvey tells me you came back a couple days early. He said you have ants in your pants. What gives?"

"Later on I'll ask you about your fishing trip, Colonel. But right now I have a kind of worry that requires advice from you."

"To do with flight readiness? What's the topic? You're making it sound mysterious."

"You know my wife and I went to China on vacation."

"You told me. I knew it. Actually I was a bit surprised that you got travel visas from the Chinese."

"We traveled all over. My wife thinks she's...that she might like to be a Buddhist. We visited the south, the center and went as far west as the westernmost province, Xinjiang."

"That's mostly desert isn't it? What's to see out there?"

"A lot of desert. That's for sure. But also a lot of mountains, and that means snowmelt and that means oases."

"So why did you come back early?"

"While we were visiting a remote site at the desert's fringe, we were buzzed by a pilotless drone."

"Hmmm. Pilotless. How could you be sure?"

"It came over at low altitude...at high speed. That gets your attention."

"Even so, Jeffrey. How could you be sure that you were seeing into the cockpit?"

"Look, Colonel, this bird, whatever it was, made four high speed, low level passes over us at a very remote location. At a dead end road on the desert's fringe. Fifty miles from the nearest town."

"Even so..."

"And at the end of each turn, the plane made an Immelmann followed by a snap roll to reverse direction."

"Even so...pilotless? This sounds like some crazy hotshit pilot showing off to prove himself—where no one can chew his ass."

"Colonel, the last pass overhead was inverted. That cockpit was empty. It was a drone."

Joseph Harmoukian was the kind of CO, or boss if you're a civilian, that many of us have encountered. He did not want to make waves. Ever. And his favored mode of dealing with potentially vexing situations, such as this one, was to act as what he described as "the devil's advocate." He rarely stopped to think that the devil needs little assistance to perform his own work.

"Jeffrey, I believe that you think you saw a pilotless plane. Perhaps what threw you off was that unique straight wing profile. It stands to reason. You see that slender, glider-like profile and your brain thinks drone, drone. You see what you want to see."

"Ah, bullshit, Colonel. No disrespect intended. This drone had swept wings, it was going half again faster than the Reaper or you can have my paycheck. And the plane was being controlled by someone who was not aboard. Period. I saw it for quite a while, looked at it carefully, and I have 20-10 vision. Both eyes. OK. So you don't believe me. But I would like to make a formal written report, describing what I saw, when and where I saw it, including how I happened to be there. I'll make the formal report to you and then I'll just try to forget about it. Is that acceptable to you?"

The last two sentences were the kind of words that gave Colonel Harmoukian occasional bad dreams. His brain was racing. But there was no way he could get in trouble if Anderson wrote his report and he bucked it upstairs without delay. *Damn, did he really see a swept-wing drone in China. How could this be? Isn't the Reaper lead edge? Maybe there are swept wings on our drawing boards. But in China? Last I looked the PLA was still riding camels in their deserts. Their space program is moving along...but pilotless jets...? I'm skeptical.*

"Tell me again, Jeffrey. Where exactly did you see this aircraft? Go back to the beginning. I need to let this sink in."

When Captain Jeffrey Anderson finally completed his report, it was fourteen pages long and it was directed specifically to his commanding officer, Colonel Joseph Harmoukian. It was immediately classified SECRET and was bucked up the chain of command to a limited distribution. Two days later a copy of the captain's report was in the hands of Colonel Roger "Slick" Richardson at the Air Combat Command in Langley, Virginia. Slick Richardson read the report twice. Under his breath he muttered *Holy fuck.!* Then he buzzed his secretary. "Try to put me through to General Harman."

Once the formal report was completed and Jeffrey Anderson realized that it had been immediately classified SECRET, the fighter pilot captain relaxed and the change in his karma was immediately apparent to his wife, Claudine. She was happy to have him back and she was only too eager to overlook some of the better known Buddhist teachings with regard to annihilating desire.

When Captain Anderson's report was finally placed in the hands of analysts working for the Air Force, one of the steps that followed immediately was an effort to estimate where the flight might have originated. Air Force intelligence, based on satellite data had pinpointed the locations of most Chinese air bases, but it was not apparent where the drone's base was located.

As a starting point, analysts estimated that the cruising range for a first generation swept-wing drone might fall somewhere between the range of Predator and Reaper. A first gen drone, with kinks to iron out, might have a range of a thousand miles. Out and back....that might suggest examining possible launch sites within a 500 mile radius from the point of observation.

For a first cut, they began by examining a radius of 350 miles. Several cities had good commercial airstrips—Hami to the north, Jiayuguan to the east, and Dunhuang itself. From a terrain standpoint, Dunhuang was clearly the end of the line. To the west, there was not much going on. To the east; population, agriculture, industry. To the west there was nothing. Only the oceanic vastness of the Taklamakan. There was no proof. But most of the analysts agreed. The drones were flying from a base in the desert.

But where?

"The softest thing in the universe
 Overcomes the hardest thing in the universe.
 That without substance can enter where there is no room.
 Hence I know the value of non-action."

Tao Te Ching
Lao Tsu
(translated by Gia-Fu Feng and Jane English)

CHAPTER 10
Curious Thoughts in Kuqa

On their second trip to China, Walt and Tara stopped at Kuqa on the circuit around the northern fringe of the Taklamakan Desert. Kuqa is an oasis town of about 70,000 people. It was an independent state until the 8th century, after which it fell under Chinese domination. Historians find the town interesting because it was a stopping place for Xuanzang in his 7th century travels to India.

Today, one of the main reasons for tourists to visit Kuqa is its proximity to the Thousand Buddha Caves, located in the red rock cliffs of Kizil, about 40 miles from town.

Walt and Tara had booked into a hotel, and their Chinese guide and driver had opted for other arrangements, to save money. The hotel was small, and marginally adequate, but there was adequate hot water and Walt was able to get a shower after rising.

The preceding day had been tiring, they had arrived late, eaten late, and tumbled into bed like a couple of teenagers. Walt's itinerary called for them to spend the following day in Kuqa. He had planned a visit to the caves, in order to make a determination concerning the appropriateness of this town, and possibly this hotel, as a stopping point on trips with students. His mind was racing with things that he wanted to accomplish during day.

After waking, he had wrapped the elastic bandage around his stump and strapped on the prosthesis. His pair of wide-leg khakis had been selected because they could be pulled on after the device had been attached.

He knew that Tara had slipped into the bathroom ahead of him, but she hadn't shut the door so he figured that she might be brushing her teeth. He walked into the bathroom and was surprised to find her looking in the mirror. She was crying.

"What's wrong, lotus blossom?" he said, concerned. He had only seen her cry once before—when Flo had been rude.

"Nothing," she stammered with an embarrassed smile.

"Why are you crying?"

She turned to him and he took her in his arms. She nestled close against him, burrowing her face into his neck. Nuzzling.

"Why the tears?"

"It's nothing," she said. "I'm just so happy. To be here with you. Sometimes it feels overwhelming. All this."

"C'mon. 'Fess up. Is something bothering you? You can tell me. You're not still thinking about all that crap from Florence? Tell me. "

"No. Really. It's nothing." Now she was starting to laugh. "It's just you, you big, sexy brute. Sometimes I worry if I'll be enough for you."

"Tara...Tara. Look at me. That may be the dumbest thing I've ever heard you say. I might not even be here if it weren't for you. Don't talk stupid."

She buried her head against his neck; then turned abruptly and bit him on the left shoulder. *Damn! That hurt!* But he didn't say a word. She turned back to his neck and clung like a limpet as he tried to figure out what had just happened. He held her for a long moment.

"It's still early," he said, releasing her. But she clung to him. "I'm going down for coffee and to clear my head for a spell. Come down when you're ready. You could get another thirty or forty minutes of shuteye if you wanted."

"Maybe I might," she said, ungluing herself and sliding back into bed.

In the lobby Walt headed for the coffee maker and found that it was just perking, waiting for his arrival. The small dining room was almost empty. He headed for the quietest corner and sat down to enjoy the coffee and to clear his head for the day's activities. The hotel's sound system was pumping out some type of Chinese music that, mercifully, wasn't so loud as to be intrusive, but clear enough to be pleasant. He took out his pocket notebook and a ball point pen. His intention was to write about his expectations for the day—what he expected to find at the Thousand Buddha Caves—and his criteria for making a decision concerning a stop for his students.

To his discomfort, his brain wouldn't focus on those topics. As he sipped the coffee—very good actually—he found himself thinking about the bite mark Tara had just left on his shoulder. Her teeth marks had been clearly visible and he was going to have a bruise.

It was curious. He had never allowed himself to think about it too carefully. But in the few years he had been with Tara, scarcely two months passed when she did not bite him. Sometimes she bit him pretty hard. On at least three occasions he could remember she had broken the skin; drawn blood.

He had never spoken to her about it. They had never discussed it, and after biting him she had never brought it up. Never. Not once. Certainly, she had never apologized. As he allowed himself to think about it—analytically, in this exotic location, halfway around the world—he found that he was actually pleased that they had never spoken about it.

Still...it was clear that she realized what she had done every time she did it. Once, when she bit him on the collarbone, it had left a bruise that lasted for at least two weeks. So she had to be aware of what she was doing, and of its consequences. He sipped the strong coffee, black with no sugar, and tried to focus on expectations for a day at the caves.

Outside the dining room, on a small enclosed terrace, some kind of caged bird was singing. It was a bird that Walt could not recognize—perhaps some kind of blackbird, black, with yellow on the wings. He needed to think about their day ahead, but he kept coming back to the marks on his shoulder. *OK. Let's think about it for a few more minutes.* He closed his notebook and took another sip of coffee.

The first time she had bit him was the first time they had slept together. *Without making love.* That much he remembered vividly. That first time, he remembered, she had bit his mouth, surprising him. Later, on other occasions, she had left teeth marks on his shoulders, collarbone, and hip bones. Once at the bottom of his rib cage. More than once she had drawn blood by biting his lips. But more often her bites were catlike, she would simply hold him with her teeth.

There were only a few people in the dining room, and one of the groups of four near the coffee urn appeared to be the quartet of Australians who had checked in about the same time. Until the Aussies came in the music on the speakers had been Chinese, but someone had changed the tape to western music and Walt realized it was a tune he knew. It was a curious piece of music, one which he had never particularly liked, and couldn't peg to any particular era. Yet, he knew some of the words to this tune. What was the name? *Lollipops and Roses.*

He could even remember some of the words.

Tell her you care,
Each time you speak,
Make it her birthday
Each day of the week.

God, what corny words. Why had they stuck in his brain? They got even worse

Carry her books,
That's how it starts.
Sixteen to sixty
They're kids in their hearts.

The tempo of the Chinese version seemed slightly off, but that was the song, all right; no mistake. Lollypops and Roses. That was all he could remember; and he didn't have the slightest notion of where he had heard the song in the past.

Roses and lollipops. And lollipops and roses. More words popped up in his memory.

Some days she'll laugh.
Some days she'll cry.
Minute to minute
You'll never know why.

Something like that.

Who would have ever expected to hear this tune in gritty Kuqa, on the northern fringe of China's Taklamakan? While drinking coffee and looking at some kind of caged blackbird? The world was strange. Mysterious. And wonderful. What was he thinking about before the music?

A couple of times she had bit him during orgasm, and that part he could understand. That made sense—but the other times were often puzzling. Was it an affectation? Conscious...or unconscious? Was it some unconscious way to demonstrate possession? *What the hell is going on in her mind when she does it? Why would she bite me on the hip bone. That time left a bruise that lingered for nearly a month. Actually, it was just over a month.* He didn't know how to explain it. In any event, it was a form of personal signature, making her unique and unforgettable.

Now, sitting alone, in a town few people at home had ever heard of, he realized with a shock that he didn't mind. And, although his knowledge of women was far from encyclopedic, Tara was showing him a behavior of which he had no prior knowledge. *I can't say I like it,* he mouthed the words silently. *But she does it...so I can't say I don't like it.* He reached up and rubbed the spot on his shoulder where the mark was still tender. And he smiled. *Jesus, what is happening to me?*

He thought about Florence, the woman to whom he was still married, now sleeping with another man, a married man, and apparently eager to sever her marriage to him. *Eager...but not too eager.* He had been in love with her at the beginning, only to be done in by his injury.

Just thinking about his loveless years with Florence made Tara's possessiveness valuable beyond measure. *No matter if she devours me, I'm never going to complain.*

The music changed and now some Chinese group was playing Beatle tunes. He was getting up to get more coffee when Tara joined him.

"Hi, sweetie," she said. "Did you eat yet?"

"Hi, lollipop. No, I was waiting for you."

"Lollipop?" she said, laughing. "That's new. Where did that come from?"

"Right out of the ether," he said. "C'mon, Let's get some breakfast."

"We are all of us made by war, twisted and warped by war, but we seem to forget it."

Doris Lessing

CHAPTER 11
Interview

Immediately after Walt and Tara returned from their second visit to China, word got out on the JBU Campus that the Silk Road Professor was planning to extend his program to begin from the eastern end of that fabled trade route. While the number of those who could actually participate in the program was relatively small, the impact of his tour classes was disproportionately large. Students who visited Central Asia came back with photos and stories. Word spread quickly around the campus and Walt's classes became very popular.

The demand for spaces on his tours to Central Asia had grown to be greater than he wished to accommodate. As a consequence he had needed to determine a selection process to cut the number of potential travelers to a manageable herd. After considering a number of options, he finally selected a simple lottery, held in the Student Union building six weeks before the end of the spring quarter. Only candidates having a C plus average, or better, were eligible to enter his lottery.

Based on the comments he was receiving concerning his proposed expansion to include China, it appeared that he was likely to have more applicants for the eastern—Chinese—end of the tour than for Central Asia. Already, even before he had taken his first working excursion for credit, it was common knowledge that he had established connections with two Chinese Universities who were helping him with his program arrangements in exchange for some type of *quid pro quo* for Chinese academics.

Between his teaching schedule and his planning activities in support of his trip, he and Tara were kept very busy. His secretary, whose services he shared with the department head, Dr. Li, was less helpful than he might have wished; due in part to her age, and her loyalty to her old boss. But Tara was a brick. She could do just about anything. She had told him in the past that she had *ensorcelled* him, and he was coming to believe that it was really true. He depended on her.

On a wintry day in February a student whose face was unfamiliar showed up in Walt's office. The young woman was a senior in journalism on an assignment for the magazine published by the Alumni Association.

JBU's Alumni Magazine was titled "**Wheatland Sage**, James Buchanan University, A magazine for Alumni and Friends," and it came out four times each year.

The youthful journalist had proposed an article on Walt and his Silk Road Program, with particular emphasis on his plans to extend these tours to include China. The girl, Maxine Allison, was personable and she told Walt that she believed that it would take no more than two hours of his time. She proposed to schedule it for any time that suited his convenience. But she asked him if he could work her into his schedule in the next two weeks, based on deadlines for the spring issue.

"Are you willing to come to my house on a Sunday afternoon?"

"Of course. And may I take a few digital photos of you as we're talking?"

Maxine Allison showed up at the appointed time and her questions had been well thought out in advance. Walt escorted the young woman into his study and Tara came in for an introduction, returning in a few minutes later with a tray filled with tea things.

"I can make coffee if you prefer, but we've been drinking coffee all morning and I thought this would be better. Green tea in the green pot, hot water in the white one and tea bags as you choose."

"Tea is fine. Thanks." And Tara was gone. Maxine explained that she would write a few paragraphs at the front and back ends of the interview, but that the bulk of her piece would be based on their conversation—which she did not prefer to tape.

JBU: Thanks for agreeing to his interview, Professor Roberts. Your programs for taking students on tours of the Silk Road are very popular. And they're unique to JBU. How did this idea come about?

Roberts: One of my first classes in the Department of Central Asian Studies was titled "Legacy of the Silk Road." It was a place I had visited as a young boy and been fascinated. The idea just came to me naturally, and with the approval of our visionary president I put our first tour together. It was very popular from its inception.

Q: The Silk Road covers such a vast range of territory. All of Asia. How did you determine which places you would visit?

Roberts: From the beginning it was obvious that I would have to be selective, that we couldn't eat the whole camel at one bite. So I chose to visit countries that were former SSRS, Soviet Republics, known colloquially as "the Stans." These countries today are known as CIS, Central Independent States. They share common attributes and problems. I began by focussing on Uzbekistan, Turkmenistan and Kazakhstan. Mostly because they were easiest to enter. And also because I have some slight familiarity with the languages.

Q: Did you have any problems at the beginning with entry visas for multiple independent nations?

Roberts: Entry visas are frequently a big headache. But not always. Fortunately there are service bureaus that can help with this process. For a fee, of course. It's always important to start the process well in advance of need. So far we haven't had any major problems. I will add that border crossings can often be a hassle. It helps when students have a good sense of humor—and don't get impatient.

Q: Most of the countries you have visited in the past are Islamic republics. In light of the world situation, has this presented any unique problems?

Roberts: This is a legitimate concern, but good manners and common courtesy usually prevent any confrontation. I try to prepare everyone in advance with regard to clothing and head gear. Things like...no shorts. No halter tops, no scoop necks, no exposed bra straps. It's mostly common sense—and good manners. Students are provided with guidelines for acceptable behavior in mosques, tombs or religious shrines. No preparation can anticipate every potential form of fanatical behavior. We haven't had any problems to date and hopefully that record can continue.

Q: Are we correct in our understanding that you are currently planning to expand your tour to include China?

Roberts: This is a dream I have had from the beginning. We began our visits with heavy emphasis on the cities that many westerners associate with the ancient Silk Road; places like Tashkent, Samarkand, Bukhara. Also Khiva, Merv and Ashkabad. All the way to Turkey sometimes. But on the other side of the world's roof there are other cities—in China—less well known—that played an equally important role. Places like Xi'an, which once might have been the world's largest and richest city. Or Lanzhou, Jiayuguan, or Dunhuang. Remote oasis towns, such as Turfan, or Kashgar. The extreme western provinces of China have substantial Muslim populations, mostly because of the Silk Road trade routes. These cities and towns, large and small, are fascinating places to visit. Some of these places closely resemble the towns of Central Asia. Their populations include Uighurs, Huis, Kazakhs, Kirghiz and other ethnic groups that are not culturally Chinese. *I'll spell all these names for you Maxine. Don't worry about it now.*

On and on! Maxine plowed methodically through her notes. How much of China will you plan to visit? Do you expect any problems in obtaining travel visas for your groups? What cities and places will you plan to visit in China? Will your tours ever be extended to cover the entire Silk Road in one long visit? When do you plan to begin your China course? How often will they be offered? How many people are involved in the management and coordination of your tours? Do you work with conventional travel agencies or tour companies? Are these classes expensive? How can most kids afford extended stays in foreign countries? Are these trips just available for students with wealthy families?

The girl had done a good job of preparing her questions. If Walt had made the list himself he could hardly have done a more thorough job of covering the key points that would be of interest to parents. For the better part of an hour she pressed on with most of her questions. Occasionally, Walt's careful answers would cover her next question. He already had formed a picture of the key points he wanted to cover, and was prepared to work them in at the end. He was pleased that the girl's list covered the meat and potatoes, but he was beginning to wonder if he was repeating himself.

Q: How many students do you take on your trips, and what are the criteria you use to select them?
Roberts: We like to keep the groups between twelve and fifteen. Less than eight is less fun for me. And more than fifteen can be difficult to manage. It's hard to talk loud enough and fast enough to hold everyone's attention. Fifteen is a good size for a group. I tried eighteen once and it was not much fun. You start to feel like a sheep dog. Don't put that in, please. And we always hire Chinese guides.

Q: Considering the way the world is today, some students might be apprehensive about this part of the world. What has been the most significant problem you have encountered in the past? Are there any dangers to be particularly avoided?

Roberts: Our Silk Road journeys take a very small segment of the JBU student body, so our experience must be regarded as anecdotal, but so far no one has been hurt or injured during our programs. Parents who might worry about their children should be far more concerned about binge drinking during Pledge Week, or bad behavior during Spring Break. We count on young men and women from JBU to behave like adults. So far, they haven't disappointed us. Our most common problems are usually diarrhea or stomach upsets. By the way, if you interview some of our returning travelers I think they'll all tell you that this is not the easiest four credits that they ever earned. There is a lot of work involved. Before and after the trips.

Walt was beginning to wonder if she'd be given space to cover all this detail.

Q: Is it harder, more difficult, more complex to travel in China than in the other countries of the Silk Road? For example, are there problems with food? Or water?

Roberts: One thing that makes it more difficult for us is the lack or absence of language skills to communicate when we're away from hotels and major cities. I would love to be able to speak Chinese. While many Chinese are proficient in English, good speakers are hard to find in some places. Hard? Make that impossible. Chinese food is, for the most part, excellent. But occasionally we encounter strange dishes. Drinking water always requires caution. We see intestinal problems on a regular basic. But a bit of careful preparation usually ensures that we have what we need to take care of any problems. We haven't had to send anyone home for an illness, but on occasion our timetable has been disrupted.

Walt turned to see if Tara was in his line of sight. On one of his early visits to Central Asia she had come down with diarrhea and been bedridden for a couple of days because she took the wrong medicine. Walt had changed his schedule so that he found himself alone with the girl for several days, and she had wrapped him up like mayfly with a spider. But just at the moment, Tara was out of sight in the kitchen. Maxine plugged on with her questions. He was beginning to get restless.

Q: How do students sign up to visit China's Silk Road? Is it necessary to take your classroom course in order to go on your expedition?

Roberts: The classroom prepares students for what they can expect to see during the journey once limited to camel caravans. Often, during a busy day, we're on the move and there isn't time to go over everything we're looking at. If we stay at a site for three hours and we're walking most of the time, there's no way to impart a lot of information. The short answer is 'Yes!' Do the prep work and then take the trip. By the way, only a small handful of people have ever asked to take the trip for what I consider the wrong reasons.

Q: Now you've made me curious. What would you describe as the wrong reasons for taking an exciting voyage to a famous destination and getting college credit for it?

Roberts: Maybe I should modify my previous answer. To be eligible, students must have a C plus average, or better. Occasionally students from wealthy families have tried to sign up, with little or no interest in the Silk Road, or anything else except a vacation on another continent. I get to make the choices and I call them like I see them. So far I've traveled with a highly motivated and exceptionally talented group of young people. I want to keep it that way.

When she came to the last question on her list, Maxine folded the sheets together and let them fall on the floor. In the kitchen, Tara, who had been listening for the interview to come to an end, slipped into the living room and hit the play button for a CD she had placed earlier.

"Well professor, I've gone through my list of questions. I brought a few more, but you've covered most of them already so I guess I'm done. Unless you can think of something important that I neglected to ask, I believe I have more than enough to put together my piece for the *Wheatland Sage*. I appreciate your time, and the exposure to your fascinating tours. I think our readers will enjoy these insights into your program. I find myself wanting to go along. Especially to China."

"You're certainly welcome, Maxine. I've enjoyed it as well. Good luck with the piece. Let me know how it turns out."

"I certainly will, professor." She stood up and turned her head to see where the music was coming from. "Y'know what's different about this interview, Professor Roberts? This is the fifth time I have interviewed a faculty member. And every other time, the individual wanted to see my completed piece before it could run in the magazine. You've never once asked to vet my piece."

Walt laughed. "You look like a big girl to me, Maxine. Of course, if you want me to, I probably could. But otherwise..."

"No. But thanks for that offer. I appreciate it." She had been gathering up notebook and question sheets into her shoulder bag and she stood up to leave.

"One more thing, professor. That music in the background? It sounds Chinese. Very interesting."

"Yes. An all-girl band of Chinese musicians, all playing traditional instruments. The piece you're hearing now ties right into to our interview."

"Interesting. How so, might I ask?"

"The name of that last piece was *Dunhuang*. Where we'll certainly be going." They were at the door and he was helping her with her coat.

"And what was the name of the band?"

"Twelve Girls Band." He laughed. "Actually, they have thirteen musicians. That's China. Inscrutable."

As Maxine's car pulled out of the driveway and disappeared, Tara came out of the kitchen and put her arm around him. "How did it go, sweetie?"

"My god, Silky; that is likely to be the most boring article her magazine will ever see."

When the magazine came out a few weeks later, Walt realized that the cat was now out of the bag. Expectations had been set and now the work would begin in earnest.

The magazine had been out less than a month when the call came from Washington. He was not really prepared.

"The Reaper can fly three times as fast as a Predator and carry eight times as much weaponry, such as Hellfire missiles, the Air Force said.

The Reaper's greater range and speed make it better suited than the Predator to Afghanistan with its vast, rugged terrain. The Reaper will also be deployed to Iraq. Its speed and arms will let it track and kill moving targets able to elude a Predator...."

Faster, deadlier pilotless plane bound for Afghanistan
Tom Vanden Brook
USA Today, August 28, 2007

CHAPTER 12
Langley Air Force Base, Virginia

The group of senior Air Force, Navy and Marine Corps officers gathered in the comfortable conference room at Langley represented the cream of America's military flyers. There were 20 men in the room, and all of them were general officers. Their flight records, considered all together, had spanned more than 200 models and variants of aircraft purchased by the Defense Department over four decades.

A few of these venerable aviators had been the children of fathers who brought down Japanese airmen from the cockpits of Vought-Sikorsky F4U Corsairs or Grumman Hellcats. Some had occupied cockpits in squadrons of F8U's flying from carrier decks at the time of fighting in Lebanon. The F8 Crusaders flown by some naval aviators had, at least since 9-11, been recognized as having a name that was now politically incorrect.

These officers were elderly men, approaching retirement now, but, as has always been true, it is old men who send young men out to make history— and sometimes to die in the process. This group was not insensitive to the responsibilities they bore, because most of them had, at some time in their past, been responsible for sending men younger than themselves to face the possibility—some times the certainty—of an unpleasant death. They had made these decisions and learned to live with them. And they had reaped the rewards that accompany the ability to live with this knowledge.

Air Force General Warren Bloodsworth stood up to address the meeting that had been scheduled to extend over three days. During his active years as a pilot, Warren Bloodsworth had flown the biggest planes in the Air Force inventory. He had ferried military equipment from Japan and the Philippines to scores of distant locations around the Far East. He had also been involved in making improvements to storm tracking planes. Few men had deliberately flown into worse weather than this decorated veteran. Since receiving his star he had cultivated a reputation for tenacity and doggedness that many of his superiors found valuable. Subordinates did not always agree.

One of the civilian secretaries who assisted with his staff work told her boyfriend, "The old SOB is anally-retentive."

"That sounds a bit judgmental," her companion replied.

"OK, You be the judge," she said. "Last week he pitched a hissy fit because of sign on the copy machine. The sign had said 'PERSONAL COPIES, 10 CENTS. The corner of the sheet got torn off somehow, and the sign read PIES, 10 CENTS. He made a big deal out of it. What a crock! You ask me, he's over the hill."

Notwithstanding, it was this Air Force pieman who opened the meeting.

"Gentlemen, welcome to you all. It is a genuine pleasure for me to be here to address you this morning. In spite of the serious business we have been summoned to transact. I see a lot of familiar faces, and I can't pass up the opportunity to reminisce about a few experiences I have shared with many of you."

Bloodsworth had been out drinking the night before, with several of the old friends he had flown with in bases from Japan and Vietnam, to Diego Garcia. He had used several hours prior to this meeting to polish up several of the stories they had shared the prior evening, and he used the first five minutes of his introductory remarks to rehash some of his early morning recollections.

Audience members were, for the most part, experienced storytellers themselves and they listened with tolerance to his anecdotes of experiences that were only too familiar to all of them. Finally he got down to business.

"Gentlemen, we are here for a serious purpose. We have been summoned to consider a problem now faced by the USAF, an institution where all of us have spent our professional lives. Some of you will be very familiar with circumstances leading up to this meeting. For some of you, much of what you will hear today will be new. And it is likely to stretch your credulity. Let me come directly to the point.

Each of you will be familiar with the successes we have experienced with the Predator unmanned drones. Most of these aircraft were piloted by former military men who were retrained in the techniques for maneuvering pilotless planes from remote locations.

Our second generation of unmanned drones, the Reaper models, were substantially more sophisticated. They were faster and more maneuverable, and they had longer range, greater payload capacity and commanded greater firepower. In short, the second generation more closely resembled the type of fighter aircraft all of you have flown in the past. In some cases, the capacity of these new planes exceeds that of anything you have flown in the past.

And as we speak, work is in progress on the next generation of unmanned planes that will represent a substantial advance over what we are flying today.

Nothing I have said should be, in any respect, a surprise to any of you. We are well accustomed to continuous progress and continuous advances in every area of technology, including those which apply to the military.

But these new developments have presented—perhaps I should say are presenting—us with a new type of challenge.

Our experience with the sophisticated Reaper drones has shown us that the most capable operators—I will not call them pilots—the most capable operators of these drones are not necessarily former military aviators. No. The best drone pilots don't necessarily come from the cockpits of our fighter aircraft. They come from the flying fields of our children; from the game players and computer operators of our leisured youth.

The best operators of drones, I repeat, are not experienced fighter pilots. They are young men, and, in a few cases, women, who have grown up flying virtual aircraft on flight simulators. In many cases these simulators were developed for use by hobbyists for recreational flying of radio controlled aircraft.

These conclusions are not subject to interpretation or question. Results have been verified by carefully designed experiments conducted by Air Force scientists and engineers. The results are conclusive every time an experiment is performed.

Our fighter pilots who have been involved in these tests have admitted, unequivocally, that they have been bested by, in many cases, mere children."

The last sentence provoked a response from most of the participants signaled by throat clearing, chair shuffling and changes in facial expressions. No one challenged the assertion immediately, but in the discussions that followed it was clear that most of the audience believed that experienced pilots would never make poorer controllers for drone aircraft than selected young men with no actual cockpit training.

The conference had adjourned for the day—to be resumed tomorrow—and General Bloodsworth had invited his long time personal friend, General Harley "Hawk" Wheeler to join him for drinks and dinner. In a private lounge at the Officers Club they were testing their knowledge of some of the pricier types of single-malt Scots whiskey, and practicing a brand of masculine one-upsmanship that had characterized their friendship over four decades. "It's Scots, not Scotch," Wheeler had said earlier.

In these games a certain amount of lying was permissible, even desirable, and Hawk Wheeler had just finished telling Bloodsworth about visiting the only distillery where this particular brand was produced. It was, Hawk had complained, in one of the smaller islands in the Orkneys. Hawk had been laying it on pretty heavy.

"Christ almighty, Hawk. You've gone too, far this time. You got me once before with that preposterous yarn about the Irish whiskey that was produced at a place in the north called the Butt of Lewis. But I'm not gonna be taken twice by your bullshit. Tell me that you could only get to this distillery by riding donkeys up the hill. Or maybe one of those Scottish cattle with the huge horns. Or maybe an imported yak. My god! I know that some of these small places are really located in some out-of-the-way spots. But, my god, General...."

"Eighty per cent of what I just told you is actually true."

"Yes, you bastard. That's why I bit in the past."

"Nah. That's not why. You're just gullible."

"You should have been a stand-up comic. Missed your calling."

"Just like today. Somebody's got you believing that fighter pilots may become obsolete."

"Whoa! Wait a minute. Is that what you got out of today's session?"

"What did you think I'd come away with?"

"I'm disappointed that I didn't do a better job of explaining the situation."

The whiskey in both their glasses was gone and Bloodsworth held up two fingers to signal across the room to the bartender.

"One more, and then we'll head for dinner. I've got a surprise for you. I seem to remember that you liked soft shell crabs. Getting much harder to find good ones."

"Look," Bloodsworth said, "I don't want us to talk business while we're eating. So just let me remind you of a couple of things you already know."

"Here it comes. The sales pitch."

"Just listen, and cut the malarkey. First, you know that most of the Reaper pilots in Afghanistan are not fighter pilots. And those who are fighter pilots are measurably less skilled than the kids who are at the controls.

Second, drones are cheaper to build, arm, maintain, and fly than conventional fighters. And they are rapidly approaching them in performance. The technology will probably enable most any ship to be converted to a drone, and flown from a ground console.

Third point. The lion's share of components in our current inventory of RC planes—and even some components in military drones—are manufactured in China. Even those that are made in USA could be obtained from China if Congress didn't intervene. It follows that China could catch us in drone production very quickly. Hawk...are you sticking with me?"

"Go ahead. Make your next point. I'm listening carefully."

"The next fact that we need to fit into the equation is that kids can fly these things from consoles—with zero feedback except through their eyeballs. In the cockpit, pilots are frequently at or near the threshold of sensory overload. Engine noise, vibrations, g-forces, awareness of all the shit we have to wear. G-suits, helmets, flotation gear. Heat from the sun, glare, a hundred things are impinging on all our own sensors. Shit, I don't have to tell you. You've been shot at. But with drones, the controllers are in an air-conditioned space. Pull any maneuver and if the wings don't come off, you're home free. Feel nothing. There is no feedback. None."

"OK! Conceded. Nothing to tug on your ass. So what's your point?"

"Point is that the controller thinks only of the maneuvers he wants to make with the ship. He doesn't even have to turn his head to look left or right. All six views are right there. At his disposal."

"So?"

"Reality becomes unreal."

"Maybe I shouldn't be sipping this third scotch. I still don't follow."

"Everything we learn in the cockpit is intended to prepare us to fight with a human adversary. It's dangerous, uncomfortable and sometimes scary as hell. But when it comes time to pull the trigger; or launch, we're trained to take out our opponent because we know it's him or us."

"Christ, Warren. You're making me feel stupid. Tell me what's your point."

"The young men we have flying these planes haven't been trained or conditioned to be killers. We ask them to take out a target, and there is no risk or danger to them. They can drop six 500-pound bombs on a village and take out 20 people, and five minutes later their bird is back at its designated base. And they're eating ice cream. It's not real for them. It's a big game. But they know, they learn, they get confirmation of what they have done. And they aren't prepared for it."

"When are we scheduled to eat? I'm hungry."

"Last year we had three Reaper controllers commit suicide. And eleven more have requested reassignment. Nobody anticipated this."

"OK. Now I'm listening."

True to his earlier word, General Warren Bloodsworth didn't climb atop his soapbox during the meal; which was excellent. But after dinner they both indulged in a generous snifter of brandy. Don't worry. Neither man was driving. While they were sniffing their drinks and allowing their crabs to settle, Bloodsworth relapsed and picked up where he had left off.

"Unmanned flight is coming. Like it or not. It's cheaper eight ways from Sunday. In addition, it's well suited to the type of unsymmetrical fighting we're seeing these days. Mark my words, Hawk. In five years from now every service will be flying drones. The Navy will be flying them from carriers, and from fast attack ships. The Coast Guard will be flying drone helicopters to drop life saving gear to people in the water, or aboard distressed vessels. Try to imagine what the beach landings of WW II would have been like with drones like Reaper. Guys sitting in England could have taken out most of the German's long range guns—and bunkers. The world has changed; and it's still changing. Goddamit, Hawk, I need you to get on board with me. We need to be on the leading edge of unmanned flight. Right now, we are, but that could change quickly."

"OK, General. I've listened. And I'm open-minded. Now tell me about what you've been doing for fun. If you can still remember what fun is."

"You know—we've had to imagine the war here, and we have imagined that it was being fought by aging men like ourselves. We had forgotten that wars were fought by babies. When I saw those freshly shaved faces, it was a shock. 'My God, my God—' I said to myself, 'It's the Children's Crusade.' "

From "Slaughterhouse Five"
Kurt Vonnegut

CHAPTER 13
Jawboning

General Bloodsworth had called several colleagues to join him for lunch in his conference room. He had made arrangements for lunch to be brought in and he had invited two of his naval colleagues, Admirals Frank Daugherty and Thomas Perry. In addition he had asked Marine Corps Brigadier Avery Harrington to sit in. Harrington had brought along his boss, General Tomas Rodriguez. The agenda? An exchange of information they might find interesting, with the expectation that more discussion might follow. An information exchange. That's all he had communicated. They all knew each other. They all showed up.

The meeting was about drones, about the potential that drones offered for to the American military, about the risk of delaying development for too long, about the potential for any industrialized nation to catch up rapidly, about the threat from terrorist organizations having access to this technology. But Bloodsworth tried to be careful. He didn't want to seem like he was selling. He wanted to seem like a dispassionate observer. *We have a problem here, guys. Whaddya think we ought to be doing.* He wanted them to feel some ownership. The general was no dummy. He knew he could never sell this problem as an Air Force problem, It had to be viewed as a national problem; one which could be presented in closed testimony before the Senate Armed Forces Committee by a multi-service group, and he didn't want to seem like the recruiting sergeant.

Nevertheless...

The presentation was compelling. It began with some of the spectacular successes enjoyed by the Predator. Then, the Reaper was shown as the next generation. Its initial applications were impressive and most of the group had not viewed this footage before; even if they had heard of it. Still—a picture was worth ten thousand words. And the views from Reaper's cockpit were impressively clear and unambiguous. Targets seemed to vaporize.

Then the footage switched to views taken inside the command modules, to images of the youthful controllers maneuvering their aircraft to deliver the final strikes. There were several sequences, clearly being taken from different locations. The implicit message was clear, if unstated. These vehicles of death are being flown by youth. One might almost say, by children. Bloodsworth was determined not to touch that aspect with a ten-foot pole. It was left unstated; as an exercise for the viewer.

Near the end of the presentation, footage consisted of scenes shot at amateur flying fields, of helicopters in inverted flight, performing a variety of maneuvers that caused one Marine general to sit up in his chair.

At the end of the meeting as the lights came up, Bloodsworth stood before the group—silent—waiting for some reaction from his audience.

Rodriquez, the Marine Corps general, was the first to speak. "Do you really believe that drone helicopters will be able to perform the maneuvers we were witnessing at the end?"

"They're doing it now. Talk to me after this meeting. I'll tell you where the flights are being conducted. Go see for yourself. Look, gents. All of you in this room are my friends. That's why I have called you together. Because you all know me. I have a message to deliver. But unlike Billy Mitchell who stuck his neck out to get it chopped off, I'm a career man. Air Force. Born and bred. I want to do my duty but I don't want to be a hero if that means telling everyone upstream that they're a bunch of dumb bastards. I'm no Billy Mitchell.

"If Billy had never been born, we'd still have tactical and strategic bomber squadrons. He just stepped up the clock. That was courage. An attribute we are paid to encourage.

"You've seen the footage. You have formed an impression of what these vehicles are capable of performing. You can make informed decisions. But there is one late breaking piece of information that couldn't be included in this presentation."

He waited for the unspoken question to be formulated in their minds.

"China is already hard at work on unmanned aircraft."

He paused again, waiting for it to sink in.

"China already supplies most of the servomechanisms and small scale aircraft used by nearly every hobby flyer in the U.S."

The message was still penetrating several centimeters of American bone.

Finally, the Marine Corps general spoke up. "Surely full scale helicopters can't perform the maneuvers of shown by these hobbyists."

"They can, General. They are. You might wonder why. But they are doing it. Your sons and daughters." He paused. "Also the Chinese."

Years ago, Admiral Daugherty had been the CO of the carrier that was, at the time, the queen of the Navy's fleet. In many ways it was the high point of his long career. Some of his fondest memories were of hours on the bridge of the world's most formidable warship—an experience that placed him, even though his name was unknown to most Americans, in the pantheon with Alexander, Timur, Genghis Khan and Eisenhower. Lord of the Universe. He had been seated in—as Robert Service had once described it—*the house of high control.* For his brief moment he had *regulated the spheres.* And things had been calm on his watch.

The admiral had a question. But it was not a question he wanted to ask. He wanted to squeeze out an answer without having to frame his question. "A lot of the world's tensions are ameliorated because we can take off from the deck of a carrier."

This was stated with a large degree of legitimate pride, and with a certain amount of smugness that could not be concealed.

Bloodsworth smiled. It was like he had a straight man. "Thank you Admiral Daugherty. A perceptive observation." He paused.

"Pilotless helicopters can take off from the deck of a carrier."

"Helicopters,"—he paused again, for dramatic effect—"and fighter aircraft."

There was a stir, signifying skepticism, perhaps even a degree of incredulity, in the room.

"We were not able to include all of the most recent developments in this video. Nevertheless, anything that human pilots can perform in the cockpit, their counterparts can perform in pilotless aircraft... operated remotely. This may well be the future of aerial warfare. You, gentlemen, may have been vouchsafed a view of the future, and you might well be judged on your reaction to what you have seen here today."

"The reference paper quickly spawned seven "integrated product teams" to conduct additional analysis, and these teams in turn gave birth to further spin-offs. In no time there were no less than fifty study teams, "breeding like drunken muskrats," according to one official, in many cases duplicating one another's work. Rumsfeld's instructions were expressed vaguely enough to allow special interests to use them for massive raids on the taxpayer's wallet. A team with strong naval attachments, for example, used a clause in the reference paper calling for forces stationed overseas to be able to defeat the enemy with minimal reinforcement to urge that the navy's fleet of aircraft carriers (each of which cost roughly $4.5 billion without planes or escorts) be tripled to thirty-four."

Rumsfeld, His Rise, Fall, and Catastrophic Legacy
Andrew Cockburn

CHAPTER 14
An Offer That's Hard to Refuse

The call caught him off guard. Walt had not spoken to Paul Chapman since he and Tara had gone to dinner with him in a Washington restaurant. At that last meeting Walt had tried to make it clear that he didn't want to be involved in any of the covert activities cooked up by Chapman's agency. He thought he had made it clear that he had paid his dues. "No more calls," he had said.

And now, here was Chapman again. On the phone. And he had to be polite. "How have you been feeling, Paul? No more ticker problems?"

"Fine, thanks. Nope. I had a clean bill just two weeks ago. I don't have to go back for six months. I am cutting back on the scotch though—and that can't be good for long term health."

"You never did hit it too hard, Paul. Don't let the doctors *make* you sick," Walt said with a laugh.

"Look, Walt. Something has come up, and it would be very helpful if you could come down to Washington for a few days. I know you told me not to call you again. But this request didn't come from me. In fact, it originated a couple of levels higher up." Chapman hesitated, then continued.

"From another branch of government. I was surprised to learn that they wanted to talk to you. I still don't know were they learned your name," he lied. "It seems that your reputation has been spread around."

"My reputation? What reputation? C'mon, Paul. You don't have to blow smoke up my ass."

"This is on the level, Walt. Look. We go way back. And, yes, I admit to having planted Katya with a view toward using some of your expertise in Central Asia, but honest, this request wasn't initiated by me. And I'm not going to talk about this on the phone."

"Well, Paul, I suggest you just tell these mysterious big shots that I'm not available any more. I'm retired."

"Only, they know that it's not true. And these are not people you can say *no* to. They're kinda like an *integrated product team*. They don't take no for an answer. Really. I don't think you have an option."

"Excuse me, Paul. Am I hearing correctly? No option? Excuse me? Operator? Operator? I'm trying to get the USA."

"I can understand that you might be pissed. I'd be angry, too. If I didn't understand what was at stake. But once you understand—and I know the way you work, Walt—once you understand, you'll do the right thing. For the country, and for your own conscience. I know how you work when the chips are down, Walt. So, stop struggling and come down for a listen before you decide to go to the mattresses."

"Goddammit, Paul, why won't you...."

"Bring Tara. You can make it into a fun weekend. We'll put you up in a nice place in Georgetown and you can take her to see the sights after you've heard the pitch these guys want to give you. Car and driver at your disposal."

"So if you're not involved, how come you're making the call for them? Speak for yourself, John Alden."

"Well, Priscilla, they thought you might be a tough nut to crack, and they knew that I had been successful before, so they pulled me in on the periphery. I know a little. But I don't know everything."

"Here's what you probably don't know, Paul. These guys most likely came after me for some activity that has to do with Central Asia. With some of the "stans." Or maybe even Turkey. But what they don't know is that for the past eighteen months I've been changing my focus. I'm looking at China now. They need to get another fall guy to carry their bags."

But this time, Paul Chapman's next words would ring in his ears long after their conversation was done.

"Trust me, Walt. These guys know about you and China."

There was a long pause while this sank in. Chapman could almost hear him thinking.

Walt mind was racing through a gamut of scenarios and none of them were to his liking. *These bastards have been spying on me again. When will this stuff ever end?* He was trying to think if anyone in his classes could have been planted—the way that Katya had been sent in as a grad student. But although nobody stood out immediately, that meant nothing. He knew that he was subject to the Law of Inadequate Paranoia. *Those bastards.*

"So give me a date, my friend. A date and time. I'll have a limo and driver there whenever you say. The people who want to talk to you meet three days a week, Mondays, Wednesdays and Fridays. They'll talk to you on the day that's most convenient for you. Probably not more than three hours. Count on half a day. You don't need to bring anything. Just your own smiling self. I'm hoping you'll bring Tara. And though I know that you will probably be a grumpy SOB for most of the time, I'm actually looking forward to seeing your gorgeous lady friend once more. Give Tara my best, Walt. I'll call again. After six p.m. on Sunday. Unless you tell me otherwise. Please Walt, come up with a date for me. Otherwise, the next call will be from someone who you probably won't know."

That night as they were preparing for bed, Tara kneeled behind him and rubbed his shoulders as he was unstrapping his prosthesis.

"You were kinda quiet tonight," she said. "Like you have something on your mind. Am I reading it right?"

"Pretty much on the mark. Something unexpected has come up. And I don't know what to do about it."

"Is it something we can talk about? It's not to do with Flo is it?" Her forehead wrinkled.

"No, no. Nothing like that," he said. "We can talk about it. You'll be involved as much as I will."

Tara sat up straight in bed, propped her pillow against the headboard and drew up her knees almost under her chin. He had her full attention.

"You remember Paul Chapman?"

"Of course." She hadn't seen Chapman since that time in Washington when they had dined together after she and Walt had returned from Central Asia. But she didn't know if Walt had spoken to Paul in the intervening months.

"You may remember that I asked him not to call me again."

"Um, yeah. You were pretty emphatic as I recall."

"He's called again. Wants me to come—us to come—to Washington to discuss some other activity those guys are cooking up. I said no. But he is insisting, and says the request didn't originate with him. Hinted that it's from fairly high up. Whatever the hell that means. But how can that be? It's not like anything we did was earthshaking."

"Could it have anything to do with our plans for China?"

"That's what I've been wondering about. That must be it. But how could they know what we're planning? Our plans haven't exactly been in the news."

"Duh!" Tara laughed. "And you the professor! Do I remember that we each have travel visas for China, Kazakhstan and Russia? Think anybody in government might know about that?"

"Shit!"

"And what about your interview?"

"Shit! Shit! Yeah, well, apparently a lot of people know. I think we'll just have to face into this. Make a trip down to Washington and see what they have in mind. "

"Me, too?" she said, clapping her hands like a child. "Goody. Maybe you can rent a car and take me over to see Mount Vernon."

"I don't want to get involved in any of their bullshit schemes, Tara. No kidding. I want out."

"I know. I know. But don't start fretting before you know what they want. Anyway, whatever they want, you can deliver. You know that."

"I'm glad you're so confident. OK. If you're with me, I'll call Chapman and set it up. I'll make everything contingent on getting you to Mount Vernon. C'ome on. Turn out the light. Let's go to sleep. "

"I'll turn out the light. But you're not going to sleep."

PART 2.
GOVERNMENTS AT WORK

"The Navy sees the UCAS (unmanned combat air system) in the vein of the EA-18G Growler and the E-2B Hawkeye, as a specialized support plane flying intelligence, surveillance and reconnaissance missions, says Work. Once naval aviators are convinced that the UCAS can operate safely on a carrier, he believes the Navy will want to add long-range capabilities to its surveillance function.

For example, UCAS could be loaded with advanced medium range air-to-air missiles and fly in a persistent orbit to hit targets, and conduct close air support and interdiction operations."

"Navy Still Years Away From Deploying Attack Drones..."
www.nationaldefensemagazine.org
September 2007

CHAPTER 15
China's UAV Advocates

Major Ju was not an aeronautical engineer, but he was a competent pilot of fighter aircraft. He had not been trained as a helicopter pilot. For this reason, his selection to head up the PLAAF's program to demonstrate an unmanned helicopter came as a surprise to him. Actually, he was the hand-picked choice of General Zheng.

For a time Ju considered the possibility of applying himself to learn how to fly helicopters, but he realized that it would take a while for him to gain the same level of proficiency that he had with fighters. The more he thought about it, the more puzzling it became. Finally, he accepted the fact that his superiors had tapped him for the job because of his long-standing advocacy for unmanned flight.

That was only one of the factors that had led to his selection. Over the years of his service it had become clear that the major was good with details, good with people and he had a finely developed sense of judgment that made him an excellent manager of complex, poorly-defined projects.

It was clear to him from the outset that the Baby Dragon program was simply a low-budget demonstration of the potential for unmanned flight. His exposure to various committees in Beijing had convinced him that there was considerable resistance to unmanned flight at higher levels in the PLAAF. The old generals and colonels at the top were reluctant to peer into the future. There were a few visionaries—men like General Zheng, who had traveled widely and who stayed in touch with the latest developments in other countries.

The most exciting work was going on in the U.S., but there were also a number of significant developments coming from other countries—notably Russia, France, England, Germany and Israel. Italy was also involved. In particular, the U.S. was pushing to extend their stealth technology into un-manned flight and they were making good progress.

This was the area where Major Ju felt that he had most to offer. But for the time being, his first job was to demonstrate what unmanned helicopters could do in a battlefield situation.

Ju's team included a handful of senior Russian consultants and a mixed bag of Chinese engineers, technicians, mechanics and the infrastructure to support them in the field. All told, the hardworking major was directing the efforts of just over 400 people.

At meetings back in Beijing, a committee of senior PLAAF officers established criteria for Ju's demonstration program. The modified Kamov was to be given the code name Baby Dragon.

First of all, it was agreed that the primary task would be to modify several helicopters for unmanned flight. This would consist of extensive modifications to control systems through the addition of servomotors, sensors and computer controls. The platforms to be modified would be a single model of the Kamov K-26 helicopter, a squat adaptation of an earlier design used for anti-submarine warfare in the Cold War era. The KA-26 was a later model, used chiefly in rescue work and for civilian purposes; agriculture and forestry. It had two three-bladed contra-rotating propellers and a roomy interior that was compatible with the modifications made by Major Ju's team.

Six Kamovs were purchased from Russia for this demonstration. All were modified in China to be compatible with remote control from the ground. Each ship had to demonstrate the ability to take off, fly a predetermined round trip of at least 500 kilometers and land safely, all directed by an operator on the ground.

After demonstrating Frankenstein could get up and walk around the block, Phase II would demonstrate that these ships could function as gun platforms. Rocket pods would be installed in locations once used for carrying stretchers. The Kamovs would fly to a distant target site, visually inspect a designated target at a given GPS location, hover until a confirming order was received and then fire their rockets at the target. This demonstration was intended to show the UAV's utility as a weapons platform.

The third phase of the program was intended to confirm that the Kamov's on-board systems would allow the remote operator to detect a hostile enemy attacker in the air and to take appropriate evasive action. Initially, the Kamovs would not be provided with offensive weapons against an aerial attacker, but they should be capable of a wide range of evasive maneuvers. Cameras on the manned attackers should indicate whether evasive actions were successful. It was expected that the range of maneuvers available to an unmanned helicopter would be greater that those available to a piloted ship.

After that, assuming that all tests were accomplished successfully, an investigative review board of senior PLAAF officers would evaluate program results and determine how to proceed with further UAV development.

The helicopter program progressed rapidly with few setbacks. Results from the demonstration flights met all criteria for success and the project moved into another phase that was classified and transferred to another province. Major Ju's role had been a key factor in keeping things moving and, in recognition of his success, he was promised reassignment to a program involving jet-powered fighter drones.

The fighters were modified at another site but field test responsibility was assigned to the major at his desert test site location.

"Robotic air vehicles are beginning to replace some of the Air Force manned combat aircraft. Soon, they will be handling a major share of the service strike mission. The first steps in this transition already have been taken in the field of fighter-class aircraft. Classified projects now in development seem sure to cut into the manned medium and heavy bomber roles as well."

UAVs with Bite
Air Force Magazine Online, January 7, 2007
John A. Tirpak, Executive Editor
From the Internet

CHAPTER 16

Yorktown, Virginia

General Warren Bloodsworth was married to a woman who came from an old Virginia family. When she learned that her husband was being posted to a high level, secret job at Langley Field, she went to work calling several of her female friends who were active in FFV and ended up in communication with one of the high-end real estate brokers on the peninsula. She was interested in a suitable apartment, condo, or private house in Yorktown; provided, of course, that it met two criteria. It had to have a view of the York River, and it had to be sufficiently large and comfortable to impress ladies of First Families of Virginia, whom she intended to invite just as soon as she could move in and get her hands on a roster of members.

She was a persistent worker and within sixty days the general was in comfortable digs from whose picture window Lord Cornwallis could have planned the exodus he should have made if he had been smarter—and moved faster.

The general was content to sit back and let Sheila Bloodsworth do the work. He had his sphere of activity. She had hers. Once they were settled in to the comfortable condominium, he was not averse to inviting his colleagues over for a weekend.

The first weekend guest to visit the Bloodsworths were his long-time pal, Hawk Wheeler and his wife Nancy. The Wheelers had driven down from Alexandria. Sheila had taken Nancy for a tour of the battlefield at Yorktown, and they had told the two men to fix lunch for themselves.

Bloodsworth and Hawk Wheeler were content to drink their lunch. General Bloodsworth had gone to the trouble of purchasing an unusually expensive bottle of single-malt scotch whiskey, knowing that Hawk considered himself a connoisseur of fine scotch.

The two friends were stretched comfortably on the big sofa that faced out onto the famed York River.

"I know that sometime this weekend you'll start trying to sell me again. I can feel the tension building in you."

"Fuck you, Hawk. You're not as smart as you think you are."

"I know one thing for sure, Warren old pal. I am not as smart as you think *you* are."

Bloodsworth laughed. "You got that one right. One point for you. But goddam, Hawk. You can really be obstinate."

"I don't believe, nor am I likely to ever believe, that the day of the combat pilot is over. That fighter pilots are going the way of buggy whips and carriages. No. I don't believe that."

"Have you ever been out to Creech?"

"Of course. You know that. I was out for two years during the eighties. We were...."

"No, not in the past. Have you been out recently. Since the Predator? Since Reaper?"

"No, Warren. There's been no reason for me to go. I'm up on the Predator. I was briefed just last week. I know that current plans call for there to be fifteen Predator Squadrons in service by 2010."

"Goddammit, Hawk. Are you listening to me at all? The fucking Predator, right now, is obsolete. In three years from now we'll have fifteen squadrons flying an obsolete drone. Kids will be flying more sophisticated aircraft in their backyards."

"Don't get carried away, Warren."

"Look, the Reaper is already operational and it's faster, higher, longer range, longer dwell and ten times more lethal than Predator. And its replacement is already in development. The Navy has got it figured out that drones can take off from carrier decks and they're working like blazes to catch up. It's no telling what the Russians or the Chinese are doing. France has a super drone in the works. My god, when they come out with it, they'll probably sell it to the highest bidder."

"Are we gonna watch a ball game today?"

Warren could see that Hawk was determined to resist any overture he proposed. "How about we go for a ride after we catch some lunch?" Bloodsworth said. "There's an air show in Hampton and I think you might enjoy it. They'll have an interesting collection of scale models of old warbirds; Fokkers, Nieuports, Camels and one of my favorites, the Pfalz, And even some old multi-engines. Old bombers. Including some models that Germany used to bomb England."

"I'm up for that. We can stop by Langley and eat at the OC. OK?"

Hawk Wheeler had to admit that the hobbyist's air show was more interesting than he had expected. The Hampton flying field was located near a small pond, and some of the remote control aircraft were seaplanes; including some fascinating old warbirds. Many of them were unusual designs that he hadn't thought about for decades. One of the ships that fascinated him was an old German Hansa-Brandenberg float-plane that had an interesting configuration with a retractable pontoon.

He was intrigued by the aerobatic maneuvers performed by the flyers. While all ages were represented, some of the flyers were just kids, a few barely more than twelve years old. He had to admit that they were good. Near the end of the program a young boy, perhaps fourteen or fifteen, put his aerobatic plane through a series of improvised maneuvers that were challenging to follow. As the young controller pushed his plane off the field, Hawk met him behind the flight line.

"That was an interesting set of maneuvers you made up, son. What made you think of stringing them together like that?"

"That was a programmed routine sir. I was practicing for a meet next month in South Carolina," the youth responded.

"You're telling me that you were following a set series of maneuvers?"

"Yes sir. That last sequence was the Dixie Death. It's one I'll have to do next month."

"You weren't just hacking around?"

"Dixie Death, sir. I've pretty much got it down pat if there's not much wind. In a little cross breeze—like today—it's a bit more difficult. That why I ended my routine with it. Just for practice. Toward the end I was starting to drift out of the box."

"Wait, son. Hold up a sec. You mean to tell me that you can repeat that exact maneuver? Exactly like you just did it?"

"It's just Dixie Death, sir. No big deal. Like I said, it's kinda tricky in a cross wind, but, yes sir, I've got it down pretty well."

"Son, let me...are you here with your parents? Let me walk back with you." General Bloodsworth joined his pal as Hawk and the lad were taking the plane back to its assigned station behind the flight line. The two Air Force officers, inconspicuous in mufti, introduced themselves to the boy's father and Hawk expressed an interest in seeing the boy fly his plane through the same series of maneuvers again.

"I'm willing to stick around until this event is over, if it wouldn't inconvenience you too much," Hawk offered, with a glance at his friend who was technically his host. "I was fascinated by that last series of maneuvers," he said.

"Oh yeah. Dixie Death. He's been practicing six or seven of those programmed maneuvers until I'm sick to death of them," the father said. "Yeah, we can stick around. He likes the attention. I think that's why a lot of the kids work so hard to get their skills up. But we don't have to wait until the end of this meet. There's another flying field just over to the right, past those bleachers. We can fly off the athletic field if you like. They let us use it when they aren't practicing."

The boy and his father drove over in their van with the plane. Hawk and Bloodsworth walked the short distance. The boy took off and put the plane through the maneuver he had described as Dixie Death. Bloodsworth had not seen his original flight. The sequence of maneuvers included three loops, followed by three rolls, all implemented during a steady climb. At the end of the third roll, the plane nosed down, performed three spins, pulled out just in time, and landed. The young pilot taxied the ship back to the assembled quartet.

"And you can do that again?" Hawk said, incredulous.

"Yes sir. The breeze has pretty much died."

"Would you mind?"

The engine revved and the plane turned to repeat the maneuvers that had two Air Force generals watching with intense interest.

Back at the Yorktown condo, the two generals found that their ladies had still not returned from their outing. "We're gonna have to take these girls out to dinner. There's not much chance they'll want to fix anything after a day of roving around."

"Not to worry, Hawk. I know a great seafood place not more than thirty or forty minutes away. I think Nancy will like it, and I know you will. In fact, I think you've been there before." Their plans for dinner came together within minutes.

While Warren Bloodsworth was drizzling scotch that cost over fifty dollars a liter over a couple of ice cubes, General Hawk Wheeler finally gave him the OK he had been seeking for weeks.

"That kid today was impressive."

"Thousands just like him. You ready to go?"

"And that kind of flying can be extended to almost any fighter jet?"

"Pretty much, yep. We're doing it now."

"OK, you persistent bastard. You probably engineered this whole afternoon. OK. Tell me how I can help."

Bloodsworth was chuckling. "You and Nancy like planked shad? Damn, Hawk, I've got to get you back out to Creech."

"WASHINGTON—Airport security screeners stepped up scrutiny of remote-controlled toys Monday after authorities said terrorists could use them to detonate bombs. 'Credible specific information' indicates that terrorists are looking at using remote devices that can trigger an explosive, the Transportation Security Administration (TSA) said in a statement."

Remote-control toys latest TSA worry
Thomas Frank
USA Today, October 2, 2007

CHAPTER 17
Hatching the Dragon's Egg

At the eastern end of China's Taklamakan Desert, the oasis town of Dunhuang was once an important decision point for merchants traveling the Silk Road. From here, travelers headed west must decide whether to skirt the northern or southern fringes of the Taklamakan.

Today, thousands of tourists come to visit the famous Mogao Caves, a repository of ancient Buddhist paintings and art objects. The city's prosperity is linked to tourism and it has a commercial airport. In a very real sense it is still the end of the line. A few miles to the west, the endless dunes begin. A few ancient ruins thrust through the sand in places but even the tourists mounted on camels rarely venture deep into the Taklamakan.

Dunhuang's domestic airport was a factor in its selection by Major Ju's team as a test site for their unmanned helicopter tests. True, the town's constantly changing tourist population was a factor that argued against its selection, but in a sense this could become an advantage. Any interest shown by outsiders in activities conducted by PLAAF would stick out like a sore thumb and could be dealt with immediately. Additionally, the test site would be located miles from the town, deep in the desert.

The major had insisted that all of his detachment be exempt from wearing military uniforms while in Dunhuang. The plan put together by his office called for a self-contained facility, initially comprised of 75-80 engineers, mechanics and technicians, closely guarded but unfenced. Part of the contingent would be quartered in Dunhuang, and would make arrangements to be fed by local establishments. A normal duty cycle would call for soldiers to alternate their time between duties at the test site and at facilities in the city. The focus of their efforts would be to conduct a series of tests, including daily flights of varying duration, in every season of the year. The modifications to the Kamov helicopters selected for initial evaluation would be performed by teams composed of Russians and Chinese.

This was likely to prove a difficult assignment, and was recognized, as such, by senior PLAAF officers. The idea was not only to prove capabilities but to identify and highlight specific problems and deficiencies.

The control stations were designed to fit within standardized short-length shipping containers, modified internally, but maintaining external dimensions. Heating and air-conditioning were essential; not just for operators, but for the reliable performance of on-board equipment. Weather extremes in the Taklamakan were punishing.

Unmanned helicopters had been test flown in several configurations. It was clear to Major Ju from the beginning that these tests were only precursors to more sophisticated fighter aircraft, probably with jet engines. It was the implied promise of this work that motivated the major to take the assignment.

He envisioned that China first original production model would be a unique Chinese design, conceived after a careful study of the performance specifications for both the USAF Predator and Reaper and every other scrap of intelligence they could collect. In his imagination, the Chinese model might be intermediate in size to these two planes, currently operational, but would be superior in performance. In particular, it would be superior in speed, maneuverability, range, payload and firepower. The clearly stated goal was to have, from the beginning of any confrontation, a capability that was greater than that possessed by the USAF. If there was to be a variable, it would have to be the skill of operators. PLAAF did not intend to be inferior in weaponry. Or even at parity.

Unlike the US planes that had long, straight wings with no exaggerated dihedral, the Dragon's wings would be swept, and its top speed was 450 mph. The configuration was selected by Chinese engineers with assistance from a select team of Russian aeronautical designers working under tight security.

The Dragon's payload capacity would also be intermediate to the two US planes. She would carry just over 2400 pounds of weaponry. But her range would exceed that of the American Reaper. The exact range and nominal time on station were classified, but they were generally believed to be in the vicinity of 25-40 percent greater than Reaper.

An upgraded version of Reaper already existed on the drawing boards, but for the time being, no new hardware was being built in China. Major Ju dreamed that he would be assigned to this first program. It was the promise of this reassignment that made him drive himself.

Meanwhile, the team would also evaluate a remote-controlled helicopter design capable of carrying a variety of payloads. This next model was called a weapons platform named Taifu—Typhoon. In addition to the team of

PLAAF personnel who would be reassigned to the Dunhuang tests, Major Ju's advance team provided additional accommodations for up to twenty Russian aeronautical engineers who would visit the site from time to time. And for another thirty Chinese civilians who were, at the time, unidentified.

Major Ju was one of only a handful of people who knew the identity of these civilians, several of them just boys. They were selected after consultation with selected senior managers of eight of China's largest manufacturers of recreational aircraft, and the engines that powered them. They were the young men who tested the equipment that ended up in European and American hobby shops.

"...*The Gutless Wonder*. It was about a robot who had bad breath, who became popular after his halitosis was cured. But what made the story remarkable, since it was written in 1932, was that it predicted the widespread use of burning jellied gasoline on human beings.

It was dropped on them from airplanes. Robots did the dropping. They had no conscience, and no circuits which would allow them to imagine what was happening to the people on the ground."

From "Slaughterhouse Five"
Kurt Vonnegut

CHAPTER 18
Setting Expectations

The guiding force at Air Combat Command (ACC) was its commanding officer, Lieutenant General James Anson Maitland—"Jam" to his long time friends. Unlike many of his cohorts whose ascents to star rank were based on early exploits as fighter pilots, Jam rose to the top after a beginning in the biggest planes in the Air Force's inventory.

The general had won his spurs flying aerial tankers. Fighters over Vietnam relied on Jam and others like him to refuel in the air. As a result, his name and reputation was well known to a generation of fighter pilots.

Later in his career he championed the building and acquisition of huge airlifters, such as the Hercules and the generation planned as its replacement. For most of his flying career, Maitland had flown large cargo planes, beginning with his early experiences at North Carolina's Pope Air Force Base. He had participated in many drops of airborne infantry and had been flying with the 101st Airborne Division out of Fort Bragg when a plane in his squadron, a C-114, lost an engine and descended through a stick of falling paratroopers, cutting several of them out of their chutes. That was an ugly episode in his long career. He had seen, and survived, many problems that fighter pilots are unlikely to encounter.

Partly as a result of his experiences, but also as a consequence of his personality, Jam Maitland was a guy who spent a lot of time thinking about the future. For several years now he had been speculating and reading and studying about the future of aerial warfare, and he had concluded that there was a very important role to be played by drones, flown from the ground; UAVs.

The generation of young men and women who grew up playing computer games could provide a substantial talent pool to be tapped by the Air Force. One of the key roles for the Air Force was to recognize the need for this talent and to develop programs to recognize, reward and train young people in the skills this branch would require.

Maitland was no dummy. He didn't rise to three stars in the Air Force without some well-developed political skills, and he would have made a great congressman if he had chosen that path. But the Air Force was his life, and he had a vision for the future. There were not many people with whom he could discuss his concepts.

One of the people was, interestingly, a civilian. More interesting, this civilian was a woman. There were several civilian members of the staff at Langley's ACC Headquarters complex, and his highest ranking civilian was Dr. W. A. Kaminsky. Wanda Kaminsky had her PhD in Political Science from UCLA. Like a few other females in high government offices, Wanda Kaminsky spoke Russian. She was also competent in French and she had lived in France for three years. Currently in her mid-fifties, Wanda could easily be taken for an attractive woman several years younger. She had been at Langley for over four years before Maitland was assigned to the command of ACC. His wife, Clara, had died three years earlier from leukemia, and he was, despite his rank, prestige and rugged good looks, starving for female companionship. And he was temperamentally unsuited for one-night stands. His wife, a sweetheart from his college days, had been an exceptional woman, one he knew would be hard to replace.

He was slow to warm up to Wanda Kaminsky whose sharp intellect scared the pants off ninety percent of the men she contacted daily in her work for the government. The males with sufficient egos to approach her were usually too immature to capture her interest.

She and her boss circled around each other like cautious wolves for over a year. By the time they were on a first name basis, each had done enough research on the other to fill a couple of notebooks. Jam knew that she had divorced her husband back when she was thirty-five. Wanda knew that his well-loved wife had died on him, that their two children lived on the west coast and were involved in their careers, and that he had never been seriously involved with another woman. Maybe there had been a couple of contenders; that part was hazy. But she already knew that he was sufficiently romantic that a lot of his personal tastes were not openly shared with fellow officers. She knew, for example, that he was fond of operatic music, with a preference for romantic works—La Boheme, Carmen, Lakmé, Thaïs.

When she learned from one of the general's secretaries that he had two recordings of *Lakmé* by different artists, and had just ordered a third, that made up her mind to be approachable—if he was inclined to approach. She had never known another man who had even heard of *Lakmé*.

She was eyeing him warily. He was eyeing her hungrily. But despite his gentlemanly demeanor and chivalric reserve, Jam Maitland was not the man to pussyfoot around when he saw something he wanted.

After one of their strategy planning sessions, Wanda stayed around after the meeting broke up to ask a few questions. Less than ten minutes later, General Maitland had invited Dr. Kaminsky to spend a long weekend with him at the Homestead in West Virginia. She said, "Maybe," and he had been around the block enough times to know what that meant.

The general gave his driver the weekend off and he drove his personal vehicle. That was how it started. Both adults took pleasure from the meaningless coincidence that his nickname rhymed with the first syllable of her last name. When they were alone, he called her Kami.

As a result of this mundane affair between two middle-aged people, each comfortably established in a responsible position, he came to rely on her as a sounding board in matters of policy and strategy. Her judgment was sound and she was unusually well informed. When she knew he was interested in a topic, she made it her business to keep up to date, and her security clearances made this relatively easy.

Jam Maitland began to discuss some of his theories about UAVs and their potential for future aerial warfare.

"It's the wave of the future, Kami. It seems clear to me. Not that it will replace...but it's certain to supplement conventional aviation. Just in the same way that helicopters found, and served, their own unique niche."

"I think you're right, general. Of course, the start has already been made. The Reaper is certain to be a big factor when the next big show begins."

"What worries me is that many countries who now have little or no air war capability can catch up quickly. We have a lead, but we could lose it quickly. Maybe not lose it...but another country might reach parity quickly. China, for example. France. Russia."

"That's certainly a valid concern," she replied, leaning forward to refill his glass.

They were chatting on the deck of his porch overlooking the Chesapeake Bay, enjoying the last half of a shaker of Bombay martinis.

"My own opinion is that China will be the nation that's quickest to catch on. If I'm right, they'll move quickly to gain a capability to match ours. How fast they move will depend on the vision of their leaders. Could be slow. Or fast." He was reclining on a chaise. The sun was warm, but the air was cool. A great day to be outside. He was totally relaxed, and he felt like he was talking to someone who really understood him.

"It seems to me, Kami, that our ability to move so quickly with our UAV programs stems from the fact that we have a whole young generation who have grown up with computer games. We're learning that these youngsters are quick to understand the basics of air war. Sometimes, I think they learn too quickly."

"I know what you mean. They grow up with access to keyboards, screens, control panels. Not the way we came up. I think your vision is on the mark."

"And the hackers.... There's another group who grow up immersed in, and surrounded by computers and computer technology. I really can't understand this group very well. Their interests and skill levels are beyond me. But I've seen some of these kids. They take great glee in hacking into military base communication systems. We spend a lot of money just to be aware of what they're trying to do."

"Yes, I know. I have seen some of the expenditure breakdowns. Also, it's not clear that any of these hackers actually have malicious intents. From what I learn, they are often impelled by the challenge to do what is supposedly undoable."

Dr. Wanda Kaminsky was wearing a light sun dress, perfectly appropriate for the day. She had put it on after arriving at the general's house for lunch prepared by his long-time, aide, MSgt. Michael Keever. After lunch served on the porch, MSgt. Keever had taken off for the afternoon, and Kami had slipped into Jam's bedroom to change into the sleeveless dress.

"Can I refill your glass?" she said. "I think we're coming to the end of this batch." When she bent to pour the last of the martinis, he could see—between her breasts—halfway to her navel, and it was a view he enjoyed.

"Y'know, Kami, it's a real pleasure talking to someone who understands what I'm talking about. Half the old farts in our planning sessions must still be back in the days of the Flying Tigers. They're looking for pilots like John Wayne. Maybe that's an exaggeration but, my god, some of the best controllers I've seen in the past couple of years still have acne. Don't shave. They listen to music by groups with names like Gumbo Dwarfs, Foo Fighters, Plastic Surgery."

"I'm hearing every word you're saying, General." Her ankles were thicker than Clara's had been, but her legs weren't bad and out in public she was very classy dresser. Understated. He liked that. And the noises she made! That was an extra bonus. She made him feel ten years younger. No, make that twenty.

" We really don't know shit about what is going on in many other parts of the world. Relative to UAVs, that is. Here, we have a talent pool that's growing steadily, and it's one that might be augmented rapidly in case of a national emergency. But I have no idea of the equivalent situation in other countries of the world. None at all."

"*Terra incognita.*"

"Do you? You read all kinds of things. What's your impression?"

"*Terra incognita.* We just don't know."

"When I bring up topics like this at any of our planning sessions, I can see the old guard types' eyes film over. They don't get it."

"No question, general. You're out in front." Her response wasn't all unadulterated flattery; she really did think he was a clever fellow.

"I just wish there was some way we could get better intelligence. Better information."

"You'll think of some...."

"Did you see, last week, the letter that came across from an Air Force officer vacationing in China? Who thinks he saw a Chinese UAV?"

"Did I? I can't recall. It sounds vaguely familiar."

"This guy thinks he saw a Chinese military jet that had been converted into a drone fighter. He was out in the desert somewhere."

"I might have seen it ."

"We ought to be on top of stuff like this. So far our satellite intel isn't telling us everything we need to know."

This time, Wanda laughed. "Intel never tells anyone all they need to know. You know that, General. That's why you guys hire people like me."

Suddenly things became very clear to Wanda Kaminsky. Clear, beyond any shadow of doubt. She was thinking...*I can make you do outrageous things, James. I can make you do things that you would never think of doing on your own. You are a good man James, but you are putty in the hands of someone like me. Did your wife understand that? Yes, I'm sure she must have.*

The general, comfortable, was enjoying this pleasant, sunny afternoon with a mature, intelligent woman who, he was confident, would spread her legs and welcome him into a warm, exciting interlude that would help him to forget some of the things he preferred not to remember. He was thinking—*I can make you moan and gasp and say things you would never wish to repeat in polite company.* He was particularly excited by the noises she made that sounded as if she had a bone caught in her throat.

For several moments their conversation ceased as they watched the sky. A fish hawk flew overhead, headed in the general direction of the Yorktown Bridge where there were several large nests atop the light poles. Then Wanda spoke.

"You could get good intel from China if you sent some young people who know what to look for."

"I don't have the slightest idea what you're talking about."

"Send kids who are adepts. At computers, games, radio controlled flight. Send them to China. Let 'em loose on their own. Americans may not speak Chinese, but plenty of Chinese kids know a bit of English. Internet cafes. Hard Rock. Youth talks to youth."

"That's not an original concept. I've heard it before. You really think we could learn something this way?"

Wanda knew she was on the right track. "Youth talks to youth. They don't have the hang-ups of our generation. Do you think anyone under twenty-five has any concept of the meaning of the phrase, *Little Red Book*? They don't even know the name Chairman Mao. Chiang Kai Shek? You might as well be talking about Clara Bow, the It Girl."

"So how do you see this happening?" he said, intrigued. *This gal is really clever. Plus..she is just about as horny as I am. If she had bent over three more inches I could have seen to her bush. The gods are smiling on me.*

"This is purely theoretical, Jam." She could see that he was in the bag. "But suppose you sent a group of young Americans into China? To meet and talk with kids just like themselves. They could probably tell you if China was moving toward parity. After they had rubbed shoulders with some college kids their own age. Look, this isn't well thought out. We're just talking. In the sunshine."

"But it's an interesting concept. If we screened them first—gave them some sort of an indoctrination— so they knew what to look for...." She could see by the changes in his face and body language that he was actually interested.

"If you'd like, I could flesh it out for you."

"Ah," he said, diverted. "Flesh. My lovely girl. You have said the magic word."

Dr. Wanda Kaminsky smiled. "That sounds wonderful. But give me two more minutes."

The next two minutes actually took about twenty, during which time she outlined a program to screen for talented high school seniors with backgrounds in RC flying, computer hacking, or both. Once identified, they would be enrolled in a unique, non-military indoctrination program that would ultimately lead to a college education at an institution of their choice. They would be escorted to China for several weeks and allowed to mix and mingle with their age cohort. They would find internet cafés on college campuses, karaoke bars and all of the myriad places where young people meet and mingle. They would have been trained to look for signs that could point out emerging trends. The cost would be minimal, and—even if the resulting information was limited—the risk would be minimal. She had actually been thinking along these lines for some weeks and had written a couple of scenarios that she was confident he would find interesting. Now, on the fly, she had attempted to summarize her concepts. Inadvertently, she had said the magic word. But it wasn't all that bad. This was a situation she could work.

The general was interested all right, but not, right now, in her scenarios. When Kami had turned up for lunch, he had taken the opportunity to pop—discreetly—a little blue pill, and his clock was running. He could hear part of what she was saying, but his brain had headed south. "You've got to put all this in writing. I'll need to see it. C'mon."

For Wanda Kaminsky knew, as her general did not, that within the government there are pools of funding waiting to be tapped for an almost endless array of half-baked projects that might, conceivably be of some utility. All that was needed was the knowledge of where to apply. And she knew. *My god,* she thought, falling back. *I love this job.*

That's how the whole program got started.

The general was lying on his back and his eyes were still open. Wanda assumed he was still awake.

"Look, Jam, if we send kids to China, they can't be conventional spies. They can't look like espionage agents. They will just be serious hobbyists, who are competitors with the Chinese and others from around the world. In a setting of international competition. They're simply hobbyists. Enthusiasts. They want to know what their competitors are up to. If we choose kids whose reputations can be verified on the Internet, no one could possibly have a legitimate concern. They may run up against the Chinese kids they'll talk to—who knows where? Berlin, Budapest, Las Vegas? Leave this to me General. This will never look like an Air Force Project. Leave it to me. I know how to do this.

Now... what were you going to show me? Ah, *merde!* Have you been listening?"

Dr. Wanda Kaminsky was not one to let grass grow under her feet. One week later she had a program mapped out and three of her staff were working to identify the top one hundred RC pilots in the U.S.—between the ages of 18 and 22—based on their performances in competitions. "We'll need background information on families, school histories and data on outside interests. No known or suspected drug users to be included."

She created a three-person committee to select ten candidates for a unique Air Force educational program. Parental approvals required to participate. Two weeks of training seems about right.

"The important thing to keep in mind," she told her staffers, "is that they are just kids, not intelligence agents. They'll talk to other kids, Chinese kids like themselves, hopefully on university campuses. And they'll get a sense of what's going on. We just need to put a bit of body English on the kind of topics that will interest them. We only want kids that have the ability—even if not the desire—to be trained as AF controllers. It would help if they're also interested in photography."

Two of her staffers, Air Force captains, were women. "Make sure," she coached them, "that at least one third of our candidates are women. Girls. Intelligent; and sharp. Then we'll need to conduct some screening interviews."

"Nearly 8,000 sailors aboard the Kitty Hawk and its battle group observed Thanksgiving at sea. Wren said that about 290 families had flown to Hong Kong to spend the holiday with the sailors, who weren't due back in Japan until Dec. 1. "It was a bit disappointing," he said. "But we are good sailors, and we will do what we need to do. One of the great things about the Navy is our flexibility. We can go anywhere—except Hong Kong."

"U.S. carrier returns home to Japan after snub in Hong Kong"
Eric Talmadge
The Associated Press (November 28, 2007)

CHAPTER 19
The Challenge

Within the Headquarters of the PLAAF in Beijing, the makeup of the committee representing the General Logistics Department was skewed toward men who were over sixty-five. In other words, if China had followed the practices prevailing in many western nations, most of the committee who made crucial decisions on expenditures would have been retired. Like much of the equipment employed by the PLAAF, they were in good shape, still in good working order—but they were obsolete.

Still, they were the men entrusted with making many of the crucial decisions concerning expenditures. Of course, most of the details behind the specifics of budget allocations were made by the army of staffers, mostly younger men, who labored diligently to assemble the budget recommendation packages.

Lost in the details of these expenditure figures, the funding allocations required to expand China's program for unmanned aircraft were embedded in other categories, such as "research for unconventional aerial defenses."

Much of the work on Chinese aerial drones had been conducted at two airfields in the Guangzhou Military District. The research had been started in that district because of its proximity to China's rapidly expanding electronics industry. Prototypes could be revised and redesigned with greater speed in Guangzhou. As designs hardened, and selected models showed promise, small quantities of development machines were shipped to the Lanzhou district where airbases at remote locations enabled a wide variety of long range tests. Sites in Lanzhou were less likely to come to the attention of foreign visitors whose presence in China was increasing all the time. And, as the 2008 Olympic Year drew nearer, the number of foreigners in the country was certain to increase dramatically.

After the hearings in Beijing, the discussion of the possible future for China's unmanned aircraft program did not end. Three of the committee's senior members had once been in the same squadron that flew over Vietnam. These old airmen had once been young fighters who took great pride in competing against the best aviators that the U.S. Air Force could throw at them. Some had more than one successful kill under their belt. Over half a century they had risen slowly through the ranks, and though their careers had often placed them far apart, now in the waning decades of life they were once more together, in secure administrative positions in Beijing. Their lives and fortunes were secure, and they had, without any formal arrangements, once again re-established the type of bonds that once they shared when they wore flying jackets and g-suits.

In short, they were now old drinking companions. Scarcely a week passed that these once formidable aviators did not get together at someone's home or at a private establishment where they could enjoy other types of companionship. Although these old men usually got along well with one another, they did not always agree on everything. Within the top group of five old friends, the most progressive and forward looking was PLAAF General Zheng Ju-Baio. As a fighter pilot Zheng had not been the most aggressive of the five, but nevertheless he had managed to down two American aviators. But in the field of planning and budget allocations he was clearly the most outspoken in favor of ideas that his colleagues frequently considered too new or too daring.

Zheng's father had been a civil engineer whose specialty was bridge design and after attending a technical university in the old Soviet Union, the newly fledged engineer had been fortunate enough to attend a graduate university in Switzerland. From his father, Zheng had learned habits of thorough examination and analysis, and they had stood him well in every phase of life.

At the opposite end of the spectrum, Quan Yang was clearly the most stubbornly conservative of the elderly PLAAF fighters. If Quan Yang's recommendations had prevailed, the Chinese Air Force would have been completely dependent upon Russian aviation manufacturers, Quan was stuck in a time warp, and to Zheng Jubaio's way of thinking he was an ancient turtle whose back had grown slick with moss. Each man knew and understood the other's differing points of view and their arguments were, for the most part, brief and good-humored. But each, in his own heart, quietly believed the other to be—while brave and deserving,—a fool with regard to the ability to make strategic plans that should impact China's Air Force.

They disagreed vehemently on the potential of unmanned aviation in modernizing the PLAAF. It is only to be expected that their friendly banter tends to degenerate into argument when they are, as happens on occasion, consuming Maotai.

Zheng: "In the near future we will see aerial combat between high-performance aircraft in which the combatants will be on the ground, at distant locations."

Quan: "We will not live to see this. It is a dream of a time, perhaps, when dragons return to the earth."

Zheng: "It could happen very soon. The technology exists today. As we speak the U.S. is working to make this a reality."

Quan: "Then they may be preparing, I would think, for civil war. To fight against one another. Their red states against their blue states possibly. No one else will have such vehicles."

Zheng: "We have them now. They are flying above the deserts in Lanzhou."

Quan: "You should have watered the Maotai, old friend. This cannot be. Tiny toys, perhaps, but not planes such as those we flew."

Zheng: "The payloads and armaments are comparable. Even superior. You have not been paying attention to developments. And the range of these drones makes them formidable as weapons of aggression."

Quan turned to their host, Min Tsao and pointed to Zheng's glass. "Take our friend's cup and bring him some green tea," he said with a sneering laugh. "He has addled his wits."

It was not the words that Zheng found offensive, but the expression on Quan's face, the face of an ancient turtle, was extremely annoying.

"To see a camel and take it for a horse with a double back..." he said, emptying his glass. It was an ancient Chinese insult to a person who was believed incapable of seeing the truth."

"No camel...and no horse either," Quan replied.

"Tell me, Quan, if a pilotless plane flew around Victoria Peak would you be convinced?"

"Probably not. I would be suspicious."

"Because it can be done right now. This is not for the future. This is reality."

Quan gave a loud laugh that sounded like a bark. "That is a wonderful suggestion," he said. "So now we can all see the truth or falsity of what you say. Next week my wife and I will be visiting Hong Kong with my wife's sister's family and their estate is just north of Central. They have a view of the Peak from their terrace. If your robot plane flies over the Peak we will be certain to hear of it. Then I will support your plan," Quan said, laughing.

Zheng's mind began to race as soon as he heard Quan's proposal. This might be just the opportunity he needed to influence the appropriations he wished to have approved.

"And if the plane should make this flight, I could, of course, count on your full support in approving additional funding for hardware?"

"Ha ha! Of course, of course. If it should happen. But like a man kicked to death by a duck?—there is no such thing. Of course. Count on me. Afterwards!"

Zheng rose to his feet and extended his hand to his long-time comrade.

"I believe we have made a wager."

Three days after he had laid on this outrageous bet, General Zheng had completed all the arrangements with his PLA Air Force colleagues. Most of the men involved in Zheng's wild plan were young officers challenged by the audacity of the idea, while convinced that the general's authority would be sufficient to protect them from official displeasure. It was risky, but risks appealed to many young airmen.

It was only by the merest accident that General Zheng learned that his planned demonstration would occur during a visit by the U. S. Navy's aircraft carrier, Kitty Hawk, whose stay was scheduled to place the ship in Hong Kong at the planned time for his flight. He thought about the possible consequences of exposing his ego trip to aviators of the Pacific Fleet and considered that it would not be wise. Likewise, it would be difficult—difficult and embarrassing—to call off the series of events it had taken several days, and as many bribes, to arrange. He closed the door to his office and put his head on the desk. One hour later he emerged from his office and gave his aide several phone numbers, together with a half page of written instructions.

The carrier Kitty Hawk was at sea when a message was received on the bridge. The ship was being escorted by several other naval vessels. The carrier's commanding officer, who was taking a nap at the time, was called immediately. The message was from Hong Kong's Harbor Master advising Kitty Hawk and her escorts that, regretfully, space for anchorage would not be available. No details were given, but the message ended with a sentence that additional information would be provided by a spokesman for China's Foreign Ministry within the hour. *The circumstances are unfavorable. Deep regrets.* Kitty Hawk and her flotilla changed course and made their way back to Japan, with a large complement of disappointed sailors. The cancelled visit made the pages of many American newspapers, but General Zheng's successful UAV flyover went unreported.

"Small cannot oppose great, few cannot oppose many, weak cannot oppose strong."

Meng-Tse (Mencius) c. 372-c. 289 B.C.

CHAPTER 20
Clearing the Air

Spring was in the air. At the beginning of central Pennsylvania's April, snow was gone and daffodils were up and beginning to poke through the ground. In another week they would be fully open. On a Friday afternoon, Walt was home early from his office at JBU but Tara was out, probably shopping for groceries. He was in a funk.

These bastards from Washington were making him angry. What did he owe the country? What did he owe his president? What was a legitimate price for citizenship? *I gave them a fucking leg...and no hard feelings. How much do they want?*

When they had asked him to take a herd of cats into central Asia he had agreed. It had not exactly been a bed of roses, but he had agreed. And he had done the best he could.

Still, it wasn't enough for these bastards. Now they wanted him to reprise what he had thought was the final act. *One more time. One more time.*

Tara, of course, made everything bearable. But, right now, she was gone. The more he thought about this latest summons the angrier he got. His anger was compounded by a feeling of helplessness in the face of the power structures that wanted to use him. True, he could refuse, but then they could probably make him sorry.

Today, at work, he had spent some time at his desk reading the philosophy of Mencius, Meng-Tse, who had been prominent about a hundred and fifty years after Confucius. He was trying to reconcile himself to circumstances, and it was proving to be more difficult than he had expected. Tara was a help. Her practical good sense had kept him from blowing his stack more than once.

Now he was facing a trip of two, possibly three, weeks with a group of plants selected by some process known only to the Air Force—to snoop around for evidence of developments in the field of pilotless aircraft. What were these children going to learn that couldn't be learned more easily with satellites and spy planes? Or by other means? *What happened to Google fucking Earth?* He was not aware of new developments in these fields, but surely we were making steady advances, year after year. How would these kids behave when they were on the other side of the world, in a place where they couldn't communicate easily with home, and where there were no familiar convenience stores to provide them with the everyday things they took for granted?

He looked to see if Tara had left a note saying when she'd be back, but there was nothing. He dropped his briefcase on his desk and took a bottle of vodka from the cabinet.

At the back edge of his lot, the prior owners had left an old picnic table that stayed out in the weather. It was still holding together, and he and Tara had eaten dinner out there on a couple of occasions. Now, he walked to the table and seated himself so he could see Tara's car when she arrived. Then he took a big slug of vodka. The grass was starting to get tall and he would have to make sure that the contract for mowing had been renewed. While he was thinking about it, he took the memo book from his shirt pocket and wrote himself a note to call the mowing guy tonight, Maybe after supper.

In any of the cities he planned to visit, they could encounter a gamut of unforeseeable problems—that he would be expected to solve. He took another slug of vodka.

Should I go on this goofy trip? Or should I just tell these guys to screw themselves? What are the down sides if I refuse to go? What are the up sides if I actually go and the trip is successful? On the other hand, how do I even know what constitutes success? He opened the little notebook to a clean page and made a truth table. *Go. Don't Go. Succeed. Fail. This was dumb. If we don't go, success and failure have no meaning. Wait. That's not exactly true, because if we don't go, it will be a failure from the perspective of my 'clients.'*

The truth was that trips to western China were likely to become increasingly dangerous in the months and weeks leading up to the Olympics in Beijing. The Islamic populations of Xinjiang province were likely to be visited by fundamentalists, including representatives of Al Qaeda, intent on stirring up trouble. Friction between Muslims and ethnic Chinese had existed for years, but it was highly likely that events would focus attention on this region as it was increasingly covered by the world's media. Already there had been a few problems but, so far, he had weighed the risks and decided that he could continue his program. But sometimes he felt that he might be running more risk than was justified by the educational benefits. It was one thing to gamble with his own life. But risks to the lives of his students? Or Tara's? What were the indicators that would tell him to lay off these visits for a year or two? Possibly until some time after the Olympics when China might be out of the world's spotlight, and terrorists might focus on other regions?

If he was honest about it, he had to conclude that his tenure was probably—at least in part—due to some intervention by higher ups in government. So someone—possibly more than one individual—in government had spoken to the JBU administrators and had carried sufficient weight to influence his university.

Clearly, if they could help him, they could just as easily hurt him. If they chose. This was infuriating to him. I'm what? A puppet? To be manipulated by these bastards? He sat for a long time in silence, taking an occasional pull at the bottle.

He turned to a pair of clean pages and began again. He labeled one page Advantages, the other, Disadvantages. Under advantages he quickly made several entries. *Doing something I like. Visiting Silk Road cities. Investigating a different route. Funding won't be a problem.* He quickly listed eight attributes of success that might accrue to this trip. Then, under Disadvantages he listed: *No real control over selection process for my students. Trip goals are unclear to me. No way to even define what constitutes a successful outcome.* He ran out of steam when there were only six entries on the Disadvantages page. Damn! This was counterintuitive. He would have thought it would be easy to fill a couple of pages with disadvantages. But he was having trouble coming up with hard objections that should have just keep pouring out in a torrent.

Maybe it's the alcohol. This isn't like me. He tried to think of something he might have picked up from Meng-Tse that would be helpful.

Some kind of shiny green beetle was walking along the crack between boards of the table's surface. *I don't even know the name for that beetle. And he lives here. What am I doing back here, anyway. Self indulgence. That's all this is.* When he had walked back to the table, he had felt like he was full of anger at the agencies he considered were bullying him. Now, barely thirty minutes later, those feelings seemed to have dissipated and what he was feeling was a considerable disgust with himself.

He opened his little notebook to another pair of clean pages. But he was struggling to know what words to write. He removed the bottle cap and took a big swig of the vodka, but he didn't swallow it. Instead he swished it around his mouth and spit it out. Then he printed four letters across the top of a page. S E L F.

The next lines came easily. *Expect nothing! Never complain! Be grateful! Keep working Stop talking! Walk more! Love Tara!*

Nothing else flowed out the end of his pencil. He waited. But that was all. The way. The Way. Tao. Heaven and earth. Impartial. Indifferent. The ten thousand things.

Tara's car was pulling into the driveway. He put the notebook in his pocket, picked up the bottle and called to her as he walked back to the house. "Yo! Silky!" She waved and went in.

In the kitchen, she put a couple of grocery bags on the table and kissed him. "You had some vodka? Without me?"

"Sorry. I was missing you."

"I wasn't gone long."

"I was just...." He struggled to find the right word. "Shit. Self indulgent."

She pressed up against him, hard. "Poor baby. It's those guys in Washington. They're getting to you. I can tell. But don't worry. They can't beat us both."

Walt thought about the words he had just written. Be grateful. Stop talking. Never complain. She was right. Just now, his arms around her, he felt invincible.

"Thank you, my sexy kitten. OK. Put this stuff up and take us out for dinner."

"So far, Reapers have been durable. None has crashed or been shot down, North said. Each of the Air Force's ten Reaper systems cost $53 million. The Air Force says the Predator system, which it defines as four planes, ground control stations and satellite link, costs $40 million. It has 102 Predators in its fleet, records show, and had procured 258 through 2007."

"Air Force requests more fighter drones."
Tom Vanden Brook
USA Today, March 6, 2008

CHAPTER 21
Pentagon Weekend

Walt and Tara were driven to a comfortable Georgetown hotel where a suite had been reserved for them. They had dinner at an Afghan restaurant that Walt had visited in the past. The next day he was scheduled to meet the group of people who had invited him. The meeting was scheduled for 10 a.m. at the Pentagon.

At quarter past nine, a vehicle and driver arrived at the hotel and an Air Force captain in uniform showed up in the lobby to escort Walt. Walt was surprised to see the Air Force uniform. Tara had declined the offer of a car and driver for the day, preferring to be on her own.

The conference room in The Pentagon was located in the second ring. Paul Chapman was the only familiar face in the room. At the other officers wore Air Force uniforms with the exception of one Navy captain. This was totally puzzling to Walt. His military service had been with the Army. More importantly, his involvement with government agencies as a civilian had all been based on the experiences and background he had gained while in the Army. *What services could I possibly provide to the Air Force. And the Navy? These guys must really be at the bottom of the barrel.*

Chapman introduced him to the men in the room. There was one woman, an Air Force lieutenant colonel—with wings. She was the most junior person in a room full of chickens and stars. The Air Force captain who had escorted him to the conference room had disappeared.

There was a table filled with coffee urns, several kinds of pastries, sliced melons and some oversized strawberries. After the individual introductions were completed General Warren Bloodsworth kicked off the meeting.

"Gentlemen, most of you here today know why we have convened this meeting. The only person in the room who is totally in the dark is our invited guest. I believe you have all been introduced to Doctor Walter Roberts of James Buchanan University—where he is a professor of Central Asian Studies and a recognized authority on the Silk Road. These are facts that are well known. We are honored to have him with us today. Welcome to the Pentagon, Professor Roberts."

After a moment of scattered applause, the general continued.

"What many of you may not know is why we have chosen this professor who has joined us today. Let me give you a brief resume of the services he has provided for the government." He put on a pair of reading glasses and picked up a few sheets of prepared notes.

"During fighting in Afghanistan, Special Forces Lieutenant Roberts performed with distinction in the field where his language skills complemented his talent as a combat leader. He was wounded in an engagement there, subsequently receiving the purple heart and a bronze star.

"Subsequent to leaving military service he obtained his PhD in Central Asian studies and began his career in academia. So far, nothing too unorthodox. Then, a couple of years ago he was requested to lead an unconventional team of operatives into Central Asia for the purpose of...*blah, blah, blah, blah, blah...!*"

Walt was mildly embarrassed to hear a three-star general rehashing his role in leading his Herd of Cats. His role in taking town the Russian drug network had been negligible. To him it had seemed trivial. Minor at best. To make matters worse, much of what had transpired took place without his awareness of what was happening. It was almost a comedy of errors. The blind leading the blind. Happily for him, things had turned out well and he had been rewarded out of proportion to his accomplishments.

"Now, gentlemen, we learn that Professor Roberts is planning to carry groups of American students into the far reaches of western China, an area that has recently taken on increased importance to our intelligence gathering activities."

Now Walt was beginning to wonder. How in the hell did the Air Force know he was planning to take students to western China? And why did they care about the places he would visit? Oasis towns, Buddhists monuments, caves, museums?

"Professor Roberts will undoubtedly be puzzled by our motives in calling him here today. Or our interest in the places he is likely to visit. To help our guest understand our present concerns I have requested Colonel Shawcross to help us out. Colonel Shawcross. If you please."

The lone female, an attractive brunette with an athletic build, came to the podium and called for the lights to be dimmed as she motioned for the TV to be lowered. The sound track—if there was one—had been muted, and narration was provided by the colonel.

"Professor Roberts, this brief presentation is addressed primarily to you. The plane you see here is the USAF unmanned drone, designated Reaper. Currently it represents the lead edge—operationally—of the USAF's pilotless flight capabilities. While it has been spectacularly successful in the field to date, we are still learning, and we feel the capabilities of this modality have only been scratched. Some even believe that it is not out of the realm of possibility that manned flight may have reached its apogee and that unmanned flight could be the wave of the future."

The planes on the screen were performing some dramatic maneuvers, but they could hardly qualify as aerobatic stunts. Most of Reaper's dramatic performances occurred in attacks against moving targets, trucks, vehicles, and one dramatic sequence, against a squad of running combatants.

Then the view cut back to the interior of the command center from which controllers were flying the drones.

The lady colonel's pitch took about fifteen minutes and ended abruptly as the lights same up. General Bloodsworth moved to the podium.

"You will appreciate immediately, professor, that the use of drones is extremely cost effective. The aircraft are substantially less expensive, their capabilities, currently inferior, could easily be upgraded to the levels of current combat aircraft. And the key factor is the reduction in cost to be realized by avoiding the need to train, maintain, and place at risk, a combat-ready pilot.

"Now, professor—and here I must remind you that your SECRET security clearance is still in effect; and applies to everything we will discuss today—we come to the heart of today's session.

"The technology that we rely on for our drones does not currently require any breakthroughs or any quantum leaps. It is available, more or less off-the-shelf, to technologically advanced nations. This includes, as must be obvious to you, China.

"Recently, we have received intelligence that leads us to believe that China is working aggressively to develop an unmanned drone capability. Furthermore, this intelligence, which appears to be unimpeachable, indicates that they may have leapfrogged our Reaper to produce an aircraft that has superior performance capabilities. Naturally, we wish to obtain more information about China's program.

"And now, we learn two highly important facts that can assist us. One— You have a military background, and a proven track record in covert activities for the government and Two—you some familiarity with western China, where we believe some of these activities are taking place, and you have a legitimate reason to return there—accompanied by others.

"Now, Professor, we have been talking for some time. But you will un- doubtedly have some questions and concerns. Perhaps we should take a moment to hear from you. But, first, perhaps some gentlemen—and of course, our lady—would like to warm up their coffee."

While the group was milling and stretching, Paul Chapman drew Walt aside. "Look, Walt, I could see you getting pissed. Just so you have a clear picture—the report on your role with the Herd of Cats was classified and circulated to many agencies. That happened automatically, and I had no particular role in that. However—and this is where you could have a legitimate beef with me—when I learned of your China plans from your interview in the JBU Alumni magazine, I did some checking and I put your name in a classified file of potential resources. The Air Force had a problem that materialized out of nowhere and they called me. I told them you were completely trustworthy and that you could be relied on in any emergency. They took it from there. If you want to be angry with me for that—then I'm sorry for the way you feel."

"Paul, I've found a wonderful woman. And I have a job I'm good at. Regardless of what they want me to do...it doesn't fit my needs."

"You've got to hear them out, my friend. And these guys aren't used to tak- ing no for an answer. Notice that they're all in uniform. I think you know what that implies."

In the hours that followed, the Air Force plan was unrolled. It was not substantially different from the job he had done before. They wanted him to conduct another bogus tour. But this time, instead of sending him out with a group of mature adults, each with a distinct area of specialization, the group would be composed primarily of kids just on the brink of college. The oldest, they said, just turned twenty.

They were chosen based on their flying skills with RC airplanes in aero- batic contests—coupled with computer know-how. They were all bright young people, all bound for college, all with great promise and clean noses in the past. But, still, they were just kids. He had taken sophomores on his tours in the past and he had experienced problems with them. Now, they were asking him to wrangle a group of puppies with little or no interest in his field of specialization, into a part of the planet that was becoming in- creasingly dangerous—to accomplish a mission he could not understand.

Are these guys crazy?

"The U.S. military is quietly exploring hypersonic technology that would propel missiles or aircraft at up to six times the speed of sound—nearly 4,000 mph.

Known by code names as Falcon, High Fire and Blackswift, the experiments and tests are being kept closely guarded as the Air Force looks toward a future generation of air power and weaponry midway into the 21st century—or possibly sooner.

One possibly is an ultra-fast long-range bomber that the Air Force wants to field within three decades. Air Force officials hope to deploy a new interim bomber by 2018, followed by a more advanced, and possibly unmanned, bomber in 2035 that could incorporate many of the concepts emerging from current research."

"Air Force seeking missiles, aircraft that go six times..."
Dave Montgomery
McClatchy Newspapers (in Buffalo News, Feb, 2008)

CHAPTER 22
Armtwisting

The first day at the Pentagon was spent—for the most part—briefing Walt on parts of the USAF's program for drone aircraft. At the end of the day he was driven back to his hotel suite in Georgetown where Tara was waiting for him. They walked around Georgetown for over an hour, visiting bookstores and specialty shops before finding an interesting Chinese restaurant.

The second day was intended as the sales pitch. After everyone had taken their seats, coffee cups filled and PDAs prominently displayed, the hard sell began.

"Well, Professor Roberts, you have known from the beginning that we didn't invite you here to fill you in on our classified programs for a new phase of aerial warfare. We want to recruit you as a resource to help with our intelligence gathering. Your reputation has preceded you and you come highly recommended. So, if we can begin by assuming that you will support our endeavors, we would like to outline what we have in mind."

"General, please call me Walt. Just about every person in this room is senior to me, both in age and in experience, so I would be happy to dispense with the professor title. Sir, I presume that in learning of my so-called exploits, you have spoken with Paul Chapman. If so, I am certain that he may have told you of my express intention to avoid further involvement in covert or clandestine activities. I am a simple college teacher trying to get students interested in a remote part of the world, and to stimulate awareness of the history and lore of places that may play a significant part in our future."

"Walt, you are a plain speaker, and yes, it is true that Chapman has warned us that you would probably not be interested in our activities. But before closing the door, please hear us out.

"In the future, we believe that pilotless aircraft will play an increasing important role in air warfare. At the present, as we discussed yesterday, we believe that we are on the lead edge of these developments. But, our forecasts indicate that our lead is slim and— more to the point—it is also precarious.

A determined competitor, especially one with an aircraft industry, could catch up quickly.

"Any of the developed nations could, if they chose, catch up quickly. But at the present time we are not particularly concerned with the countries of NATO. Bluntly put, our primary short range concern is China, a nation where we are aware you have been focussing your attention for the past several months."

He signaled to an aide, the room darkened and a video tape began rolling. There was no title, and the sound track, if one existed, was not running. The screen showed the interior of an aircraft production line.

"You're looking at a Chinese production line for their A5 FanTan jet fighter, a design that they got from the Russians over two decades ago. It was a good fighter in its day, but time has passed it by. The Chinese still continue making a few. Recently we have reason to believe that they have converted a number of these fighters. The nature of the conversion has been to replace the pilot with a remote control system, at least six directional cameras, and other servo-control systems that permit the aircraft to be flown effectively from a remote location. China is now playing catch-up ball and we believe they can catch up quickly. The strategic implications may be immediately apparent to a man with your academic and military background."

As the morning unrolled, Walt had a sickening feeling of *deja vu*. The request being made of him was not substantially different from the program laid out by Paul Chapman a few years ago.

This time, however, instead of herding a bogus group of academics and alumni, he would be taking potential students, only they would not be actual students. They would be young men who were skilled in remote control flight as skilled hobbyists. All had been tagged by the USAF as potential controllers and had been sent though a six month indoctrination to prepare them as observers—and for further training.

And the Air Force, in its great wisdom realizing that he had no language proficiency in Chinese, had made arrangements to provide him with a skilled speaker of Mandarin—*Putonghua*—the official national language, understood in most places in China.

They wanted him to take a group of six "observers" plus one translator, across western China, with particular interest in crossing Gansu, Qinghai and Xinjiang provinces. These were the places he had planned to visit and his Air Force hosts knew that in advance. Just like in the past, they had done their homework on him and it made him angry. But this, he knew, would serve no useful purpose and when he felt himself growing angry he would rise and fill his cup half full of coffee and sip it as slowly as possible.

If he agreed to carry this first group, they didn't rule out the possibility that other requests would follow.

"How do you think my university will react when they learn that my so-called academic program has been preempted by phony students?"

The general smiled. "You needn't worry about that Walt. I can guarantee that this will only enhance your popularity with your administration."

"That's questionable. They have a reputation to maintain. And there's always the question of lost tuition fees. They don't see themselves as a public institution."

"All of your charges will be duly registered at JBU by the time you depart for your next trip. Including your translator, an Air Force officer who is relatively young and can relate to your charges. You will appear legitimate, precisely because you will actually be legitimate."

"These students will be registered in my department...?"

"Yes! Of course! And their expenses will, naturally, be picked up by the USAF. Channeled through your university, of course. Yes, they will be registered in your department. Actually, they will attend for at least part of one term. I can't recall if JBU is on the quarter or the semester system. They will be JBU students and we may want to have them tour again."

Walt's primary questions had more to do with the outlook for success of what seemed to him a cockamamie plan.

"You expect this group of young people can cruise through a foreign country, with every conceivable distraction, and successfully identify a covert military activity whose whereabouts are not even known? Doesn't this defy credibility? A needle? In a vast country full of haystacks?"

"Admittedly, a long shot, Walt. But you're assuming that you're the only game in town. Be assured this is not the case. We will learn a lot from your activity. These youngsters are sharper than you might think. They know what they are looking for, even though you, assuredly, do not."

"General, when the freshman class shows up on campus at JBU, every single boy and girl has gone through our admissions process, a kind of rudimentary screening. The idea is to weed out, if that's not too harsh a term, those who would be unlikely to graduate. The admissions process, admittedly, is a crude instrument, but without it, we would have a much higher rate of dropouts. I tend to take a high dropout rate personally—as an indicator that I haven't done a good enough job as a teacher. These kids you're giving me...what kind of screening have they been through?"

The general leaned forward on the podium and broke into a grin like General George Patton atop the high ground at Kasserine Pass. "I was wondering if you'd ask that question, and I didn't want to describe your gang unless you asked. Let me tell you a bit about who you're getting.

"We've had this group of kids identified for over a year and a half. They come from all over the country and they all have good academic records. All have completed at least the junior year of high school. So, technically, they're exceptional high school seniors, or potential college freshmen. All possess computer skills rated from very good to excellent. Some are adept at hacking. All have, at some time or another, been competitors in radio-controlled air shows. Four of your group made it to the TOC in Las Vegas. This is a big deal."

"The TOC?"

"Tournament of Champions. Amateur flyers competing for money. It's a tournament by invitation. Only the cream makes it to the top. Half of the flyers are Americans, mostly young. The other half are from all over the world. All of these kids are proficient as controllers and could easily qualify as drone pilots. With very little military training. But there is one more attribute they all share."

He paused, waiting for Walt to ask, but Walt was a classroom pro, and he could stand the wait.

"They share the characteristic that they despise and detest the discipline of a military career, a military life. This is what our psychologists tell us. Is this a good thing...or a bad thing? Who can say? It's a personal thing, but none of these kids exhibit the least desire to wear a uniform. They aren't bad kids, not unruly or undisciplined. But they don't relish standing in ranks, saluting, wearing uniforms. Otherwise, we'd have recruited them. All of these kids will probably go to college and they'll probably all graduate. But right now we have them in a special program that appeals to them, and it has some element of monetary reward."

"You have them on the Air Force payroll?"

"Not exactly, Walt. We have engaged them in a special program that they have found stimulating. I will tell you this. They can recognize any planes currently being flown by the PLAAF, China's Air Force. Most of which is still flying planes that were designed by Russian aeronautical engineers. Plus— they have all had exposure to the type of training we give our UAV operators. Familiarization only."

"When do I get to meet them?"

"They'll all be registered in your next batch of classes. But right now, how about if we take a break and get some lunch. We'll continue afterward."

Walt had made notes all during the morning session, and his questions and his host's sometimes rambling answers lasted for just over two hours. It was only quarter past two and he felt that they had told him everything that would be forthcoming, when Bloodsworth sprung it on him.

"There's one major change in your itinerary that we want you to make."

Walt sat up straighter. "We know that you are planning to take your Silk Road travelers along the northern border of the Taklamakan, and that you have been planning to cross the border into Kazakhstan. Flying home out of Almaty. But we have a different proposal that will better answer our needs, while at the same time, meshing reasonably well with your own program."

"But my program..." Walt started to protest.

"Let me continue," Bloodsworth interrupted.

"We would like you to limit your tour to China. Instead of skirting the northern fringes of the desert, travel from east to west along the northern route ending up at Kashgar and subsequently exiting through Kazakhstan, we'd ask you to return east along the southern route. Actually circling the Taklamakan. We'd have you return to Dunhuang again, along the southern edge. Back home by way of Beijing. Again.

"That's a whole different program."

"Of course. It's a loop. But we know you can do it."

"I don't have a program."

"You'll make one."

"Thanks for the vote of confidence."

"Walt, let me remind you that this first group will not be depending on you for their education. Hell's bells, professor. There's a chance you'll like the southern route so well you'll change your whole approach to trips in the future."

"That's a pleasant thought," Walt said, with just a hint of sarcasm that he immediately regretted.

He could sense that the men in the room felt that their solicitation was over; and that it was time for him to fish or cut bait. Chapman had already hinted strongly that it would be unwise to refuse.

"Gentlemen," Walt said, rising to address the assembled brass. "I am most appreciative for the courtesy you have shown me and for the careful attention you have given to most of the aspects of my educational tour program. But I would like to sleep on your proposal. And to consider some of the implications that will require more time. Possibly consult with my...associate."

"You realize, of course, that none of these particular details relating to Air Force objectives can be discussed with anyone. I don't have to remind you that everything we've discussed is SECRET. "

"Of course, I understand perfectly."

"Trip plans, of course, are your own concern. Your group will all be legitimate students. In class within a week of your acceptance. And we will assist with obtaining appropriate visas. They will come to you out of a normal student population. After you leave we will give you a confidential list of the names you will need to select from your first group of applicants. If you would like, we can ask Mr. Chapman to act as liaison after you have responded to our request."

"Clear enough. OK. I understand. Let me have overnight. May I meet with you tomorrow? Perhaps this whole group need not be involved."

The next day's meeting was scheduled for 1000 hours and it was agreed that Chapman's vehicle would pick him up forty minutes in advance. Chapman would accompany him to General Bloodsworth's Pentagon office. Chapman approached him as they were headed for the lobby to call their drivers. "You really have only one choice, Walt." That really pissed him off.

Back at the hotel, Tara was interested to learn how the day had gone. "I can't discuss it with you. You can't know anything. Don't ask. I won't tell. They know all the details of our plans for China."

She grabbed his shirt front and pulled him to her for a hard kiss. Not too hard. "No more, Professor. We take students, alumni, faculty members and anyone else. Let me know what I can do."

"Thank you for not bugging me."

She pulled him in again.

"Anyway," she said, "I know my man and I believe that you are gonna eventually tell me every secret you ever had, because you won't want to hold back anything from me. You won't be able to stand it."

"Maybe."

"Those bastards are pressuring you."

"Yes."

"You don't like their proposal."

"True."

"You want to tell them to kiss your ass."

"Yep."

"But there could be repercussions?"

"Probably."

She pulled off his tie and began unbuttoning his shirt. When the buttons were undone, she slipped it off one arm, then the other, and let it fall on the floor. Then she unbuckled his belt, pulled it out of the belt loops and tossed it on the chair.

"Look, Professor. We are a great team. You and me. Why try to fight them? Nothing they can do to you could possibly damage the man you are. And you've got me. Thick or thin. Why fight 'em? Let's go along. What the hell, my lovely man. They can't hurt you. And they might actually help you. Say yes. Say yes. I say 'screw 'em.' I'll be here as long as you want me."

He gave her a quizzical look.

"Take the money and run."

"My god, Tara. What did I do before you?"

"Come on," she said, pulling him toward her. "We've got the rest of the afternoon. We can eat late."

"Listen, Sugar Britches. We've tried a lot of ways. Planes, trains and private drivers. If we sign on for this cruise, these guys are gonna rent us a bus. And driver. All of the way or most of the way. Whatever we decide."

"You da man. Get under."

It was much easier to say yes to the USAF than he had expected.

"Back at the Nightmare Inn, we spread our Bartholomew map out on the bed. If we could get to Dunhuang, we might be able to take a road that branched southwest from the town to the Taklamakan. Our destination, as far as I was concerned, was still the southern half of the road that circled the desert. That would take us through Hotan, Qiemo, Yecheng, the same string of oasis towns Fleming and Maillart traveled through to Kashgar.

'But the truck drivers said that road is closed,' Mark said."

Night Train to Turkestan
(Modern Adventures Along China's Ancient Silk Road)
Stuart Stevens

CHAPTER 23
Planning the Loop

Back in the study of the farmhouse he shared with Tara, Walt had assembled several different large scale maps of China, and the best one was laid out on his big work table. Tara was beside him, perched on a drafting stool.

"Do you understand what they're asking us to do?"

"Professor, you've asked me that at least five times a day for the last three days. Yes. They want to meddle with your trip to China. Our trip."

"But do you understand what that means to us?"

"Duh! Gawsh, Marshal Dillon, whut cud it mean? Dammit, Professor. It means we take three weeks and retrace some of our steps."

"It means we go west by the north route around the Taklamakan, and come back along the south edge of the desert."

"We can do it. In Turkmenistan we crossed the Kara Kum twice on one trip to Uzbekistan."

"Yeah, but this is the Taklamakan."

"And we're not going across this desert."

"Take a look at this map, Tara. Forget the northern route. We've done that already, You know what we're likely to hit all the way to Urumqi. But drop down to Kashgar, Kashi on this map. And then let's take a look at the southern route that takes us back to Dunhuang."

They refolded the map to make it manageable.

"First day out of Kashi, it doesn't look like we want to go any further than Yarkand."

"That's only 163 kilometers, about a hundred miles."

"OK, Princess, you want to keep going. Where do you think you..."

"I see what you're saying . The next oasis is Hotan. Not much going on in between. Wait a minute. That's not a lot further. About 165 miles. Maybe we should try to make it to Hotan in one day."

"We may have to. The thing is...Yarkand is interesting. It would be worth half a day's stop. But we might not have the time to spare. Look at what we're facing after Hotan."

They figured the mileages and estimated driving times several different ways, with different stopping points and they both agreed that—if they pushed—it would take at least three fairly long days on the road to make it back east to Dunhuang. Bad weather might easily add a day or perhaps more, and chances were that everyone would be wrung out by Dunhuang.

On top of this, they had made their plans based on being able to use the vehicle track from Miran to the highway north to Dunhuang. They would need to replan the exact route together with their Chinese driver, who hopefully would be able to speak some English. The presence of a full time interpreter would be helpful, and that had not been the case in the past. So that was a plus.

They worked until well after midnight. Tara made green tea and they kept the Twelve Girl Orchestra cycling as they worked. They made several different timetables for alternate routes. By the time they tumbled into bed, some of their plans were beginning to seem pretty reasonable.

Walt was sitting on the edge of the bed taking off his leg as Tara slid into her pajama top. "You really understand that this place could be much more dangerous and unpredictable as we get closer to the Olympics." He said it as a question.

"Yes. Of course."

"And this doesn't worry you a little?"

"Honestly? With you, I don't worry about much of anything." He could tell by her voice that she was very tired and would probably be out in a few minutes. She hit the bed like a cinder block and backed up to make contact. She fell asleep like a healthy baby. He could almost hear her falling—feel her body relaxing. When she was almost gone, he responded.

"Funny, I feel the same way with you."

PART 3
GRASSHOPPERS

"So the message from Peking to any would-be aggressor is conclusive; if attacked, a nuclear counter-offensive would be likely. Everyone knows that China's Air Force and Navy pilots are still flying aircraft that were designed well over thirty years ago. Aware of these deficiencies, the National Defense Science, Technology and Industry Commission is busily cutting back on the dated aviation technology they inherited from the Russians. "

"The Dragon's Teeth, Inside China's Armed Forces"
Text and photographs by John Robert Young

CHAPTER 24
Weekend in Beijing

Finally. It was done. The whole sham procedure was completed. Walt felt sick about having been manipulated. Tara was a big help. She constantly reminded him that he had been asked to serve his country by men at the very highest level. Now—finally—he had the first phase of this dark chapter behind him. Walt had identified his selection of faux-candidates for his first extended trip of the eastern Silk Road. He had been interviewed on local TV regarding his new program. Much ado about nothing. Actual time for his sound bite was just over 85 seconds. The JBU Alumni Magazine had asked him to bring back photographs for a Silk Road piece.

Walt was a bit interested to learn that the President and the Provost of his University had no idea where the Taklamakan desert was located. But, after he thought about it for a while, he realized that he probably didn't know much about Duns Scotus. Everybody found their niche.

He had his six—let's call them—students. And an interesting bunch they were. He had been expecting six males. He got four boys and two girls. They had all been the result of a careful selection and screening program by the USAF. A heterogeneous group. The youngest was eighteen, the oldest just twenty-one. All of the young people selected by the Air Force were geekazoids, or so they seemed to Walt. Computer nerds, game players with some aptitude for programming. They had not been outstanding performers in school, however they all tested high in IQs. Two of the group were products of home schooling. All were experienced radio-control flyers and had won recognition as competitors.

He had learned their names, but all six of the group had been together during their Air Force indoctrination programs and, traveling in a group, they told him they preferred to go by the nicknames they had chosen for themselves. These names were easy for Walt to remember and he had arranged them in alphabetical order. The males were Ace, Boyington, Sherlock,

Tomcat. The females were Annie and Bonnie. Walt had never asked, but he assumed that Terry's nickname, *Annie*, was from Annie Oakley and Lisa's, *Bonnie*, was from Bonnie and Clyde. They were both pretty girls, Annie-Terry. a redhead and Bonnie-Lisa, brunette. Walt thought about it, and decided to ditch the nicknames.

Now, after months of preparation and shamming which had probably been as uncomfortable for them as for him, the group had assembled in JFK and boarded the flights that would take them first to O'Hare and then directly to Beijing—where preparations for the 2008 Olympics were underway in earnest. Tara checked to see that they all had passports and visas before they left for Chicago and Walt checked again before boarding for Beijing.

It was a long, miserable experience aloft. His leg would be uncomfortable and he would need to make a special effort get up and walk every hour or so. Tara was big help. *What would I do without her?* She nudged him with the now familiar elbow and simply whispered in his ear. "Up, big boy!"

During the flight both Walt and Tara were careful to spend time with Air Force Major Liang. Penny. Now they were comfortable with calling her Penny and, despite her initial standoffishness, by the end of the flight they could converse easily. During the flight she taught Tara to recognize Chinese characters for man and woman. "Toilet," Penny told Tara, "is pronounced *tser-swoh*. Once you're headed in the right direction, all you'll need to recognize is the different characters for male and female." Tara didn't bother to remind her teacher that she had already made two trips across the Inner Kingdom. Tara liked Penny and wanted to become friends.

Eventually, several movies later, after more food than a normal person could possibly consume, the lights came on and the incomprehensible messages sounded. They were descending.

Screeeeeeeech. Touchdown! The plane was on the ground in Beijing and the huge aircraft shuddered as it braked to a halt, then turned to taxi to a terminal gate.

Beijing. The People's Republic of China. These kids would have to be impressed, no matter what backgrounds they came from. They were still children. Even if they had traveled the world with their parents, visiting Beijing was still a big deal. Walt's teaching instincts were taking over despite any problems he had anticipated in the past. *Maybe this will all work out.*

After a long, tiring flight, which had ended on a weekend, Walt had planned for the next two days to be spent in Beijing. He had made arrangements to connect with his Chinese guides and drivers and to take his charges on a tour of the sights of Beijing—Tian'an Men Square, the Forbidden city, the Great Hall of the People, the City Walls. The Forbidden City, just by itself, would take half a day if their guide was a good talker.

Tian'an Men. Could these kids know what the words meant? They were smart enough. But did they give a damn? Maybe some did. But how could they possibly know? Why would they possibly care? No fault of their own.

Tian—heaven. An— calm, peace. *The Gate of Heavenly Peace. The Square of the Gate of....* It was sad in a way.

His charges were all bright kids. But they were, without even knowing it, stuck in a time warp. *Without even knowing it.* The world was changing around them and no one had bothered to tell them. *But...is it any different for them than it was for me? Or than it has been for Tara?*

From the airport they took a van to their comfortable accommodations in Beijing, courtesy of the USAF. Walt had to confess to himself that the days in Beijing might be a lot of fun. His kids were bright. Tara was at his side. *Don't forget to include that. I give thanks every time I open my eyes.* And money was not a concern. Oh, yes, lest he forgets to remind you, his health was good.

China is...interesting? Fascinating? Incredibly wonderful? What is it? Maybe it's too big and too complex and too different to be easily comprehensible.

Walt's charges seemed to expand in China. He began to look at them differently. When they were 'plants' in his classes there had been resentment on his part. On the plane, they were simply a burden around his neck.

But now, as individuals—afoot, curious, stimulated—he began trying to see them as conventional students, young people with curiosity and enthusiasm for history and culture. The first full day in Beijing with his gang of catbirds, he had to confess, was as much fun as any of the trips he had made in the past with legitimate students. Apparently, whatever training the Air Force had put them through had done the job. They showed up in the lobby on time. So far, he hadn't had to pull them away from the hotel bar and they seemed to be relatively polite and well mannered. Of course, Beijing, China is considerably different from Central Asia where Islamic conventions are always a first consideration. Things might be a bit different after they began to move west.

It was great to have an interpreter along. Penny Liang's language skills, coupled with her maturity and command presence was a tremendous asset. She could whip them into line in a moment. The kids had seen her in uniform. They had all, he reminded himself, been indoctrinated together at an Air Force facility. Walt had to admit that it was hard to picture this compact, attractive woman in a uniform, wearing the gold leaf of an Air Force major. Nevertheless, it was quickly apparent that she might be able to help him keep their charges in line.

Back at the hotel after dinner, Tara sat away from the bed and watched him as he took off the prosthesis.

"You're tired," she offered.

"It's not that exactly."

"You're disappointed with this group."

"Not disappointed, exactly."

"I think maybe it is, Professor. You're bending over backwards to give them the benefit of the doubt. But it just isn't working. You're looking for a way to hook 'em. And there isn't any. These kids didn't *choose* you. You were thrust upon them."

"You could be right. Come over here and sit by me, Silky Girl."

"No, let's talk for a few minutes. If I sit by you, you'll seduce me and we won't talk. You want to use me. To avoid thinking. I know how you are."

Walt laughed. "My god, Tara. Did your parents find you inside a peach pit?" He reached over to grab her, but she pulled back, just out of reach.

"OK," he said. "They weren't bad today. Because of the places we visited. The crowds, the food. Other kids they meet. But when I mention the Silk Road, or its connection to China's history, their eyes glaze over. They have no interest in any of the things that are supposed to be the reason why we're here. I feel like a fool for agreeing to be involved in this charade. I'm the wrong guy for this trip."

"I think you should give them at least a couple more stops, Walt. Give them to Dunhuang. If they don't shape up by then, you can just write them off. We can cover the loop by ourselves another time. If they're not OK by then, we can just go back the way we came. Get them home safely, and just say 'screw it.' You don't owe those people your whole guts. You worked hard today. I was watching you. We had a lot more fun in Central Asia. But this place is just as interesting as Turkmenistan, Maybe even more so." A pause. "Definitely more so."

That was the agreement they settled on. Walt would see how they behaved by the time they reached Dunhuang, and that would be the basis for how he would conduct the balance of the trip. Beijing and Xi'an were tourist stops. Dunhuang was the end of the line—the end of the wall, beyond that point ancient travelers had to decide whether to use the northern or the southern routes. Beyond that point, travel—even today—could be uncomfortable. Or even dangerous.

Like Xi'an, Dunhuang was an impressive destination. People came from around the world to visit the Mogao Caves. If the group responded with some degree of enthusiasm and interest, he would treat them like legitimate students for the outbound trip to Kashgar and then they would reassess. If Dunhuang was a bust for them, then he and Tara would retrace their westbound route—looking for things that pleased and interested them. His charges would be free to tag along. His Air Force employers had stressed the need to give them plenty of rope. OK. They wanted it? They'd get it.

"You've never referred to this group as your Herd of Cats," Tara said. Walt was shaving.

"This is China. Cats don't seem to fit. You don't see a lot of cats here."

"What else could you call them?"

"I don't know. Think of something for me. Something Chinese."

"Dragons, maybe? But they don't seem like dragons. Something from those Chinese zodiac calendars you see in restaurants at home. Year of the Monkey. Year of the Ox. I can't remember them all. Don't they have a tiger? What else?"

"They eat dogs. Also scorpions. But these kids aren't scorpions. How about your monkeys? Monkeys might work."

"Oh! Oh! I've got it Professor. Oh! You're gonna love this."

"Bring it on."

"Grasshoppers. Remember that program with the Kung Fu guy?"

"Done, Tara. Done, Silky. That's the winner. The herd of grasshoppers."

"Flock? Isn't that better?"

"In 1949 the newly established Communist government of Mao Ze-dong decreed that Mandarin Chinese, the 'dialect' spoken in Beijing and the surrounding areas, was to be the official language of China, and thereafter would be taught in all of the schools throughout the country.

Today, virtually all Chinese speak Mandarin Chinese, known as putonghua (poo-tongh-hwah) or 'the common language,' as their first or second language. A further boon to foreigners taking up the study of the Chinese language is the fact that Mandarin Chinese—now the only 'dialect' needed—has only four tones."

Preface to "Survival Chinese"
Boyé Lafayette De Mente

CHAPTER 25
Problems With Translation

Since his first visit to China, Walt had been interested in learning more about the language but he never seemed to be able to find time. On this trip, he had determined to learn how to recognize fifty to a hundred Chinese characters and master the tones. Of course, the presence of Penny Liang promised to make this task a bit easier, but he wanted to begin taking a few steps on his own, and on this first morning he had gone down to the dining room even before breakfast was served. Tara was still asleep.

There was usually hot water for making tea and he sat in a corner of the empty room as the first waiters and waitresses began to set up for morning guests.

About ten minutes before the announced serving time, staff began bringing out trays of hot food for the warming tables. At the same time someone began piping in soft music.

He had a pocket phrase book and he was trying to learn a few basic words hoping that Penny would help him to pronounce them correctly.

At first, lost in his phrase book, Walt scarcely paid any attention to the music but after several minutes, as he studied some basic phrases—*Good morning, Goodbye, Please. Thank you*—he was suddenly aware that the music was familiar. It was a tune he had heard years ago. Where? It was something he had heard when he was small. Somehow he associated the tune with a childhood visit in Philadelphia when a radio disk jockey had played it at least once every morning. He guessed it was a big-band novelty tune. How odd to hear this American music in central China. After forty years. As he thought about it a bit, the tune was probably old when he first heard it long ago.

How, in fact, did this hotel even come to possess it? He knew it dated from before CDs or cassette tapes. Possibly even before tapes. It was an old tune, by an old band. It dated back to the era of big discs. Thirty-three RPMs. Or possibly even old seventy-eights. Long before his time.

And then the name of the tune suddenly popped into his head. **Celery Stalks At Midnight**. But he couldn't remember the name of the band. Maybe he never knew it. The music brought back good memories of his childhood when he had traveled to exciting places with his Air Force dad and mom. Suddenly he was interested in learning the name of the band. It had to be a record on a turntable somewhere nearby. More likely a tape.

A young Chinese waitress was approaching with a carafe of hot water to see if he wanted more tea. Maybe she would know where the music was being played. She approached smiling. and he offered her his empty cup. "Nice music," he said. She smiled, but the look was uncomprehending and he repeated the words. He cupped his hand to his ear and gestured to indicate the music and she understood. She smiled and nodded. *Yes, nice.*

"Where is it coming from?" he asked, and immediately realized she had no idea what he was saying, only understood that he wanted something. She said something he could not understand, so he repeated the gesture that had meant music and said *Nali? Nali? Nah. Lee. Where?*

Ah, yes. She understood. She pointed to the back corner of the room where a speaker was mounted just below the ceiling. He shook his head and repeated the question. She smiled and nodded to indicate understanding. Nah Lee? She smiled and walked away, beckoning him to follow with a toss of her head. He rose and followed as she headed toward the kitchen entrance but then she turned and led him to the corner where she pointed up at the speaker.

So much for lesson one. OK, he said. *Cheeng!* OK. Thank you. Xie Xie, *Shay shay*. The first grasshopper pair appeared at the door to the dining room. End of lesson one. This lesson was a bust but maybe Penny could help with lesson two. Tomorrow. They would be in the bus, headed west for a long day on the road.

Penny Liang had a Master's Degree in Oriental Studies from Brandeis when the Air Force had recruited her. She had grown up in San Francisco and attended high school there before her parents moved to Los Angeles. There, she had attended UCLA as an undergraduate in Political Science.

She was thirty-five and in an intelligence position as a translator when her Air Force superiors assigned her to Walt's group as a translator. From her parents and from her education, Penny had become fluent in both Mandarin and Cantonese. She was very bright, and she was very proud of position she held in the Air Force. She was a recently promoted major although she rarely wore a uniform based on the unusual nature of her job—but she was unmarried, and although she had slept—perfunctorily—with half a dozen men, Major Liang had never been in love. She had no idea how this might feel. There was a problem, however. She was a woman and—uniformed or not—her clock was ticking.

Penny had lived her life pursuing goals and she often did not have the time or the inner resources to understand herself very well. Mission driven, the sharp-looking major was perfect for a military life but ill-suited for achieving personal happiness.

She liked Walt right away. A couple of days later when she met Tara they, too, got along well. Walt was pleased to have a Chinese speaker who would be available to him 24-7. In prior trips he had been able to hire someone for a day, or for several days, and language had not been a significant problem. To date, he had resisted the urge to look deeply into the language. His Chinese was limited to *Ni hao.* Hi! *Ni Hao ma?* How are you? And *Shieh shieh!* Thank you. Most of the hotels where he and Tara had stayed in the past had someone at the front desk with a bit of English. There were a lot of Aussies in China. Also, he was a bit surprised to learn, a lot of Germans. And Japanese.

After the initial introductions had been made, Penny had spent about two hours meeting privately with Walt and Tara. Kind of a get-acquainted session after which they went to lunch together. A Chinese restaurant.

"I don't want to get all pushy, so please don't misinterpret," she had said. "But since we'll be traveling together, I may, at times, become annoying if I'm telling you things you already know."

They liked her already.

"Don't worry," Walt said. "We're gonna get along fine. Tara is tough as nails. And she's teaching me something new every day."

"He's a fast learner," Tara laughed.

"This, you probably already know, is *chai*. You know, of course, that Chinese is tonal. A tonal language. You say it like this. *Chai*. But we are drinking now, black tea. *Hong chai*. Say it !"

The three adults sipped their tea. Ate their Chinese food, and made their initial connections. It was a pleasant meal, unremarkable, and the memories soon faded. Weeks later in China, when the headaches of dealing with six grasshoppers caused Walt's patience to fray, Penny Liang would be a rock.

From the beginning, Penny did not seem to relate to the grasshoppers as well as she connected with Walt and Tara. Maybe it was an age thing. Penny was an adult. Walt and Tara were adults. The grasshoppers were still kids. Penny was impatient with them. To her, coming from several years of military discipline, they seemed crude, rude, unruly and lacking in discipline, insensitive to the culture of their host nation. They seemed that way to her because...that's how they *actually* were.

At their very first stop in Beijing, Amory, the 19 year-old, put a move on Penny and she was offended. Tara could probably have stopped him in his tracks and set back his development three or four years, but Penny was not quite so well adjusted. Also, her assignments, mostly in Washington and at the USAF Academy in Colorado Springs, had been relatively sheltered from hormonally inspired advances. Actually, as passes go, Amory's was relatively innocuous.

Fueled by nearly half a pint of maotai, Amory had told an USAF major, mufti clad, that he would like to "try her muff." Inspired by her lack of an immediate response, he had been even more specific. "We can take as long as you want. All night. You are so pretty. I want to hear you moan." He would remember nothing in the morning.

Penny was offended. Well, she was *pretty much* offended. Or at least she wanted to be offended. She left the bar immediately and she debated whether or not she should bring this up with Walt. After thinking about things for over an hour, she decided to manage the news and see whether Amory would be an ongoing problem.

That proved to be a good decision because the boy didn't act out again. But Penny was now on guard and this did not make for warm feelings toward the group Walt called the *Grasshoppers*.

Amory had called her pretty and that was how she thought of herself. But like many Chinese women, she thought that her beauty would last for about forty years or so, after which she would slowly morph into a hag or a crone. She was, in fact, quite attractive, even though she did very little to enhance the features nature had given her. In the right hands she might have become a "stopper", but nothing was further from her mind.

So, from the first days in Beijing, Penny developed a slight prejudice against the grasshopper team. Of the two grasshopper girls, she liked Lisa best. But both girls seemed to be OK. She was aware that Terry had already paired off with Warren, and that was a bit hard for her to sanction.

The kids were spending their nights in Internet cafes where they could meet Chinese kids much like themselves, many of whom had moderate command of English and were happy to act as translators. When she got the grasshoppers together she tried to teach them a bit of survival Chinese.

"Ni hao!" she said. This means, "Hello." Ni means "you." Hao means "well." Together it means "Hello." Try it.

Shit. Within two days they were well beyond "Hello." They were saying *Ni hao ma?* when they came down for breakfast. One morning, Terry said to Warren, "You had me from *Ni hao!*" and others in the group had laughed.

When the grasshoppers were loose in China they frequently split up in pairs. There were two boy-girl pairs, an outcome that—astonishingly—*seemingly*—had not been anticipated. *Really?* And one boy-boy pair. They took off in different directions. An outside observer might have suspected the devious involvement of Dr. W. Kaminsky, the USAF advisor who had insisted on female participation in this program.

"In a certain district, a traveler had heard this ominous voice uttering his own name, but being a stranger, he failed to understand its significance. On reaching his inn, he told his tale to the landlord, who at once informed him that he had become the victim of the poisonous Python, which would infallibly call and devour his heart at the third watch of the night.

This cheerful intelligence was, however, accompanied by a valuable prophylactic—to wit, a small box, which the traveler was to use for a pillow. In this box, he was informed, was a pair of jade Centipedes of the flying species, which must by no means be released from their imprisonment, lest they do serious mischief. At the proper time they would come out of their own accord.

The traveler carefully observed these instructions, and sure enough at the end of the third watch there was sound like that of wind. This was the arrival of the Python. At that instant the little box opened, the Flying Centipedes emerged, and promptly disappeared through a window. The Serpent, on meeting his enemies was powerless, and was immediately vanquished by them in the manner described. By daylight his struggles were over, but the Centipedes, having enjoyed their freedom, had no idea of returning to their coffin, but flew away and were seen no more. As they cost originally fifty ounces of silver, their loss was naturally a source of grief to the inn-keeper. His sorrow was, however, much mitigated by the fact that the Serpent, dead in his yard, had as many joints as a bamboo grove, and each joint consisted of a magnificent pearl, which when sold, made the net profit about one million per cent on the Centipede investment!"

Proverbs and Common Sayings from the Chinese
Arthur H. Smith
American Presbyterian Mission Press, 1914.

CHAPTER 26
Surprise!

Second full day in Beijing. Yesterday his charges had visited Tian'an Men Square, The Forbidden City and the China National Museum. Today he had something different in mind. They would get away from the big monuments and spend most of the day walking around Jing Shan Park. Prospect Hill. They would eat someplace along the way.

To get things underway without delay, he planned for them to breakfast together in the hotel dining room. He and Tara came down twenty minutes early to make sure the arrangements were in place. This morning he wanted them to all be together at the same table. Walt was totally unprepared for the surprise start to his day.

As he and Tara walked through the lobby he saw a face that was vaguely familiar. Damn! That old fellow looks almost exactly like Flo's father. His wife—who had left him for a time to live with another man—had, after being dumped by her married paramour, gone to live with her widowed father. Her father, a very successful corporate lawyer had doted on his pampered only child and he had warmed up to Walt as much as he was likely to warm to any male who carried off his little girl.

Daddy had been misled concerning the circumstances surrounding his breakup with Flo. Misled is not exactly the right term. Florence had lied to Daddy. Big, whopping lies in which she was depicted as the wronged partner and the culprits were the oversexed, immoral coeds who made up a substantial portion of the JBU student body. Walt—because of what she called "his handicap"—had been particularly vulnerable to the blandishments of these predatory females.

Her lies to Daddy had been swallowed, hook, line and sinker. Yes, she had told him, other men had *pitied* her, and she had been tempted. But the flesh was weak, and she was, after all, only a woman. Daddy, who had enjoyed a reputation as a ruthless SOB in his negotiations on behalf of corporate clients, was a real wuss when it came to his daughter. Florence could play her old man, as the saying goes, like a cheap ukulele.

All this flashed through Walt's mind as they walked past the seated gent who was reading a copy of the English language *China Times*.

"Hold up, Tara. That chap we just passed looks like somebody I know. It can't be him, but I've got to take a look. Hold a moment."

Daddy stood up as he saw Walt approaching. "Well, hello Walt. I was certain this was where we would find you. They told me at the desk that you were here. I waited to catch you instead of calling. You were a day ahead of us. We arrived yesterday."

We? Has he found a girl friend? A traveling companion? Walt's head was spinning. *Jonah Tarkington? In China? With Florence? This is too bizarre!*

"Hello, Jonah." Walt extended his hand and the older man took it. "I certainly never expected to see you here. I can hardly believe it. I never realized you were this much of a traveler."

"No, no. I'm not. But where my daughter is concerned...." Walt's heart sank.

Tara walked up to join them. "Hi," she said. "I'm Tara."

Daddy touched her hand briefly like it was a hot potato.

"You two know each other? What a coincidence. In Beijing." She had never met Florence's father.

"Tara, this is Mr. Tarkington, Jonah Tarkington. Jonah is my..." He started to say father-in-law, but it was too distasteful for him to get it out. "...my wife's father. I certainly never expected to see him here."

They stood for a brief moment, speechless.

"What does bring you to China, Jonah? I haven't seen you in—what?—about three years?"

"We've missed you, my boy. But I look forward to seeing you again."

We? Missed you? What the hell was this? Don't tell me.... Walt felt like he had just been sucked into a black hole.

He was wondering about the penalties for murder in China—if you weren't Chinese and only killed a couple of foreigners. If he could be out in a few years, it might be worth it. Tara looked like she had been hit between the eyes.

"I was hoping we could have breakfast together, Walt. There are several things I'd like to discuss with you. Then, maybe later, Florence can join us."

Walt was beginning to see red. "How did you learn where I'd be staying, Jonah?"

"Now, Walt, don't take anything amiss. You know that your program has been reviewed in several of the publications coming out of JBU. And you made the newspaper in Harrisburg."

Tara tugged Walt's sleeve. "You want me to go on in and check on our table, Professor?" Walt nodded. "Nice to meet you Mr. Tarkington." And then she was gone.

"Listen, Jonah, if you've brought Flo all this way to torment me with some conditions, it seems like an enormous waste of money. She could torture me just as well back in Pennsylvania. Anyway, I'm on a schedule. My charges will be here any minute and we have a tight timetable."

"Walt, listen. I have spent a lot of time talking with Florence. I have convinced her that your marriage is the most important single thing in her life. She realizes how important travel is to you, and that she may not have been sufficiently supportive in the past. But she can change. She wants to change. She has changed. And this visit to China is intended to convince you that she can support you in your academic endeavors."

"Jonah, all that is whiskey under the bridge. And I doubt seriously that Flo has chang…"

"She's here, Walt. In this hotel. Isn't that enough to convince you? She has followed you across the globe. Like a good wife."

"Jonah, I don't have time to talk to you, but your whole plan is crazy. I can't believe that she sold you this bill of goods. You're a professional man. Presumably with some ability to see through baloney."

"I love my daughter, Walt. Her happiness is important to me."

"But being married to me makes her incredibly unhappy. Couldn't you ever see that?"

"Walt, these young girls…. They have turned your head. I can understand that. I'm a man of the world, too, Walt. Yes. Though you might find it hard to believe. So I understand your temptation. But Walt, now that you are going to be a father…."

Jesus H. Christ! Walt was stunned. What kind of toxic soup had she been feeding him? He was corporate *lawyer? Trained to be skeptical?*

"Look, Jonah. I can't do this. I can't do it now, and I can't do it ever. And, right now, I'm leaving. I don't want to be rude to you. We've always gotten along well, and I respect you—your position, your attention to your daughter."

"Your wife."

"Until the divorce is finalized."

"Your wife. The mother of your child."

Oh shit. So that's what this is about. She must really be desperate. It was instantly clear.

"Jonah, please don't embarrass yourself. You've heard of DNA. She knows, as you ought to know, that she is not having my baby. It's easy enough to find out who it belongs to. I'm sure you know this already."

"You would do that? Put her through that?"

"Hell yes. Would. Will. Intend to—if you persist in this insanity."

"Walt, will you agree to meet with me this afternoon? This evening? With us? When you return?"

"No, Jonah, I really don't want to talk to you again. You are not behaving rationally. You've been fed a pack of lies."

"She's changed, Walt. Look. She's here. In China. She came. To be with you. To be supportive."

"Get real Jonah. You've been conned."

"When can you meet me this evening?"

"You're not listening."

"She enjoys traveling."

"I hope you brought a good supply of toilet paper."

"Give me a time, Walt."

"Goodbye, Jonah. Have a nice visit. Take her out to walk on the Great Wall. That ought to open your eyes." Walt turned and walked into the dining room. *Oh, my god. Flo pregnant. How did that happen.* Had she done it deliberately in an attempt to get Waasdorp to leave his wife? There must have been some motive. And why had she told her father such a demonstrably false lie? He almost felt sorry for her. But it was sorrow mingled with rage. They had talked so often about having children and she had been adamantly opposed. And now. Under these circumstances that were totally bizarre.

Despite the honest concern he felt for the difficulties of her situation, it was actually laughable. Flo. The perfect woman. The paradigm. Product of Smith. Letter perfect. Facing the prospects of being an unwed mommy. And having to explain to Daddy. But what the hell was Daddy going to do to get rid of her?

This was a real mess that Walt couldn't face right now.

In the dining room his charges were already working on breakfast. Tara looked like the victim of a bomb blast.

"Did you know that they were coming?" she said in a small voice.

"Tara, look at me. I'm as flabbergasted as you are. Let's get out of here and walk. I've got to get my head together. This is worse that you can even imagine."

"I thought all the legal stuff was done."

"It is. It is. But she decided she wants to be difficult. And the old man is a lawyer. Plus he dotes on her and she has fed him a pack of lies. Tara, I'm look-ing at you. Don't be angry with me. This is totally out of my control. I would have bet everything I own that Flo would never come to China. She's here on the old man's nickel and I can tell you it's gonna cost him through the nose."

"But this isn't the best hotel in town."

"It's the hotel where we're staying. The old man tracked us down. He's a real fox."

Walt could hear himself talking but it sounded like echoes reverberating down a long hall. All the time he was talking he was looking at Tara's eyes and she looked like a puppy that had been hit by a car. He was angry at the woman who was still his wife—who had followed him to China—and he was angry at her lawyer father who had enabled her to make a trip she would never have made alone. The anger he felt had a component of violence in it, based on their behavior which was both dishonest and unfair. But in pursuing him halfway around the world, and accusing him of something he did not do, they had, intentionally or not, wounded Tara who was innocent. Maybe innocent was the wrong word.

Fuck! This whole tangled situation was beyond his ability to sort neatly but it was certainly clear to him that he was not the father of any child that Florence was carrying—and from the evidence available to him, it appeared that she had told her father several colossal lies.

All this tangle could be sorted out once everyone was back home, but nothing was never going to be worked out in—*good grief*—China.

"Look, we've got to leave, Tara. Flo has gotten herself into a terrible mess that she can't handle and now she wants to use me as a way out. Her boyfriend has gotten her pregnant. She had to have done it on purpose. He may not even have known. More likely she was trying to use pregnancy to force him to leave his wife. Now she must be desperate if she's coming after me. I scare the hell out of her.

"We need to move right away. First thing tomorrow. Don't look so stricken, Silky. You're making me feel even worse. You know I wouldn't lie to you. And right now I need you to help me speed up our timetable. I'm not talking to either of them. I'm done."

Tara sniffed hard and punched him in the ribs. "Then let's get started."

The grasshoppers and their leaders were underway by 8:30 the following morning.

"Clouds bring back to mind her dress, the flowers her face.
Winds of spring caress the rail where sparkling dew-drops cluster.
If you cannot see her by the jeweled mountain top,
Maybe on the moonlit Jasper Terrace you will meet her."

P'u,Ch'ing P'ing Tiao
Li Po (A.D. 701-762)
In "A Collection of Chinese Lyrics"
Alan Aying and Duncan Mackintosh (assisted by F. T. Cheng)

CHAPTER 27
Loose Ends—Chinese Travel

Walt's group were settled in their Xi'an hotel by late afternoon. Their driver and Chinese guide had been released for the day and the grasshoppers were still in their rooms getting set to go out for the evening. Walt, Tara and Penny had convened in the hotel lobby to relax for a bit after a day of scrambling with travel arrangements. Penny had persuaded a waiter to bring them tea and a thermos of hot water, but she finished her tea quickly and told the pair she was going for a walk.

Walt was already beginning to think about the details for tomorrow's events and Tara was watching him carefully, trying to determine if his leg was hurting or if he might need an aspirin. For several moments he appeared to be lost in thought, focussing on nothing in particular, but then, he appeared to snap out of his reverie and he began looking around the lobby in a systematic manner. Tara watched his eyes focus as he sat up a bit.

"My god," he whispered.

"What is it, Professor?"

"Look over to your right. Against the far wall. At the girl working with the lap top."

"I see her."

"In the lilac dress."

"I see her. What about her?"

"Are you looking? If she's wearing a stitch of anything under that dress, I'll eat it. With or without soy sauce."

"Oh yeah. Gotcha. Wow!"

"Wait until she stands up. Good grief. Plus—on top of the fact that it's better than if she was naked—just look at her. She's drop dead gorgeous."

"Yes she is. Yeah! Wow! I'm impressed...and I don't even like girls."

"That's why, for a time, the old Romans outlawed garments of silk. It looked immoral. This from the Romans. Go figure. How do you think the grasshoppers would react if they saw her?"

"Aaah. I don't know, Walt. They might surprise you."

"Just the boys, I mean."

"They're the ones who might surprise you."

"I wish she'd stand up and face this way. You'd see what I mean."

"Duh! I think I know what you mean, professor."

The Chinese girl appeared to be in her early twenties and she was absorbed in some task at her laptop which was a late model, ultra-thin design—for which she could easily have been the spokesperson-model.

Walt and Tara lapsed back into their conversation about plans for the following day and fifteen minutes later they were joined by the grasshoppers. The youth were traveling in a pack tonight, but they stopped for a few minutes—a perfunctory courtesy—to exchange a few words with Walt and Tara before heading out for the evening. It looked as if they had planned to go roving without Penny's assistance. This probably meant that they were headed for the environment of the local university, where experience had shown that they could count on finding kids their age who spoke passable English.

Walt knew that his hoppers would only sit for a minute or two and he was debating with himself whether or not to call the lilac girl to their attention. Then, inexplicably, lilac girl closed her laptop, put the case strap over her shoulder, and begin walking across the room. Right on cue.

Holy mackerel! Breathtaking. It's better than being naked, and just as revealing. Here she comes. Just as these guys are getting up. Perfect.

She walked right past the six departing grasshoppers and none of the boys even turned their heads. Terry was the only girl who reacted to the transparent lilac scrim with a take. "Wow," she said to no one in particular. "Great stuff." And then they were gone.

Walt turned to look at Tara who was laughing silently.

"I guess I lose that bet," he said.

"Come on," she said. "Let's go see if there's any hot water left in the shower. Maybe you can think of a way to pay me."

"The Chinese know...the more you depend on technology, the more vulnerable you are."

Sami Saydjari
Cyber Defense Agency
Quoted in "Enemies at the Firewall"
Time, December 17, 2007

CHAPTER 28
Plot Changes

In the dining room of the Xi'an Hyatt hotel, Walt and Tara had just walked up to the breakfast buffet table when they were joined by Penny Liang. "Good morning, guys," she said cheerfully, as she fell in line behind them. The morning crowd was beginning to build.

"Did you guys see the celebrity in the lobby?"

"What celebrity?" Tara said.

"I don't know who the heck it is. But I'm guessing he's some kind of professional athlete. A really, really big man. Black. Dreadlocks."

Walt and Tara looked at one another and did a take.

"He's gotta be famous—the way the girls are hanging on him."

Walt handed Tara his plate. "Go on ahead," he said. "I want to see this for myself. I'll catch up in a minute." Tara took his empty plate and he headed for the lobby.

He got there just in the nick of time. The big rasta-guy had two Chinese beauties hanging on him like a parody of a porno film and he seemed totally oblivious to their presence. They were headed for the exit. Walt watched as he slipped something to the doorman and the three people slid into the back of a stretch limo, something not often seen in China.

Back at the table with Tara and Penny, Walt said, "I think you hit the nail on the head. He's probably famous somewhere. I just don't know where. He does look big enough to play basketball."

Penny laughed. "He's big enough."

"What made you notice him?" Walt asked. "Other than his size, the dreadlocks and those Chinese dumplings on his arm."

"It just seemed so unusual to hear a guy who looked like that speaking such fluent *Putinghua*. Mandarin. I wasn't expecting it. He sure doesn't look Chinese. Or like an old missionary."

"He could have grown up in a Chinese country. You think?"

"Tell him all of it," Tara said. Walt looked puzzled. "Tell him."

"While he was at the desk talking to the clerk, another man joined him. A white man. Smaller. The black man said something to him, and the clerk at the desk couldn't understand what they were saying."

"That is odd. Most of those people at the front desk understand English and speak it tolerably well."

"Yeah," she said. "But they weren't speaking English. Or Mandarin. They were speaking Cantonese, which I can understand. Except, I couldn't hear everything they were saying. And I was standing pretty close."

At that moment, three of the six grasshoppers showed up, looking they had just been dragged through knotholes. Walt was still in a bad mood from the appearance of Flo and her father, and he was in no mood for conversation with his charges who were already starting to annoy him. He nodded with a perfunctory smile and left Tara to remind them of departure details.

"The Silk Road...started from Ch'ang-an, present-day Sian, and struck north-westwards, passing through the Kansu corridor to the oasis of Tun-huang in the Gobi desert, a frontier town destined to play a dramatic role in this story. Leaving Tun-huang, and passing through the famous Jade Gate, or Yi-men-kuan, it then divided, giving caravans a choice of two routes around the perimeter of the Taklamakan desert."

Foreign Devils on the Silk Road
Peter Hopkirk

CHAPTER 29
Curious Coincidences in Xi'an

Consider, for a moment, a hypothetical concatenation of events. Pretend for a moment that a college professor with an interest in the history and culture of Central Asia conducts groups of students along the route of the ancient Silk Road. U.S. government agencies pressure him into conducting a bogus group of "educators and alumni" on this trip in order for them to gather intelligence on drug trafficking. In the course of their travels they encounter a Russian criminal, fleeing from his gang boss, who is a kingpin in a vast network for distributing drugs. The travelers apprehend the criminal who later reveals details of the drug cartel that enable it to be seriously disrupted. What are the odds that this bizarre approach to crime-fighting could be successful? Maybe in Hollywood.

Wait! you say. Walt's group isn't looking for drugs. They want information of UAVs. Drones.

Stick with me for a moment longer.

At the conclusion of the—let's call it "takedown"— of the Russian drug organization, our college professor makes it clear that he doesn't want any further involvement with similar missions.

But, over his protests, a certain amount of high level arm-twisting takes place and the professor—whose interests have now shifted to the Silk Road routes in western China—finds himself pressured into a new mission, based on the success of his prior experience. This time the USAF seeks information bearing on China's capacity to quickly ramp up their utilization of UAVs. Once again, this academic, reluctantly recruited, begins his mission which will take him across the western reaches of China—largely in Xinjiang Province, the westernmost region—a province that shares borders with eight—count 'em—eight sovereign nations.

What, in this whole outrageous chain of events, is the likelihood that his second mission could bear the slightest connection to the first? Bear in mind that real life is always stranger and more bizarre than anything possibly contained in fiction. OK. Now back to our story.

Walt had made arrangements for his flock of grasshoppers to stay at the Xi'an Hyatt Regency located inside the walls of the ancient city. Had his group been traveling under normal circumstances, he would have selected less expensive accommodations, but considering the circumstances, this would all be picked up by the American taxpayer. The Hyatt was, unquestionably, very convenient.

On the previous night he had told his grasshoppers to feed themselves wherever they wished, always traveling in pairs, and to assemble in the lobby at 10.00 a.m. China's time system was weird. He had them all synchronize their watches and reminded them that everything in the country ran on Beijing time.

He and Tara were up early and they walked around the city for over an hour. The perimeter of the ancient walls was only about nine miles, and if had been on their own they would have made the whole circuit just to have it in their memory. But they would have been nine, slow-going miles. The city was jammed against its walls.

As it was, they visited two of the wall's four gates. They were back at the hotel almost two hours before they had agreed to meet their charges.

Before going into the dining room for breakfast they sat for a few minutes in the lobby, cooling off, and watching the interesting flow of people. Both of them were interested to see the huge, black man again, dreadlocks to his shoulders. He looked like a professional athlete from America. A basket ball player, perhaps. Well over six feet—maybe six-six—and probably somewhere about two-twenty or two-thirty. No fat.

He was wearing a shiny suit of a material that was a gunmetal blue-gray color. As big as he was, the suit looked as if it was one size bigger. Loose fitting. Underneath, a shirt that appeared to be blue silk. Everything about the big man stood out from the crowd, Skin, hair, suit, shirt.

Walt studied him carefully, then looked at Tara who was somewhat goggle-eyed. Her face was funny enough to make him laugh. Then she looked at Walt and blinked her eyes twice.

"Whaddya think?" he whispered.

"Atlanta Falcons? Miami Dolphins?" She laughed. "Let's go eat. I'm hungry."

At 10 a.m. four of the six grasshoppers were ready to go, but two of the boys were still in their rooms.

"Diarrhea," said Warren. "They went out last night and had a few drinks. Not too many, I think. It might have been the ice cubes." Walt had to go up and check. Sure enough, both boys were still in bed. He checked to see that they had Imodium or Loperamide and plenty of bottled water. Before leaving he told them not to leave for the evening before the group returned in the afternoon.

To heck with them, he thought. *We're going without 'em.*

For this visit to the Terracotta Army, Walt had engaged a local travel agency who insisted on providing the tour guide. Ordinarily, with regular students, Walt would have managed to interpolate his own topics with those of their Chinese tour leader. Now, with his flock of grasshoppers, he was indifferent.

Their bus carried them a short distance to the museum site for the famous Terracotta Army, a necropolis-tomb complex that wasn't uncovered until 1974.

On the way, their Chinese guide filled them in on some of the details concerning the discovery of the warriors, some of their ancient history, and the care taken by Chinese authorities regarding their restoration. The grasshoppers didn't appear to be listening closely to the guide, whose voice had gotten a bit sing-song and mechanical. Minutes later, when she came to the part about forty-eight of the emperor's concubines who had been interred alive with the emperor, their attention seemed to snap back, and by then, the museum complex was in sight.

The tour was pleasant and uneventful. Walt was pleasantly surprised to see that most of the key points he was concerned with, were eventually covered before the tour was over. Considering that Grasshopper interest in the region would be minimal, he started with the premier attraction, the 6,000 man army uncovered in Pit One. Betty Boop, his private name for one of the girls, Terry, commented that all the soldiers looked the same.

"No, you're not looking carefully. They're all different. Look at the faces. Look at the details." The boy with her, the one who seemed to be always at her elbow, Warren, seemed unimpressed.

"My folks have a statue just like these in their back yard, by their rhododendrons. Theirs might be a little smaller. What were these all these things used for anyway? This almost looks like it was a manufacturing plant. Did they make them here?"

From Pit One they proceeded directly to the Exhibition Hall, but his group seemed even less interested in the chariots and other buried objects from the tombs than they had been in the ranks of spearmen and archers. He loaded his charges back in the minibus with a minimum of interpretation and they headed back to Xi'an for lunch. Tara tried to keep any expression off her face. She was trying to gauge Walt 's mood, his reaction, to see how he was going to respond to their indifference. To her, it seemed as if he was monitoring their responses and was giving them the benefit of the doubt before he finally made up his mind.

As was usually the case, she had read him correctly. On the ride back to town she had little to say and she fancied that she could hear him thinking. Before heading back to the hotel, the tour guide announced that the bus would be making a brief stop at a factory making a variety of terracotta replicas of the figures they had just seen. These figures were available for sale in several configurations, from full size to half size, usually used in the U.S. as lawn ornaments or accent pieces. The stop would enable visitors to use toilets, grab a fast snack, or place orders for shipments back to the states. This stop had been mentioned to Walt briefly but it had not loomed large, and he had viewed it as little more than a pit stop. Which, considering his group, is exactly what it would be.

The factory workshop was located within a few miles of the museum and the grasshoppers seemed to be just as interested in seeing the inside of the factory as anything else they had seen. The replicas did, in fact, look just like the ancient figures they had been viewing.

Walt and Tara didn't take the factory tour with the rest of the group. They remained outside the factory entrance, seated on a bench in the small, enclosed courtyard that was colorful and fragrant with clumps of petunias and some type of flowering vines. Beside the entrance to the workshop, several other rooms opened onto the small yard. On one door, Walt saw a sign with three characters, one of which he recognized as the character "bian" meaning *shop* or *store*. He assumed the following character meant *office*. While he was watching the door, it swung open and people began to emerge.

"Tara, look down," he said out of the side of his mouth, "and put on a head scarf."

The girl responded with a sideways glance. Walt's head was down as if he was retying his shoe. When he didn't sit up immediately, she sidled closer and whispered, "What's happening?"

"Keep your hair covered up, and don't stare—but take a look at who just came out of the office. Just to the left."

A group of five men had emerged from the door Walt had been watching. There were two Chinese and three non-Chinese. Two white men and one black man. The black man was huge, with dreadlocks and a shiny blue suit.

Today he had on a different shirt. Deep blue with a white collar and a white tie. He was carrying a briefcase. The men were smiling and shaking hands all around.

"'It's the same guy we saw earlier," Tara said.

"Gotta be. Keep your face from showing. If we remember him, he could remember us."

"So what are you thinking, Professor?" She was looking down. Still whispering.

"If I gave you just one word right now, what would it be?"

"Drugs?" She paused. "Drugs."

"Keep looking away."

Thirty-five minutes later the grasshoppers were back in the courtyard, laughing and swatting at one another. The group piled into the bus and forty minutes later they were back at the hotel in plenty of time to grab a quick nap, wash up for dinner, and walk around the old town inside the walls. On the ride back the guide asked the group if they had enjoyed their visit. *And the workshop? Was that not interesting?*

One of the girls was curious about the shipment of figurines to the U.S. and other countries. "Don't those things weigh a ton?" she asked. Their tour guide laughed. "Not so heavy as you think. Mostly empty inside. What is word? Hallow?"

"Hollow."

"Yes, thank you, hallow. Mostly hallow inside. Not too heavy. But strong. They can last for long time."

Walt and Tara never saw the unknown black man again.

They took a long, slow lunch at the hotel—a meal that was perfectly adequate, but far from what he would have chosen with a different group. With conventional students he would have asked the driver to pick out a Chinese eating place near the University. Any place other than a hotel. Already, Tara could sense that he was displeased with this bunch and he was grudgingly conceding them a trial period to see if their interests might pick up—more in line with his program. For her own part, she was trying to deal with the unexpected presence of his wife in China. He had assured her that father and daughter would never follow them out of Beijing and she chose to believe him.

He still had no real concept of the indoctrination and training the grasshoppers had been given by the Air Force. All he knew was what they had chosen to tell him. In the afternoon they carried the group out to the city

walls, first built around 1370 A.D. by the first Ming Emperor. Walt had
planned the afternoon so they could walk for just over an hour, covering
several miles. Slightly uncomfortable for him, but an interesting opportunity for him to talk about the old city, back when it was Chang'an, the
largest—and richest—city in the world. He couldn't really expect them to
connect at any level with the Tang dynasty; or the fact that the city had once
attracted Manicheans, Zoroastrians, Buddhists, Nestorian Christians and
Muslims. Not to mention home grown Taoists. But he could expect them
to respond to the notions of *biggest*...and *richest*. And to be impressed by
nearly ten miles of fortified walls and watch towers without equal anywhere
in the ancient Americas. He might as well have saved his breath. On the
walk, he did notice, with some degree of surprise, that they seemed to make
connections easily with random Chinese youth encountered along the way.

"Rather like chilies, dog meat is considered 'warming' in Chinese medicine, and also a remedy for male impotence. The meat is often served in a hot pot. However, visitors shouldn't worry about being served dog meat by accident, as restaurants specializing in such dishes usually make it very clear by displaying the carcasses outside their establishments."

China
Eyewitness Travel
Guides

CHAPTER 30
Dog Meat

It was a problem that had never come up before. Of all the contingencies Walt had considered, but this one never made the list. For a score of evenings preceding this trip he and Tara had challenged one another to come up with the gamut of potential disasters that their young charges might expose them to, this one had never made the list.

Now Amory, *the Red Baron*, had freaked out, and was threatening to go home. It was sad. It was a real problem, and yet, it was all Walt could do to keep from laughing.

Part of the problem stemmed without the least doubt, from Amory's background. His parents were dog breeders specializing in Irish setters—a touchy breed—beautiful, quirky and much loved by owners. Irish setters, with their handsome red coats, were dogs that wrapped owners around their fingers. *Make that paws.* They were intelligent in the same way that people are intelligent. Smart in some areas, stupid in others. Their personalities were not only human; they were Irish. If dogs could get access to alcohol, Irish setters would, without doubt, be alcoholics. Lovable, intelligent, unpredictable, addiction-prone.

Amory grew up with these dogs. In a sense, he might have been a dog himself. He lived with dogs, slept with dogs, ate with dogs, and—about some topics—he might even have begun to think like dogs. But one thing he had never considered was eating a dog.

In parts of China, dog meat is a delicacy. Some restaurants—especially in the southern provinces—specialize in dog meat dishes. But in the north of China, dog meat restaurants are like barbecue joints in northern cities of the U.S. They're there, but the food may not be quite the same.

Now—in the same way that places with barbecue usually carry a big sign saying BAR-B-Q—Chinese restaurants with dog meat specialties will carry a sign with the characters, meaning—no surprises here—*dog* and *meat*. What else? But they don't always hang the dogs up outside.

Unfortunately, if you can't read Chinese characters you might not know what you're getting. Walt had asked Penny to stress the single character *meat*, so that grasshoppers could raise the question.

It's probably safe to assume that Amory didn't eat Irish Setter but he definitely ate dog, and what's more, he got it all down without the least difficulty. Such an experience is not unique. In the recorded history of the world, there have been recorded instances where parents dined on their own children before having the details of dinner explained to them. It was something like that for Amory.

When apprised of the facts, he hurled.

He barfed, not once, not even twice, but several times, until it felt as if his stomach was trying to turn itself inside out. When he got over being sick he was angry and it quickly spilled over into belligerence and hostility. "I want to go home," he snarled. "I want to go home now. This place is barbaric."

"Take over," Walt said to Penny and Tara.

"Come on Amory. We're taking a walk to figure out how to do this." Although Walt had eaten worse things than dog and the young man's reaction was hard for him to understand, he had to admit that the boy was really a mess. They were gone for nearly two hours before Amory straightened out..

After two days in Xi'an, culminating in the boy's unexpected meltdown, Walt was happy to get back on the road. Their next major destination was Dunhuang at the western end of the Great Wall.

PART 4.
TAKLAMAKAN—NORTHERN ROUTE

"BEIJING—China, already the world leader in cell phone use, has surpassed the USA as the No. 1 nation in Internet users. The number of Chinese on the Internet hit more than 220 million as of February, according to estimates from official Chinese statistics by the Beijing-based research group BDA China."

China vaults past USA in number of Internet users
Calum MacLeod
USA Today, April 21, 2008

CHAPTER 31
Insight at Jiayuguan's Fort

The grasshoppers had spent the day touring the area's prime attraction, the Jiayuguan Fort, situated at the western end of China's Great Wall. This impressive structure, built from rammed earth, dates from 1372 and was intended to guard the Jiayu Pass. At one time this spectacular site, flanked by snow capped peaks of the Altyn Shan Range, was considered the most strategic pass in the world.

The day had gone smoothly and their local guide's English was good, so Penny Liang had nothing to do but enjoy the trip. By four-thirty the group was back at their guest house accommodations and by five the grasshoppers had showered and were already on the prowl.

Sometime around five-thirty Walt and Tara had cleaned up and were ready to go for a walk. They hadn't rambled for more than a quarter mile when they came upon a cafe with outdoor seating under an arbor. Three of the grasshoppers were having an animated conversation with four young Chinese about the same age. They had pushed three tables together and were drinking beer. The Chinese boys seemed to have a workable command of English and everyone seemed to be having a good time.

"Hi guys," Walt said.

Kevin stood up and introduced Walt and Tara to the youths at the table.

"Pull up and join us," Kevin said, and immediately two Chinese rose to pull another table into the configuration.

"We don't want to interrupt you guys. It looks like you're having a good time."

"Yeah, but we're telling these guys that we believe we can kick their butts."

"Whoa, wait a minute," Walt sputtered.

"In an aerial combat."

The boy who had been introduced as Zhang held up his hand for silence.

"It's no problemo, professor. Zhey zhink zhat zheir skills are superior. We do not share zhat view. So we are examining our options. How can we put zhis difference to zer test. Please. Sit. We would welcome your partizipation. And perhaps you and Miz Tara would take zer beer wiz us?" Zhang beckoned to a waiter and pushed a chair towards Tara.

"Let's listen in on what's going down, Walt," she said.

It was nearly two hours and exactly three beers later when Walt and Tara got up to take their leave and go look for something to eat. In that interval, the remaining three grasshoppers showed up and were involved in the conversation, which was nearing a conclusion. A Chinese boy was making arrangements—by cell phone—with a location where they could find computers supporting the software they were seeking for their proposed competition.

Walt's head was reeling. During the give and take—in which he had taken no part—he had frequently scribbled some notes in his pocket notebook. He didn't understand the tenth part of what he had heard and it bothered him. Tara was in the same boat, except that she couldn't care less. Privately, she was amused to see Walt puzzled that his charges possessed skills of which he had been totally unaware, and of which he was completely ignorant.

"My god, Tara, did you hear the stuff those kids were talking about? It sounds like WW III is gonna start right here."

"They were talking about a game, lover," Tara said, forking an unruly gobbet of noodles into her mouth.

"Have I been asleep, Tara? I felt like Rip Van Winkle as we listened to those kids."

"Yes to your question. But no, you are *not* Rip Van Winkle. It's a big world and no one can keep up with everything. You're supposed to know this. You're the professor. The first thing you've got to find out is that you'll never know everything."

"Eat your noodles. You're no help."

"Remember this moment," she said, laughing. "You'll thank me later."

Back at the guesthouse it was beginning to get dark when they ambled through the moon gate. They sat on a bench in a small garden beneath several gnarled trees. The air carried the smell of dust and ozone. It held the promise of impending rain. They watched the light fade against a backdrop of the Jiayuguan skyline. They were sitting quietly, speculating about the possibility of rain, when Penny Liang walked up.

"Join us, Penny," Walt said. "I was hoping I'd see you tonight."

"What's up?" Penny said, as Tara scrootched over to make space.

"We were out with the grasshoppers earlier and they had met up with a quartet of Chinese kids. They were all fluent in English and everyone seemed to be having a good time—in the way of kids that age."

"So what's the problem?"

"Well—I didn't have a clue as to what they were discussing. But I think it was a lot of air force lingo. I was an Air Force brat, so I heard a lot of acronyms, but not more than two or three were familiar to me."

"OK. Try me out. I know a few."

Walt pulled out his notebook and flipped a few pages. "This one came up several times. FLIR. And DLIR."

"OK, FLIR means Forward Looking Infra-Red sensor. It's oriented to look straight ahead. DLIR is Downward-Looking Infra-Red sensing. On the bottom of the fuselage. You can't shoot 'em until you know where they are. What's next?"

"How about IRST?"

"IRST? OK, that one is for Infra-Red Search and Track; a long range weapon for target detection and identification beyond visual limits. You can see the immediate utility of this capability. This is part of what we call EOSS, Electro-Optical Sensing Systems, constantly being improved to see who and what is out there."

"This one was also thrown around a lot. I've heard it before but I can't remember. JDAMs."

"Yeah, that's one for the public. Joint Direct Attack Munitions. This applies to a whole family of smart bombs, sometimes called *bunker busters*."

"I should have known that one. So what about TSSAM?"

"OK. This one is less well known. Tri-Service Standoff Attack Missile. This one is relatively new. It's intended for a new generation of bombers with heavy lifting capability. For use in a defensive mode. These missiles are intended to stop unfriendly incoming. Before they make it to their target."

"These are all technical Air Force acronyms, right?"

"Yep. You already knew that."

"So why are these kids slinging them around so casually? They're using more acronyms than my dad used to use when he was drinking with a couple of his pals. Hell, they're using military acronyms like kids at JBU say *fuck*."

"You've got to remember Walt, these kids are used to playing the part of aviators in aerial combat. To serious players, this game is at least as intense as chess. They have to master the same level of complexity as actual aviators if they expect to survive. Actually, it becomes an interesting philosophical question. What if you could play your life as a computer game? What does it mean to gamble your life if it's not actually at risk? I can't talk intelligently about this aspect."

Walt closed his notebook and put it back in his pocket. "Thanks, Penny." Tara pinched him on the arm. *Chill.*

"One more question. If that's OK?"

"You're the boss here," Penny said, with an enigmatic smile.

"What the hell is a Herbst? I think that was the word."

"Aaah!" Penny said. "That's a good one. The Herbst maneuver. OK." Now she was flying with her hand. "Developed by a German guy working for Messerschmitt firm, MBB. Fly the fighter into a high angle of attack. Seventy degrees or more. Slow down. Put plane into a stall. Tail just mushes on through. Then use a set of paddles to execute a rapid roll. Tail will swing through and plane will exit after the roll, headed in the opposite direction. I think of it as an Immelmann-like maneuver performed by a crazy person. A maniac. But it's effective; a wild, fast, tight, turn solution to tight spot."

"And where did our kids learn all these details?"

"On flight simulators. I thought they told you all this stuff in Washington. By the way, just to reinforce what you have already heard.... When these kids fly their virtual aircraft, they aren't directing bricks. They choose a particular aircraft with specific characteristics of speed, maneuverability, armaments and performance envelopes; including range and fuel capacity. From their console, they can't make the plane do anything it wouldn't do in an actual flight. They are in specific aircraft that can only perform in precise ways. Same thing is true of their aerial foes. They need to identify what they're up against. Based only on what they see on their instruments."

"I may not have thought about this carefully enough," Walt said.

"And they also learn to maneuver RC model aircraft on flying fields all over the U.S."

Tara pinched him again.

"Thank you, Penny. I've got to think about all this. It's a lot to chew on. We'll see you in the morning."

Back in the room, he sat on the edge of the bed, rubbing his head. Tara sat beside him and put her arm around his shoulders. "You look like you're in overload, Professor."

"This is a lot different than I thought it would be. Why me? Why not just Penny? What the hell am I doing here?" he said.

Walt's party had put up for the night in a marginally acceptable guest house in Jiayuguan. In consultation with Tara and Penny Liang a decision had been taken to detour slightly to visit the Jiayuguan Fort, an impressive complex at the western terminus of the Great Silk Road. As if the massive tamped-earth walls of the fort were not sufficiently impressive, the entire fort complex, with its towers, temples, gates and halls, was backed up by spectacular ranges of the Pamir Mountains, each range progressively steeper, culminating in the snow clad peaks stark against the distant sky. They just keep climbing. Seventy-five miles away—out of sight—the peaks of the Qiliań Shan soar to heights exceeding 14,000 feet.

The three adults agreed that the fort was too good to miss when they were so close, and Penny felt that the grasshoppers were just as likely to meet Chinese students with shared interests in Jiayuguan as anywhere else they had visited.

Their stopover for the evening had the unprepossessing name Edge of Civilization Guest House, and the hot water ran out before Walt finished shaving, something he had been putting off for the past three days. He could hear Tara squealing in the cold water as she showered and he thought about Florence and what her reaction might have been in the same circumstances.

On the following day, the group breakfasted early and their driver had them at the fort shortly after the gate was opened for visitors. During breakfast, Walt had tried to lure his grasshoppers into asking a few questions concerning the fort's age, purpose or history. But it was no sale. This group had been a hard sell from the beginning and their indifference to the sights and sounds of China acted as a goad, prodding Walt to try harder to capture their interest.

On the day of their visit, there were several busloads of students that appeared to be from Chinese high schools or possibly vocational training schools. Penny confirmed that one of the buses was filled with nursing students from a training program inaugurated by the government. The girls seemed to be enjoying the freedom of their outing and, clad in thin dresses, they were uncommonly appealing. Walt expected that his male grasshoppers would behave in the same manner he could expect from students back at JBU. But his male charges took little notice.

The group was back in Dunhuang for a full day at the fort and its environs. Walt was already cataloging this adventure as "the trip from hell" and thinking about what he might want to say to his sponsors back in Washington.

Tara was the bright spot. As they were getting ready to go down for break-fast in what would be a rest day in Dunhuang, she took his arm as he was going for the door.

"Sit down for a minute," she said. "We need to talk."

"Is something wrong?"

"Maybe. In a way. Listen at me for a minute." She paused until he was facing her. "I know you're really pissed at these kids. As well you should be. They aren't perfect by a long stretch. But you're also being unfair to yourself by being so judgmental about them."

"Tara, you know I have...."

"Be quiet, Professor. Be quiet and let me talk. They have been pains in the ass. Yes. I know. I've been here, too. Remember? All the way. But they're really not adults, despite their ages. They're still kids. And Walt, they're not bad kids. Or evil. They're certainly not stupid. All of these guys are very bright. Dumb, maybe. But not stupid. Whatever that means."

"Tara, I appreciate what you're try...."

"Be still. You're starting to sound like your president. Listen to me. This is not about the grasshoppers. It's about you. It's about what you are car-rying in your heart. Listen to me. I love you. I love the man you are. And I don't like to see you bottling up anger. Especially when it's misdirected. I know you feel put upon by those military guys. But they think they're doing their job when they sent you here. These kids were dragooned into this misadventure—same as you. They are as innocent as you are. Dammit, Walt. I can hear your brain spinning. I know that you're already thinking about what you'll say to Chapman and that room full of generals. You're choosing your words to let them know you think they're all assholes, with-out actually having to use the words."

Walt laughed. "What else am I thinking?" *She got me on that one.*

"You're thinking, how quickly can I dump this bunch of kids so that I won't have to deal with them again. C'mon, Walt. Pay attention to these *children*. They're frightened. They were sent here to find out something and they have had an amazing, all-expenses-paid vacation to places that their parents may not even have imagined. It's been exciting and sometimes scary for them. But what have they accomplished? Squat. They have roved around a lot of back streets. And even some of these Internet cafes have a few spooky characters. These kids may seem blasé, but all this is a big deal for them. Back off a little. I know your heart is bigger than you want them to see. Big enough to show them a bit of...empathy. I know it."

Walt stood up slowly and, keeping his eyes on the girl, moved backwards into the bathroom. There he turned on the water in the sink and splashed cold water over the top of his head. Then he came back the room and stood in front of the girl for a long pause.

"Thank you, Tara, *Shieh Shieh!* That was good. I needed to hear that."

She stood up and put her arms around him.

"Lyublyu tebya," he whispered. "You Ukrainian witch."

She took his earlobe in her mouth. "If you say it like that again, you're gonna have to do me," she whispered back.

"Come on," he laughed. "Let's eat."

At breakfast, the entire party gathered at a single circular table in the corner of the crowded dining room. There were quite a few foreign tourists in the room including a group of four Australian couples and a Japanese tour group.

Walt had listened to Tara's little lecture carefully and he had realized there was a lot of truth in her observations. Keith was seated to his right, and Walt decided to try out a new kinder, gentler persona.

The youth returned to his seat with a plate heaped with more food. "Are you finding this trip interesting, Keith?"

"Interesting?" he replied. "Oh yeah! We made a bunch of new friends. I think I could learn to speak Chinese. I'm thinking I might look for a Chinese girl friend when I get home."

"I know you can't talk about what kind of training the Air Force put you through. Or whoever it was that trained you. So I don't want know anything about that. But I am interested to know how you got interested in aviation."

Keith laughed and choked on a mouthful of food. When he finished coughing, he said, still chewing."

"Radio controlled flying!" Walt waited for the boy's food to go down.

"You were a model builder, then?"

"Yeah, I learned from my dad. He's a model maker. Was. He could build anything. He got me started and I moved into RC flying before I was in the first grade."

"Your father was a hobbyist?"

"A model builder. He was a professional model builder. He did some stuff for Disney Studios. We lived in Anaheim then. Him and me.

"So what kind of models did he build? Did you build...?"

"Anything. Everything. He was a great scratch builder. Not just airplanes, either. When I was little, he built simple stunters that were easy to fly. Undemanding. I kinda grew up with the sport and as it grew and improved he and I were on the lead edge. It's what he did for a living and he thought I might grow up to be a skilled builder like him. But by the time I was thirteen or fourteen it was clear that all my interests were focused on flying and less on building. So we fell into a pattern. He built. I flew. It was just the two of us. Actually, he was more like a big brother."

"No siblings? What about your mom?"

"She ran off when I was small. No sibs. Just the two of us. He made a good living. Actually he built a lot of shit for movie studios, too. He was a real professional. We had fun."

"And where did you fly your planes?"

"All over. We went around the country. Western states. I competed in Arizona, New Mexico. In Colorado. I think we flew in at least twelve or thirteen states."

"So what was the most exciting thing you remember about all that flying.?"

While they were talking the others finished eating, mumbled something to Penny, and returned to their rooms. Only Walt, Tara and Keith remained at the table.

"Oh yeah, Lemme tell you about that. This is interesting. In the last two years before he got killed I was flying multi-engine planes in competition. He decided to make a model of the Flying Wing. You know this plane?"

Walt nodded noncommittally. It sounded vaguely familiar. He wasn't sure.

"Northrop designed it. The XB-35. A heavy bomber. The actual plane was flying back in the mid-1940's. My dad built our model in the winter after 9/11. Said he needed something to distract himself. Four pusher propellers. It was impressive. Wingspan of almost eight feet."

"He built this from a kit?"

Keith laughed. "Are you kidding? No kits for that monster. It was scratch built all the way. He scaled the drawings himself."

"He built it. You flew it?"

"Yeah. It took a long time and I did everything very, very slowly. People loved to see it flying. I was like the star of a lot of shows."

"That's a great story, Keith. Thanks for sharing it with us. It was really interesting." Walt pushed his chair back to leave, but Keith wasn't finished.

"I didn't tell you the most interesting part yet," he said. Walt sat back down.

"We were at a meet in Arizona. I was scheduled to make like three flights. Like flights at ten, one and four o'clock. Crowd pleasers. I had finished the first flyover and a couple of maneuvers and was leaving the field when this gray-haired guy came up to congratulate me. You could tell he had been military. But he was in civvies. *Great flight, son. A beautiful model.* He followed me back to our station where my dad was waiting and they talked. The old guy had been excited to see that it was an XB-35. *You gentlemen might be interested to know that I once flew this very plane,* he said. No shit. It was cool. He and dad were having a good conversation together and dad was telling him about his work for aircraft companies. North American. Hughes. Then the older guy turned back to me. *You've been flying a long time?* he asked. *Most of my life, sir,* I told him. *I watched your maneuvers,* he said. *Very impressive.*

"*Thank you sir.* I said.

"*Son,* he said, *Have you ever stalled this model?*

"*Yes, sir, I have. But it's ugly and I don't do it at air shows.*

"*But you've stalled it and recovered?*

"*Yes, sir,* I said."

"I could tell he didn't believe me and he looked at Dad who was listening and smiling. He gave Dad the look. *Is this true?* and Dad nodded back, *Yep.*

"The old guy reached in his back pocket and pulled out his wallet. He took out two one-hundred dollar bills. Franklins. I had never seen one before. Then he looked at my face and took out another one. He folded the three bills and put them in his shirt pocket.

"*If you stall this model in your next flight, and show me how you recovered it, these three bills are yours.* I looked at Dad, he looked at me. *No problemo!* I said. *But I don't want you to risk your ship to do it,* the old guy added.

"At one o'clock there was a pretty good crowd. I did all the regular stunts, then the flyover with smoke, and then I circled the field while climbing and got sufficient altitude to recover the stall. Then I leveled off high above the approach lane and put the wing into a stall. That sucker was falling like a dead leaf. The crowd was gasping. It looked like disaster in the making. It's like a bird that's been shot. Then I powered up one side first, and then the other one, and slowly recovered lift. It was dicey. When she finally leveled off, she was off the end of the runway so I had misjudged that part of it. I had to circle the field before landing.

"The old guy was really excited and he was shaking my hand and pressing in the money. *That was wonderful,* he kept saying. *Great job, son! Great job. I couldn't believe you'd be able to get out of it.*

"*You don't* get out of it, sir. *You fly it out,* I said.

"He gave my dad a business card. He was an Air Force general. I don't remember his name, but there were two stars on the card. A major-general."

Keith paused, story over, and stood up abruptly. "But I'm holding us up, I know."

The hall was empty as Walt and Tara returned to their room. A maid had been in to make the beds and it smelled like camphor. He remembered that he had failed to ask Keith what happened to his dad. "Thank you for your lesson, my love, " he said, kissing her. "You are a treasure."

"I know," she smiled. "Think of an appropriate reward."

"'Because it was the point where the northern and southern arms of the Silk Road converge,' Hopkirk wrote, 'all travelers coming to or from China by the overland route had to pass through Dunhuang. As a result of this heavy caravan and pilgrim traffic, the oasis itself acquired considerable prosperity over the centuries....'

Reading about Dunhuang—that pleasant oasis of 'considerable prosperity '—and walking through it induced a schizophrenic confusion that I was coming to expect in China."

Night Train to Turkistan
(Modern Adventures Along China's Ancient Silk Road)
Stuart Stevens.

CHAPTER 32
Dunhuang to Urumqi

From Dunhuang to Urumqi the road was bleak and the views were, for the most part, depressing. This was the mountainous prelude to China's desert. In the first 120 miles they encountered Bei Shan, which Walt interpreted to mean Beautiful Mountains. On this trip they seemed to be misnamed.

Xinjiang province is the most sparsely settled region of the country and there is good reason. Before the Communist takeover, the province was known to the world as Turkistan, or Chinese Turkistan. It was populated mostly by tribal people known as Uighurs and Huis, who bear little resemblance to most Chinese. They were descended from herdsmen and horsemen from Asia's vast plains, and they had, centuries earlier, been converted to Islam by conquering Arabs. They spoke—still speak—a Turkic language which they write in Arabic script.

In dress, customs and language, the Uighurs and Hui of Xinjiang were much closer to people of central Asian nations like Turkmenistan, Kirghizstan or Kazakhstan than to the Han of central China. Despite China's large number of ethnic minorities, the Han, ethnic Chinese, account for 97 percent of the population.

After Chairman Mao came to China's helm, many Han or ethnic Chinese were relocated in an overt effort to dilute the population while developing the region's resources. Since new arrivals were relocated permanently, the demographics were effectively altered, to the point where the Han were at parity with non-Han. The region had limited natural resources and agriculture, except in oasis regions near the surrounding mountains, was limited by the harsh, dry, cold desert climate. To offset Xinjiang's prevailing poverty, the central government was attempting some improvements. The grasshoppers were surprised to see hundreds of giant wind turbines harnessing the relentless winds.

The ride across Xinjiang Province from Dunhuang to Urumchi was the grasshoppers' first real taste of China's great desert. True, they had looked at miles of dunes, but the difference was analogous to looking at the ocean compared to traveling over the ocean. Their first major stop would be at Turfan, a region that was well below sea level; one of the lowest places on the planet. Walt's charges were surprised to see that vast wind farms had been erected along the eastern fringes of the desert road.

Warren yelled from the back of the bus. "Hey, Professor. What did you say was the name of this town where were headed?" He had a map opened on his lap.

"Urumqi. It's the capital of the Uighur Autonomous Region. Heavily Muslim. You guys will have to be on your good behavior."

"Is that the same place as Urum-key? This place looks like it has a different name."

"Go sit by Penny for ten minutes and let her explain how to pronounce Chinese words that are written in Pinyin. Yes. It's the same place. Urum-chee. See Penny."

This was about fifth time he had said the same words to Warren who seemed to have a remarkably short attention span.

"So will there be anything for us to do in this burg?" Warren continued.

"I would think you could find something to occupy your time. This burg has two million inhabitants. You should be able to find a gym where the Chinese Bikini Team is toning up for the Olympics."

"Woo, woo, woo, woo, woo." Keith started the whooping but all the grasshoppers joined right in.

"Sounds like the chimpies are out of their cages," Tara said with a laugh.

Outside, the bus was entering a region that appeared to be an ancient river valley with steep banks of red clay—or possibly loess—to the north of the road.

"Look at all the caves," one of the grasshoppers called out. "Holy crow. It looks like hundreds of them. As the terrain leveled out, the travelers settled down to the routines of the road.

Before reaching Urumqi, the group was passing through one of the lowest spots on the planet, the Turpan Depression. Turpan was the center of a grape growing region, reknown since ancient times for its wine. But it was also a stopping point for tourists visiting the Bezeklik Caves, a place Walt had considered for his students. He decided the group would take a day in Turpan.

Penny agreed. "You're in command," she said.

"Flaming Mountains—The road east to Bezeklik leads past these sandstone mountains, made famous in the novel *Journey to the West*, a fictionalized account of the journey of the pilgrim monk, Xuanzang, to India."

From *Xinjiang*, in "China" Eyewitness Travel Guides

CHAPTER 33
An Unforeseen Complication

When his wife and her father showed up in Beijing, Walt had been dumb-founded. Then he learned that she was pregnant, and that she had led her father to believe it was his child. Fantastic! But of all the conceivable problems or situations that his imagination could conjure, Walt could never have imagined the little headache that revealed itself in Turpan. *Sometimes called Turfan.*

Turpan, an oasis town on the northern route around the Taklamakan, has given its name to the region known as the Turpan depression, one of the low-est places on the planet. The city of approximately a quarter million people is predominantly Islamic, made up of Uighurs, descendants of nomadic tribes from Siberia who settled between the 5th and 7th centuries. Backed up against the breathtaking Tien Shan Mountains the elevation in the vicinity of Turpan is about 150 meters—below sea level. Approximately 490 feet.

Despite its location between mountains and desert, Turpan is well watered and this whole region of Xinjiang Province is noted for the production of grapes...and wine.

Walt had made a practice of learning the population of cities where he planned to spend a full day touring, and listing the names of a few American cities of comparable populations. The idea was to give his students a frame of reference for the places they would be visiting. Turpan was roughly the same size as Orlando, Florida. Slightly larger than Providence, Rhode Island. But his grasshoppers seemed singularly disinterested in this type of informa-tion. And after one of them made a mocking aside, he resolved to stop the practice.

Back in Dunhuang, the group had been observed by a man they believed to be a member of the Chinese Security Police. He had been friendly but business-like as he had interrogated the group at one of their brief after-dinner meetings. Mr. Huang Wang-Ming had just showed up wearing civilian clothing, but formal, with a distinctly military bearing. He quickly made it clear than the grasshoppers could leave but he requested Walt, Tara and Penny to accompany him to a small, private dining area where they could continue his questioning.

It wasn't completely clear to Walt what he was trying to learn about the group because his English was barely adequate, but he and Penny could talk away in Mandarin. Walt was gathering from her smiles and body language that Mr. Huang's interest was superficial and nothing to be worried about.

Huang Wang-Ming was a large man, even for this part of China where people tended to be larger than on the coast, possibly because of diet, or climate. Mr. Huang was over six feet tall and he was powerfully built. Judging by the fit of his clothing, he might have been a body builder, although that seemed unlikely. He was almost certainly a military man of some type, although he identified himself as a security policeman, a designation that was sufficiently vague.

In spite of the absence of badges, credentials, or any other form of identification that might have been offered in the states, Walt did not want to challenge Mr. Huang. Warily, he was just letting things proceed along at their own pace.

Watching Penny, he was slowly beginning to become less concerned than he had been when Mr. Huang first approached the group. He had no idea of all the places his grasshoppers might have visited, who they might have spoken to, or what they might have said.

But now Penny was beginning to smile a bit, and she was talking animatedly. More animated, now that he noticed, than her usual demeanor, which tended to be somewhat serious and business-like.

Penny was wearing a plain white blouse that buttoned up the front, and a drab, black midi skirt of some type. Normally, Walt paid little attention to what people wore, but on this one evening, as he and Tara sat watching the conversation between Penny and Mr. Huang, Walt could see six or eight inches of Penny's throat.

Unless he was mistaken, her skin was flushed. This was an observation that he had never shared or discussed with anyone, but both his wife, Florence, and his miracle lover, Tara, flushed during sexual arousal. He had no idea if this was universal, but he was relatively certain that it was a dependable indicator.

Truth to tell, Mr. Huang was uncommonly handsome. A lot of good-looking Chinese males were showing up in popular movies in the U.S., and although Walt didn't know the names of these leading men, he could see that Mr. Huang's looks would appeal to many American women.

From time-to-time, Penny would pause and translate a few sentences of the conversation, which was increasingly punctuated with smiles and laughs.

"Mr. Huang says that our group has made quite a few friends during their trip to China. He says that the Chinese students, in particular, have enjoyed meeting Americans with whom they share interests."

"Yes, tell him that they are all my students, and although we are looking at the cities of the Silk Road, they are all very interested in computer applications."

"He says they are also knowledgeable about the radio-controlled airplanes that people fly as a hobby."

"I am not surprised, tell him. That is a very popular hobby back home. Although, tell him, it tends to be enjoyed by people in wealthier families. It's a somewhat expensive hobby. Most of my students come from families that are well off. So that does not surprise me."

Penny translated, and Mr. Huang responded with a chuckle. While she was translating back to Walt, Mr. Huang, pushed his chair back and stood up to go.

When Penny finished speaking, he said a few words, included some that Walt and Tara recognized as *Thank You*, and *Good Evening*. And then, with handshakes all around, he left. The three grasshopper herders were left alone in the room. Nobody said a word for several minutes, and then Penny whispered, "Let's reconvene outside, over by the parking lot."

Outside, in the dry heat of a desert evening, Walt was the first to speak.

"Whadda'ya think, Penny?"

"I'm not sure. But I'd bet my britches this guy is in the Air Force. PLAAF. Some few words and expressions in his vocabulary. I can't exactly put my finger on it. But that's where I'd put my money. He was friendly enough, though. No bad vibes or body english of any kind from him. I say steady on course."

"Should we do anything differently?"

"I can't be sure, of course. But I'd say no. Steady on course. We just keep going. No changes."

Tara had not said a word, but she was studying Penny closely and her eyes had a look Walt had seen before. Like a hunting cat.

They agreed that the visit gave them no reason to be concerned, so no changes to plans or itinerary were made. The walked back in to the lobby where they passed four of the grasshoppers on their way out.

"What's happening?" Walt asked.

"Internet Cafe," one said. "They have some games we're good at."

"Good luck," Tara said, and Penny added something in Chinese that was probably a repeat.

All that had taken place earlier. In Dunhuang. Walt had mostly forgotten the encounter. But then, in Turpan, there were new developments.

He and Tara were back in their hotel room, putting stuff in their day packs for a short ride out to the Jiaohe Ruins and a look at the unusual irrigation systems found all across central Asia.

"Penny didn't make it for breakfast?" he asked. "Did you see her come down earlier?"

"She was down earlier. I thought you saw her. I've been waiting for you to say something."

"I never saw her in the dining room."

"That's because she walked out with the guy. That guy. Remember? They probably had breakfast next door. That place looked pretty good."

"What guy?"

"The Chinese guy. Remember? The good-looking big guy. The movie star. You know. Mister....mister...."

"Huang. The security police guy? What's he doing here?"

"Beats me. But they went out together. Actually, they looked kinda good together."

"Now I'm starting to get a headache, Tara. Penny is supposed to go with us today. I've got another guide lined up, but in the afternoon we were supposed to visit the Bezeklik Caves. Would you mind checking in her room and find out if she's planning on being with us all day?"

"No problem, Professor. Be right back."

Tara was gone for nearly twenty minutes and Walt didn't want to leave before she came back with the story on Penny. He was getting impatient, when the door opened.

"Sorry," she said. "She wasn't in her room. I had to go looking for her. She was in the lobby, talking to that guy. Wang-Ming."

"Is he here to ask us more questions? How come he hasn't talked to me? To us?"

"Walt, I think he came here to see her. I'm pretty sure of it."

"Talk to her? About what? This sounds weird."

"Walt, brace yourself. I think we have problems. Right here in River City."

"Tara, what the heck are you talkin...."

"Walt, I can read the signs. Something happened in Dunhuang."

"You are really confusing me."

"I don't know why. Look, just before we left the states to come here, I saw a word in the newspaper I had never seen before. But it was immediately apparent what it meant."

Walt sat down to wait for what was coming. This was no time to be impatient. "This is why everyone should read Lao Tsu. Take your time, Pussy cat."

"Walt, the word was 'gobsmacked.' Our miss-all-business Penny has been *gobsmacked*. I don't know, but this may be the first time it ever happened to her. She's been temporarily derailed."

"Sweet Jesus," Walt said. "What next?"

"Fresh changed in summer silks and sipping wine
And sick at heart, this time from home so emptily thrown away!"

From "Ode to a Red Rose"
Chou Pang Yen (A.D. 1057-1121)
In "A Collection of Chinese Lyrics"
Alan Ayling and Duncan Mackintosh

CHAPTER 34
Girl Talk

Tara was up early to use the toilet before Walt and she wanted to shower before this little hotel ran out of hot water. Walt was getting out of bed when she came out of the bathroom.

"I'll meet you downstairs," she said, pulling the Buchanan sweatshirt over her head.

"Yeah, OK. But don't go walking without me. We don't have a feel for this place."

"I'll see you in the dining room."

Downstairs, the dining room had just begun serving, but Penny Liang was already at a small table, ahead of the group, having coffee.

"May I join you?" Tara said.

Penny pointed to the chair opposite and a waiter moved in immediately with a carafe.

"I'll probably wait for Walt to come down."

"I would, too," Penny laughed. "Wait for him, that is." Then in a small voice she added, "You guys look so good together."

"Um." Tara waved the waiter away and turned her cup upside down.

"How long have you two been married? If you don't mind my asking."

"We're not married," Tara said. "We are, as they say, kinda shacked up."

"Oh, gee, I'm sorry if I seem...."

"Actually, Walt is still married. In the process of getting a divorce. But, for some reason, his wife is making it difficult for him."

"I didn't mean to touch on a sore subject. Just that you two look so great together.... Anyone might get jealous just looking at you. Together."

"Yeah, I hope so. He is a very special kind of guy, and I really am crazy about him. He and his wife didn't have any kids. And I could see that both of them were unhappy. In different ways and for different reasons. I just set out to get him by fair means or foul. So far, not one second of regrets."

"We don't have to talk about it."

"It's OK, Penny," Tara had already figured out where this was headed. "Actually, it feels good to have someone I can talk to about our whole situation. We want to get married, as soon as he can get free and clear. We can't figure out what's wrong with his wife. She was the one who walked out. He wanted children. She didn't. At least, not with him."

"I won't ask any more questions," Penny said.

"Go ahead," Tara said. "Ask away. I don't care. I like talking about this man, and what he has done for me. And to me. I am still, as they say, in love, and I'm sucking it up."

Penny stood up. "Let me get something from that buffet before people start coming in. Then, you can tell me how you two met. If you don't mind talking about it, I'd like to hear your story."

Back at the table with melon, grapes and rice crackers, Penny resumed her quiz. "Tell me about how you guys met."

"I was his grad student at JBU. He takes students on trips along The Silk Road, and I was on one of his trips. I got diarrhea and couldn't make the scheduled flight out. He stayed back with me for a couple of days when it was just the two of us alone. I got better and I decided to try whatever I thought might work. Honest, Penny, it was the most fun I ever had in my life. I thought I was seducing him, and he set me on fire. I can get damp just thinking about it. It was so wonderful. So romantic."

"You're a lucky girl," Penny said. "A white knight? A lot of women never have anything close to that."

Walt entered the dining room together with three of the six grasshoppers. "How come you guys are sitting over here at this small table? Some secrets? Girl talk?"

Penny laughed. "I was just leaving. I need to make a phone call and brush my teeth. See you guys at nine." She turned back to Tara and smiled. "Let's pick this up later. I still have more questions."

Tara joined the group at a big table and the rest of the grasshoppers joined them a few minutes later.

Walt's planned day was interesting, with a visit to Kuqa's main attraction, the Thousand Buddha Caves located about 40 miles west of the oasis town's outskirts. Today's Kuqa is served by a rail and bus routes as well as a domestic airport. It draws many tourists primarily to visit the famous caves, which date from the period 500-700 A.D. Frescoes in the caves are noted for their blending of Greek and Iranian influences that date from the time of Alexander. After seeing the caves and grabbing a touristy lunch their bus carried Walt's group to the ruins of an ancient city dating from the 12th century. There, the grasshoppers expressed their unanimous disinterest in the ruins of ancient walls.

By five o'clock they were back at the hotel. By six they had finished supper and the grasshoppers had changed their tee shirts. Six-fifteen and they were gone for the evening, probably not to be seen until breakfast tomorrow, after which they were scheduled to continue westward to Kashgar.

Earlier in the day, Penny had said, in an aside to Tara, "If you have time this evening, I'd like to pick up where we left off this morning. If you're free, that is."

"After dinner. Is that OK?" They agreed to meet in the lobby at seven.

Tara was slightly flattered to think that the older woman, a professional warrior whom she had seen in uniform and been impressed, wanted to talk to her. About what? Romance? Love? This trip? What? What could Tara tell this poised, mature Air Force major, fluent in Chinese, trained to command, like Walt, a college professor. At seven, she left Walt reading on the bed and went down to meet Penny. There had been a fair amount of walking and climbing during the day. Walt had unfastened his leg so it was likely that he might be down for the night.

In the lobby, Penny suggested that they grab a couple a beers and find a quiet corner to talk. This was not normal behavior for Penny Liang and Tara wondered if anything was wrong with any of the grasshoppers. She kept silent until they had located a couple of bottles of Tsingtao and found comfortable chairs.

"What's up? Is anything wrong?"

"No. Everything's fine. But I was just fascinated by what you told me this morning. That you chased after a married college professor and tried to seduce him. I mean—not to sound judgmental or anything—but didn't you think that it might have been wrong?"

Tara took a long, slow sip of beer as she tried to think of an appropriate answer. She wasn't quite sure exactly where the question was coming from. And she liked Penny too much to give her a frivolous answer. She respected her and thought that she had a great deal of class and dignity. But something about the question was faintly annoying. She belched softly from the beer before continuing.

"Did I *think* it was wrong? No. No. Not at all. Actually—I *knew* it was wrong. Whatever the hell that might mean to you. It *was* wrong. But it wasn't *as wrong* as letting a good man continue to be made miserable by a woman who didn't really love him, and who, in fact, couldn't even see what he was. Plus—on top of it—it wasn't *as wrong as* denying my own heart. I fell for this guy almost from the first time I was in his class."

"You said something like that earlier this morning. But I don't know exactly what you...."

"Penny, listen to me. Listen. Have you ever been in love? Knockdown, drag out, grown up love? Take no prisoners love?"

Penny sat up straight and her appearance seemed to change from an attractive oriental woman in casual travel attire, to an Air Force Major on duty in mufti. She stiffened.

"I'm not a virgin, if that's what you're asking."

"That's not even related to what I'm asking. No. I'm asking about smash-mouth, no-holds-barred love, that means you would sacrifice anything and anyone—yourself included—to get the one you want."

"How can you trust feelings that are so intense, and potentially self-destructive?"

"Penny, you're embarrassing me. I'm a bit younger than you, and I don't have your experience or your education. You're asking me questions that have puzzled people since the dawn of time. But my answer would be, that a person who hits her finger with a hammer doesn't have to intellectualize about pain. It hurts. You know it. No questions asked. You drop the hammer. Head for some cold water or ice. Same with the lightning bolt. You grab for the gusto. This is not a rehearsal for the play called life. This is the performance. Curtain is up. You're on. Listen, I'm embarrassed to be talking this much."

"Tara, please.... Don't be angry. Or impatient with me. Just that you and Walt together make me jealous. Please don't be angry, Tara. But I'm jealous as hell watching you. I admit it. I see how you look at him. I see how he looks at you. You guys break my heart. I haven't seen anything quite like it before, and it's puzzling to me." Tara reached across the coffee table and took Penny's hand.

Penny looked directly into Tara's eyes and her face grew stern.

"Do you know how many people live in China?" Penny asked. Tara was puzzled. "The population? Roughly? Do you know?"

"Not really."

"About one-point-three billion. That's a lot." She paused, remembering the next fact. "And they live until their early seventies."

"OK. And?"

"In this country there are over 20,000 agencies—service bureaus—whatever, that specialize in computerized matchmaking. Some of these matchmaking groups have several million clients, looking for mates. It's like those ads on TV back home. *Find your soul mate. If we don't find the one person in the world for you in six months, the next six are free. Look for the 57 varieties of compatibility.* Just like Heinz. So...there are millions and millions of people, all over the world—even here in China—are looking for love, even if they have to use computer surveys to find the right person."

"What can I say, Penny?"

"Millions and millions of people. Hunting for the one right person in all China. Paying for computer services to help in the search. Millions in the data bases. And you just walked into a classroom, and got hit by the thunderbolt. Like that guy in The Godfather?"

"As they say, shit happens."

"I know. I know. But how can you be certain?"

"Hello, earth. Tara to earth. Come in, Penny."

"Don't mock me, Tara."

"Look, Penny, how can you really ever be sure of anything? We're all just trying to do the best we can."

"Tara, I am so..."

"Dammit, Penny. You go with your gut feelings. You're intelligent, and you are beautiful, poised, independent. Why am I telling you this? You should be telling me."

"Do you remember that Chinese officer who took us to his office in Dunhuang? The big, handsome guy?"

Tara's radar picked up a bandit. *Bandit at twelve o'clock. Uh oh! This is a change of direction. Here's where this has been heading.*

"Yeah?"

"He's followed us here. But I think he was really following me. Yeah, actually, I know it."

For the next thirty minutes, the two women talked. Not everything they said needs to be repeated, but Tara told Penny several things about Walt that the Air Force major didn't know. The Air Force major told Tara one or two things that the girl would probably never have suspected. It was 'girl talk.' Some kind of a bond of trust was formed between them, even though neither of them could have put it into words.

After thirty or forty minutes, the two women walked outside and made a short stroll around the front of the hotel and past the parking lot for tour buses. Penny's eyes were wet. At the end of an hour, Tara tapped on her room door and opened it. Walt was propped up, still reading.

"You OK?" he asked. "I was starting to think I should come looking."

"I've been talking to Penny. We drank a beer together."

"That doesn't sound like Penny. Anything wrong?"

Tara sat on the bed, and leaned back to put her mouth against his ear.

It was the faintest whisper.

"Nothing wrong. But something surprising, my darling man." She waited for him to ask, but he knew she was waiting and she knew he knew.

"I think our translator has fallen in love."

Walt's book slapped shut and dropped to the floor.

"Are you kidding me? Who is it?" He was sitting up, hoping that he was not going to hear his suspicions confirmed. "Not a grasshopper?"

"Remember the big Chinese officer. The Air Force guy? The one who looked like a Soviet era statue? The perfect male? It's never happened to her before. You should have seen her face when she told me. She's gobsmacked. It's for certain."

"Oh, fuck!" he groaned. "Fuck, fuck, fuck! What next? Well, we're leaving at ten tomorrow anyway. Hell or high water."

"Every traveler in Central Asia knows (and blesses) the British Consulate-General at Kashgar, for it is a haven of comfort and a centre of hospitality to the European who tries his luck in Chinese Turkistan."

Colonel Reginald Schomberg (1933)
Quoted in: "Foreign Devils on the Silk Road"
Peter Hopkirk

"Everywhere, people were slurping fruit juice or cool jellies in spicy dressings. The crowd milled around, talking and shouting in a melodic, guttural tongue that sounded like Turkish. The air was filled with the punchy scent of cumin from sizzling kebabs.

I found it hard to believe that I was still in China. The only reminder was the occasional street or shop sign, with Chinese characters alongside the local, Arabic-based script. Kashgar, the Silk Road town where this famous Sunday market draws trade from far and wide, lies in the desert province of Xinjiang, at the westernmost tip of the country."

Shark's Fin and Sichuan Pepper (2008)
(A Sweet-sour Memoir of Eating in China)
Fuschia Dunlop

CHAPTER 35
Kashgar

Kashgar is located at the western end of China's Xinjiang Province, bordered by snow-capped Pamir mountains to the south and west and by the Taklamakan Desert to the east. It represents the terminus at which the northern and southern Silk Road tracks around the desert again converge to face the challenging roof of the world that separates them from markets in the west.

Today's city has a population of more than 200,000 people and boasts an international airport. At one stage in its history it was an independent state, ruled by a khan and known by the name Kashgaria. Because of its large Uighur-Muslim population the city bears a closer resemblance to towns in Central Asia than to China.

From Kashgar the Karakoram Highway extends southward across the Karakoram mountains, a rugged and ancient track that wasn't improved for vehicles until the 80s. It provides the only vehicle route to Pakistan and India.

Because of its strategic location at the western end of a harsh desert and the fact that it was the largest population center to be visited by caravans before they undertook the arduous passage over the high Pamirs or Karakoram mountains, Kashgar has long been an important prize for people wishing to control Silk Road commerce. For Walt it was a magnet.

Accommodations in Kashgar were delightful for Walt even though they were far from being the most comfortable his group had encountered in China. Their hotel was in the building complex that had once housed the old British consulate dating from the beginning of the 20th century. Walt made a note to reread Rudyard Kipling's Kim when he got home. He had read it years ago and it had fired his interest in the mountainous region of northern India, but his understanding of *The Great Game* had been limited by his age at the time. In Kashgar, where old consulate buildings built for

England and Russia were still standing, still in use, and still comfortable, *The Great Game* seemed all too real.

Walt's six charges couldn't have cared less about Kashgar's history. Likewise, the fact that this was the place where the northern and southern routes around the Taklamakan again converged before continuing to the west was of no interest to them. Kashgar was the most Islamic city they had yet visited but at this stage the grasshoppers had become accustomed to seeking a bit of nocturnal excitement. The spectacular scenery of the distant Pamirs failed to entrance them. After all, they had all visited Denver and Boulder. Snow was snow.

Walt arranged for a half-day excursion to the Caves of the Three Immortals but he neglected to get special permits from the Kashgar Visitors Office, so the group was prohibited from photographing any of the surviving figurines. The grasshoppers were vocal in their complaints, not that they actually wanted to take photographs but simply because this gave them an excuse to criticize Walt's and Penny's authority.

After dinner they were gone, headed for local Internet cafes, or Planet Hollywood, game parlors or Hard Rock cafes; anywhere they could find Chinese youth of their own age.

In the early evening, Walt and Tara, accompanied by Penny, visited several of the many fascinating bazaars in Kashgar's Old Town. During their rambles, they ran into Keith and Kevin at a vendor's booth where the boys were engaged in an amusing transaction. The vendor had a table full of Russia-era military badges, buckles, pins, medals and coins on display. He was trying to interest his audience in a zippo-type Russian cigarette lighter with a cloisonné insignia. The red star was emblazoned with a hammer and sickle, and a legend underneath bore a Russian word. Perhaps a motto?

The vendor kept striking the lighter, obviously demonstrating that the flint not only worked but that it had been filled with fluid. Keith had shown interest and the seller, an ancient fellow with a stringy white beard and the classic central Asian skullcap called *tubeteika,* kept up his vigorous sales pitch—with words no one could understand. Kevin was standing to one side laughing silently.

"What's happening, guys?" Tara said, as the three adults took in the scene.

"He wants to sell me this Russian lighter," Keith said. "I might buy it if I could read what it says."

Tara reached for the lighter from the vendor.

"It says Leningrad," she said.

"No stuff?' Kevin said. "Leningrad?"

"Leningrad," she repeated. "You just bought yourself a good lighter."

"One gift of years; one pulse of time; one pair of souls, we two.
Why do we let love overwhelm us, life divide us?
Eyes meet, thoughts meet, but we, we never meet as lovers do.
Heaven made the spring for someone; who?

From a Tz'u poem
By Na-Lan Hsing-Te (1655-1685)
In "Chinese Lyrics"
Translated and rendered into verse by
Alan Aying and Duncan Mackintosh

CHAPTER 36
A Night in the Desert

They had stopped for the night at a guest house in Karghilik and the grass-hoppers were out walking the streets of the oasis town with Penny. Walt and Tara were at an outside table drinking green tea and poring over a map trying to figure out a reasonable destination for the next day's drive.

"It looks like a good start in the morning could give us Hotan by lunchtime."

"I agree," Walt said.

"The old Silk Road was to the north. Out in the desert."

"Yeah. Along the line of the old abandoned ruins."

"How strict is our timetable, Professor?"

"Tara, right now our timetable is whatever we want it to be. We're just shuttling past some history of this place. I'm making a few notes, but we're missing some of the best parts. I'm not answerable to anyone for where we stop, or for how long we take. We'll get back when we get..."

"I want us to take an extra day."

"That won't be a problem, kitten. Where do you want to go?"

"I want the group to stay here an extra day."

"Here? Why here? There's nothing here to occupy them. What do you want us to do here?"

"We won't be here," she said. She wasn't looking at him. She was still studying the map.

"You're being mysterious, Silky Cat. What have you got in mind?"

"I want us to spend the night in the desert. In the ruins. Just us. You and me."

"These kids are not gonna go for...."

"Us. As in you and me—together. Alone. In the ruins of an ancient city. This one right here."

She pointed to a spot on the map labeled *Xiytiya City*. "I can't even pronounce it." It was the site of a ruined village engulfed by sand, a place of the type that a century ago had lured treasure hunters and artifact collectors from around the world. Maybe it had already lured some famous adventurer, but Walt didn't know offhand. It was a town that had been killed by scarcity of water, or encroaching sand, or both, or maybe something else. Or perhaps bandits.

"How did you pick this place, Tara? Chances are it's little more than a few ruined foundations...bricks in the sand. Maybe a few weathered sticks where there were once trees or a house. There may be nothing there but a mound."

"Don't you think we can find it?"

"We can probably find it OK, it's just south and east, and someone there will be able to lead us. And anyway, its apparently known well enough to be marked on the map."

"That's where I want us to go. You and me. Tomorrow night. OK?"

"Not tonight? Tomorrow? Sleeping out? In the open? We don't even have sleeping bags."

"We'll take today to get some stuff together. Plus something for breakfast in the morning. In case we get up early. We can always get some blankets. Even a cheap rug. Or pick up a couple of bamboo mats. They have roll-ups in most of these markets. We can find enough stuff to make it through one night."

"Yeah, sleeping gear for one night shouldn't be an obstacle. But look, what's the idea? We didn't talk about this before. The grasshoppers will be going out of their minds for something to do."

Tara laughed. "Screw the grasshoppers. This is about you and me."

"How come you never mentioned this before?"

She smiled. "I didn't think of this before. I wasn't ready to do this before."

"I'm still a bit confused. You..."

"Look. Yes or no. I. Want. Us. To spend a night in this desert. On the Old Silk Road. Completely and totally alone. You and me. Do you ever look up at the moon? I can't make it any clearer."

"Tara, I would go with you to the center of hell, if..."

"Look, Professor, don't get all philosophical on me. I couldn't stand it. Do you want a son or not?"

Walt sat up straight and shook his head as the scales fell from his eyes. He was silent for several seconds before he stood up.

"Let's go shopping."

They told Penny that they were making an unplanned detour to study the ruins of an ancient city and that they would have Fong drive them there in the afternoon. Maybe she could come along to see where they were going. The place appeared to be just out of town on the road leading south. It wasn't clear from the map what they would find, but the fact that it was marked meant that they could probably drive there. Even if Fong couldn't get them there, the road was certain to be negotiable by some type of vehicle they could find in the neighboring community.

They would go out tomorrow afternoon and spend the night in the desert. Then, the following morning, Penny would get the grasshoppers loaded for an after-breakfast departure. Fong could pick them up in time for breakfast, an hour or so before they checked out from the guest house.

On the day after Tara's request they left at mid-afternoon and Fong drove them to the sand-swept rubble pile labeled as Xiytiya City. The public was still permitted to visit parts of the ruins but they were extensive, and with a bit of afternoon searching the couple found an unvisited corner where they felt they would probably be safe. Fong could pick them up in the morning, and he agreed that it was unlikely they would be disturbed after dark. When they were alone, they found a spot near the corner of an ancient structure that might provide some protection in case of wind. Tara began to collect a pile of dried brush and Walt made a small fire. Neither them knew the name for the bushes they were burning but the aroma was pleasant and the twigs didn't throw too many sparks. As daylight faded they were able to keep their fire small and sit close.

Tara told him stories about growing up in a Ukrainian community in Cleveland. They rarely spoke about a whisper. Walt told her stories about the adventures he had experienced with Ekrem during his boyhood in Turkey. They laughed about their shared experiences with the group of operatives they had named the Herd of Cats in Uzbekistan and Turkmenistan.

"I really feel terrible about the appearance of Florence and her father in Beijing. But there was no possible way for me to know—or even imagine—that would happen. When we get back, I'll see the lawyer and..."

"Look, don't worry about it Walt. Let's don't even talk about it. I don't care about her. Or her old man. Or anything but you and me. What happens will happen. Right now, we're in the back of beyond. Nobody will ever be able to take this away from us. Or have an experience to match it."

Darkness had come quickly after the sun disappeared below the horizon. Stars were visible overhead and down the horizon in the east. As the sky darkened, several constellations of summer became visible and Walt told her the names for those he knew. The night air carried a scent of distant dust.

"A lot of our names for them come from Arabic. But there must be a lot of good Chinese names and the stories to go with them. We can look when..."

"Where did you learn this stuff?" she asked.

"Some from my Dad. Then later, from books. We have some good ones in our library back in Mercersburg. When we get back we can go out again. But we'll never have a night sky like this back there."

It was still early when they decided quit playing with their little fire and turn in for the night. Following Tara's suggestion Walt had bought the cheapest six by nine rug he could find and, although it was old, it was perfect. They spread a blanket on top of the rug and the other two were doubled on top. The night air was still warm, but the surface would cool rapidly now that the sun was gone.

Walt took off his leg and placed it where it was within easy reach. During the day it had picked up a lot of sand and it would need to be cleaned in the morning. They lay for a long time holding hands, looking up at the stars and talking little.

Once Walt thought he could hear footsteps and he got up and fastened his leg quickly. But he realized that the wind sometimes caused the sand to shift with a curious kind of squeaking sound that he quickly came to recognize. He laughed as he took off the leg and lay back down.

After a while, Tara rolled on top of him and lay with her face pressed into his neck. From time to time she would stretch her face to make their mouths meet and she would bite him gently on the lips. He held her with no demands, curious to see how long they could stay without yielding. The sky darkened slowly, slowly and he couldn't tell when he was awake or asleep. A million stars revolved above them as the temperature dropped. The whole experience had a dreamlike quality. Sometime later there was the sound of distant wind, and a far-off creaking sound of sand sliding. The steady night breeze was a presence but he couldn't be sure if it was light or soft. The girl seemed to be melting onto him. Her body was still and yet she seemed to be moving. This was nothing he had experienced before, nor was it anything for which he could find words.

Sometime during the night he was aware that part of him was wet but he was never cold and he barely changed position. It was puzzling. Usually, at night he shifted and changed position many times. But this night. No. He was waiting. Waiting. For something inexplicable to happen.

Maybe it had happened. Had he been asleep? He had an urge to look at the dial on his watch, but to move his hands was...unthinkable. He was holding her back. Pressing her to his body. Pulling. For how long? He had lost all track of time and it was impossible to tell for certain if she was awake or asleep. She can't be asleep. No. And yet So still.

From time to time—there was that gentle bite. It was like a playful cat's bite. Possessive, without breaking the skin.

At times he thought the night would never end. Then, sometimes he prayed that it might never end.

His voice was the faintest whisper.

"Are you cold?"

"Uh unh." *No.* Barely audible.

"Are you ready to get up?"

" Uh unh."

'Want to sleep twenty more minutes?"

"Un huh!" *Yes.* Accompanied by a faint wriggle.

"Not talking this morning?"

"Uh unh."

"But you still love me?"

"Un huh!" Little stronger wriggle.

"And you'll be hungry when you finally get up?"

"Un huh."

"Right now you'd like to go back to sleep?"

"Un huh!"

"OK." *God, I love this girl. What did I do to deserve her?* But he wasn't tired of playing.

"And you'll forgive me for pestering you?"

"Uh unh." Followed by an elbow jab to the ribs.

They were walking back toward the road when Fong arrived in the morning. They were back at their hotel in time to get breakfast and found that their charges were packed and ready to go. *Breakfast. Some bits of greasy lamb in rice, a type of bread that looked like naan, and bitter tea.* Penny had herded the remaining grasshoppers into the lobby, bags packed and ready to go. With or without lunch by the looks of things.

Walt took Penny to one side.

"How did it go?" he asked.

"About like you'd expect with a bunch of teen-agers. Kevin and Keith didn't come back last night. They stayed out with some Chinese kids they met locally. Keith thinks he may be in love. He's been after me this morning to teach him some Chinese."

"Overnight? And came back to get breakfast? In love?"

Penny laughed. "Don't be quick to judge, Walt. I met the girl. Xiu Xiu. That's her name. She brought him back this morning. Anyone might fall in love with her. He introduced her to his pals and they all had breakfast together. She speaks a little English. If you see her, you'll get it."

"And that's the only problem?"

"No problem, actually. I guess the parents of teens go through this on a routine basis. Keith looks blissed out. Says he wouldn't care if we stayed here for a month. They did meet some computer kids and ended up playing a few aerial games. I think they got a couple of programs on disks. But they're being cagey."

"The military is developing drones with better de-icing systems to help deal with the Afghan winters, he (Col. Greg Julian) said. Defense Secretary Robert Gates has made the expansion of intelligence, surveillance and reconnaissance capability a top priority at the Pentagon."

U.S. building air bases to support drone flights
U.SA Today, November, 11, 2008
Tom Vanden Brook

CHAPTER 37
Along the Desert's Edge

It was always clear to Walt that the route along the southern fringe of the Taklamakan would be considerably more difficult than the northern route. For that reason, his previous scouting trips had never even considered the south road.

Now, on the homeward leg, it was getting to be much more difficult. He was finding it harder to keep the grasshoppers on schedule.

They had stopped for an extra night at Karghilik, an oasis town from which some caravans had attempted to head north across the center of the desert. This crossroads town on the Southern Silk Road was only about 300 kilometers from Kashgar, and it was near the Genpan Thousand Buddha Caves which had attracted Walt's notice. Some caravans headed south from Kargilik, south into the mountains of the Kunlun Range and ultimately into India. Today a vehicle track purporting to be a road actually showed up on many maps. Despite population centers such as Kashgar, or Khotan, there were stretches that were uncomfortable, because of the lack of suitable places to stop.

This leg of the trip had few amenities. Most towns were small and poor, and the grasshoppers were getting grouchy. They were also well aware that traveling in China's west was not exactly like crossing the American west. There were substantial differences.

This morning after breakfast at the outdoor tables beside a small truck stop hotel, Walt watched as Terry came down late and turned around to speak to one of the boys before taking her seat.

He did a double take after eyeing her and it took a second or two for what he saw to register on his brain. He nudged Tara, at his side. "Tara, get up. Quick! Go get Terry out of here and give her a hand."

Tara was standing up even as she answered. "What's wron..."

"It looks like she's started her period without knowing. Either that or she sat on something red. Check her out. See what's wrong." Tara was already on her way to the girl who was, apparently, oblivious. Had she been drunk last night? This would not have been a good way to start a long, dusty day in the bus.

Walt's goal for the day was to cover a distance just over 500 kilometers. Three hundred miles. From Karghilik, they would head east toward Hotan, or maybe Yutian, roughly between five and six hundred kilometers. Beyond Yutian, near Minfeng, the Cross Desert Road split off heading north across the desert. Walt was eager to see this junction for himself.

Tara was back in fifteen minutes, and Walt had waited for her to return so they could eat together. She slipped in beside him. "You should have gone ahead and eaten that stuff while it was warm," she said; but he could tell by her face that she was pleased.

"Yep! She had started. Didn't realize it. By the way, professor, how easy do you think it is to find tampons in Karghilik?" She took a big mouthful of cold rice mixed with a chopped hardboiled egg, scallions and soy sauce.

"That's a good question, Peach Blossom. I don't think I can use it on a test, though. I never would have thought of that in a million years. But now I'm curious. These women must use something."

"Don't ask questions when you don't want to know the answers."

He laughed. "I really am curious. What do you do? What did you do? Damn. I feel stupid."

"You do the math and you bring what you'll need. Sometimes I can't believe that you really teach in a pretty good university."

"Is she OK now?"

"Oh yeah, No problemo. I had plenty extras. She was a little shortsighted in her planning. She had to change pants and her bags had already been loaded in the bus. She should be here any minute."

"Was she upset?"

"Are you kidding? I don't know where the hell these kids come from. I'm not that much older, but I just don't get 'em. She didn't know. And she just laughed when I told her. She probably could have gone all day and never even cared. Oh yeah, she would have known soon enough. After the bus got rolling. I don't believe that any of these dudes would necessarily have enlightened her."

"Thank you, Tara. I don't know what I'd do without you. C'mon, lets go check the bus."

"Me neither."

"Will you check each grasshopper? Passports, their personal stuff, baggage check, and at least two liters of water."

"OK. And a couple spare tampons."

"Tara?"

"Yes, boss?"

"Do you think this place is interesting? From a Silk Road perspective?"

"Every place is interesting with you, Professor, and I'm glad we've come this way. But does this bunch find it interesting? NFW! Not that much to hold their interest. Maybe some time if you have a graduate class. Or even some handpicked undergrads. But this bunch of knuckleheads? Forget it."

"I'm giving you a raise," he said.

"The Games have often been symbolic wars dressed in short pants. Beijing views this summer as its superpower debut, and the central government won't let separatists or free-thinking dissidents undermine its lockstep message."

> *As the Olympics draw near, China launches a vigorous crackdown on dissent.*
> From 'Briefing,' Time, March 24, 2008

CHAPTER 38
Khotan

The bus pulled into the sprawling outskirts of Khotan late in the afternoon and the driver found their hotel with no difficulty. The start of the 2008 Olympics was only six weeks away and Walt's objective was to get his flock of grasshoppers out of the country at least thirty days before the games began.

By the time everyone had their hotel room assignments and got their bags moved in, the shadows were lengthening. Walt was tired from the day's ride and he was beginning to get slightly frayed around the edges from the unusual nature of this trip. Privately, he was pleased with the thought of being in Khotan, a city he had read about, but never seriously considered visiting until this trip.

The group met in the hotel lobby and went in for dinner together. Afterwards, the grasshoppers were ready to take a look around the city; Walt just wanted to turn in and to plan for the coming day. He was fascinated by the approaches to the city and had already decided to spend the following day looking around. It would mean knocking off a rest day in Beijing on the way home. But, what the hell....

After dinner, he and Tara left the grasshoppers with Penny in the dining room and turned in early. Back in their room, Tara was watching him closely.

"You seem tired, Professor. Or maybe preoccupied. Is everything OK?"

"This place kinda snuck up on me, sweetie. I wasn't expecting it to be so big. So extensive."

"It is sprawling."

"It's bigger than Phoenix. This place has well over a million people. Almost a million and a half according to the guide books. Yet it's referred to as 'an oasis town.'"

"I like this hotel better than the one in Kashgar." While they were talking, Walt was taking off his leg and removing the elastic bandage. "Here's what

I'm thinking, Tara, if you like the idea. I'm thinking we take the day off tomorrow. Explore this place. Just you and me. Let the grasshoppers fend for themselves. They won't mind and we can get a good look around."

"Something's got you fired up. That's what it sounds like."

"This place is legendary. According to the legends, this is the place where silk was first smuggled out of China to the rest of the world. The city was known for its silk and...."

"No!" she said, pushing him back on the bed. "I want you to tell me the story in bed. Like you do. Take off your clothes and we'll get under the sheet. Remember the first long story you told me? About the Parthians? The first time you ever got me off? I still get wet thinking about that story. Lie back. Take it all off. I'll be right there. I gotta pee first."

"You really don't want to hear about Khotan," he said when she was in bed beside him.

"I really do. I do. But I want it all. I want your story, I want you beside me. I want to feel you inside me. I want to hear you and smell you. But I also want everything to last a long time. And, believe me, professor, I am listening to every word you say."

"What did I do to deserve you?" he said.

"Oh, Walt. You earned me. C'mon. Don't go all moody on me. Tell me a long story. I am so horny already I'll probably come while you're talking."

"God, Tara..."

"Do you remember that first story you told me? In Ashkhabad? In that hotel with the amusement park outside my window?"

"Oh, yes..."

"Do that to me again. Only in China. In a city of over a million people. Cos' one day I'll be old and this will be something I'll never forget."

"Tara, Tara...Tara."

"Please."

"Silky, Silky...Silky."

"Pleeeeease."

"Are you comfortable?" She moved one leg across his body. "I am now."

His story took a while. According to legends, silk culture was unknown outside central China until sometime in the fifth century. In Rome, where silk was an expensive luxury, it was believed to grow on trees. Chinese emperors, eager to maintain control over this expensive commodity, forbid the export of silkworm eggs outside their kingdoms. Secrets of silk culture and processing were carefully guarded. The Emperor had betrothed one of his daughters to a prince in the region of Khotan but had denied him the secret knowledge of how silk was made. The prince sent an emissary to the princess who planted the notion that once in her new land she would be denied ready access to silk garments since none could be manufactured there. To prevent eggs from the silk moth from being smuggled out of China, guards at border stations searched luggage with draconian penalties for offenders. But long-standing custom prevented the hair of royals from being touched.

The princess was said to have smuggled the eggs out in an elaborate hair style. Her retinue included a number of young women who were skilled in silkworm culture and in the reeling of silk from the processed cocoons.

There were numerous variations in the story and Walt explored them all.

"Tomorrow I want us to visit the local museum which is supposed to have stuff about early silk culture. Back then, this place was called Hetian. There's a Hetian Cultural Museum."

"If I can wake up. Jesus, Walt...." It was her petulant, little girl voice. "Oh! You are such a great story teller, I can hardly move." She was alternating between kissing his ear and biting his collarbone.

"Don't think you'll get off that easily," he said. "Roll over."

"I can do that," she laughed.

He was laughing, too, as he entered her. "I wouldn't want you to think I was a lesbian."

"Um!"

They were up early, first in line when the breakfast buffet began serving, and had finished eating before the first grasshoppers showed up.

"Tan Dailin lets out an audible gasp when he is told that he was identified in the U.S. as someone who may have been responsible for recent security breaches at the Pentagon. "Will the FBI send special agents out to arrest me?" he asks. Much as they might want to talk to him, though, FBI agents don't have jurisdiction in Chengdu, the capital of China's Sichuan province, where Tan lives. And given that he has been lauded in China's official press for his triumphs in military-sponsored hacking competitions, Tan is unlikely to have problems with local law enforcement."

Enemies at the Firewall
Simon Elegant/Beijing
Time, December 17, 2007

CHAPTER 39
Hung Up in Khotan

By the time Walt's grasshoppers reached Khotan, he figured that he almost had it made. True, there was quite a distance left to go, and admittedly some of the eastbound miles on the southern route between Khotan and Dunhuang were some of the roughest his group would face. But he was well past the halfway mark. It was a place he would love to visit with his legitimate Silk Road students because it, more than any other single destination, was at the heart of Silk Road legends. This was the fabled city where a legendary princess had once smuggled silk moth eggs in her hair, marking the westward journey of silk production out of China.

Khotan was sprawling. Two hundred and fifty miles to the east of Kashgar, it had always been an important oasis city and it had a fascinating history. At the end of an easy day on the road Walt settled his charges into their accommodations and told them to make their own arrangements for the evening. He was tired after Kargilik and he didn't feel like dealing with grasshopper shenanigans.

Even without the stimulus of dog meat for dinner, Tara had looked especially appealing all day and he wanted to feel her body against his. But first, he wanted to talk to her about the possibilities of this ancient oasis city as a destination for future trips. Walt was interested in taking a look into the Hetian Cultural Museum.

They went out together into the nighttime streets, trying to dress as lumpishly as possible so they would not be so conspicuously and immediately apparent as foreigners. It was, of course, a vain hope. Tara wore a headscarf and Walt had picked up a long, lightweight coat in a Kashgar bazaar that was totally shapeless. They ate at a noodle shop, had several cups of tea, asked for and received a couple of hard-boiled eggs that they cracked and broke up in the noodles. In the warm weather of late Asian spring, they walked until after dark.

Nothing they had anticipated, imagined, or even experienced so far prepared them for the next morning. When they met at seven o'clock, Lisa Partridge had some news that, at first, was only moderately worrisome.

"Professor, I think you should know. Terry didn't come back to our room last night." Walt knew for certain that Terry had spent at least three, probably more, nights with Warren, and no one had bothered to tell him before he discovered it on his own—by accident.

"Should I be worried, Lisa?" he asked.

Keith spoke up. He was Warren's roommate. "Warren didn't show up either. We think something's up."

"Well, thank you ladies and gentlemen, for bringing this to my attention. But unless I'm mistaken—and feel free to correct me if you think I'm wrong—legally, both Terry and Warren are adults. OK. In theory, anyway. They are approaching adulthood. Furthermore, this is China and we aren't playing by the Marquis of Queensbury rules. They'll probably show up just about the time they start to get hungry. Of course, I may be mistaken."

Later, he would regret those words and come to wish that he had taken a different tone.

"They left a note, professor. We think you should read it."

Where had they left it? They left it at the front desk in the box for Walt's room. There was a note on the mirror in Keith's room telling him to have the professor pick up the message at breakfast. Walt read the letter sitting apart from the four open-mouthed grasshoppers. Tara looked over his shoulder. Penny had not come down yet.

"Dear Professor Roberts, We begin by apologizing for the trouble we are about put you to. But, as I'm sure you already know, Terry and I have formed a bond; one which began before we started this trip; way back in Colorado.

You already know that our sponsers used the promise of a four-year paid education at any university to which we can be admitted. For many young people this would be a really big deal, but for us, both coming from wealthy families, it's not all that much.

We believe that we'll get the education we want whenever we choose to go for it. But now, in this remote place, we see another opportunity, which neither of us had considered before. This opportunity was pointed out to us by Chinese friends we met in Cashgar, at an Internet cafe. We met several students whose English was good.

They pointed out to us our present closeness to Tibet, a place where Terry and I had both dreamed of visiting. Now, thanks to your trip, we are close to this destination, and it is within our grasp.

Our Chinese friends tell us that our current visas should allow us to enter the borders of this once very difficult destination. We have money, we have the desire, and we are within striking distance. If we don't take advantage of this opportunity, it might never come again—at least not for several years. Our new friends have offered to accompany us to Lassa which they have visited in the past. They will help us.

So now we tell you of our intention to separate from your group. Accompanied by four of our new Chinese friends—all good kids—we intend to visit Tibet and see the Potala Palace along with other sites. Lassa has an international airport and we should have no trouble making our way home.

Certainly we expect problems from the people who sponsored us. But as was made clear to us from the beginning, we are volenteers. And in addition, we are not employees. The things that interest you about this trip, are mostly of little interest to us. No reflection on your teaching ability, but we are not historians. So Terry and I have made a decision to go on our own. Chips fall where they may.

The first to catch the fallout and flack from our decision will be you. But, having seen you in action, we are confident that you will make out OK. Still, we both do feel kind of bad about leaving you to clean up any mess.

Don't worry about notifying our parents. We'll contact them as soon as we reach Lassa, perhaps with e-mail messages. Plus, it's not likeley they will care what we do. There's a good chance we'll be home before you.

Thank you for you patience during this trip. Even though I know we were sometimes a pain in the ass, still both Terry and I feel that we learned a lot from you. Thank you. Our regards to Miss Penny and Tara.

> *Yours truly,*
> *Warren and Terry*

Both grasshoppers had signed the letter. Walt read it through twice. Then, without a word, he handed it to Tara, stood up and walked twice around the perimeter of the room before returning to his seat. Tara put the letter in his outstretched hand without a word and he read it a second time.

"Jesus Christ," he muttered. "Can you believe this?"

Tara said nothing.

"Did you read it all?"

"Yep."

"Surprised?"

"Not really."

"Not really?"

"Were you paying attention to these two?" Tara laughed. "They've been burning up the sheets since Beijing."

"Did I know this?"

"If you weren't blind."

"What the hell should I do now? Does Penny know? *Did* she know?"

"You're the doctor. Shouldn't I be asking you? Has she seen the letter?"

"C'mon, Tara. Don't be cute. Help me out here."

"OK, shouldn't you call the police?"

"Police? What police? This is China. The only effective police force is the PLA, the People's Liberation Army. I should go dump all this on Chinese soldiers?"

"Maybe you should fill in all the 'hoppers. See if they have any good ideas."

"That sounds way too much like Wikipedia. Wiki-intelligence. Dump everything into the stew pot and see what it tastes like. No thanks on that one. But you're right that we gotta tell them. Eventually. Come up with something else."

The receipt of the letter from Warren and Terry threw Walt into a blue funk and he put off their departure for another day trying to think through an appropriate course of action. Nothing he could come up with would conceivably solve the problem, but he was hoping to find some way to make the best of a bad situation. His *puppet masters* at home had told him that they were not to be contacted in the event of any emergency. His affiliations were through his university and any situations involving him or his charges should be handled through them.

At mid-afternoon of a wrecked day, he and Tara were sitting with Penny Liang at a small table drinking green tea. Walt was stewing.

"You guys understand what we're facing, don't you? Help me out, here. Come up with some good ideas." There was no reason on the planet why Penny or Tara should understand what the group was facing any better than he did, but misery loves company.

Penny was adamant. "I think we should contact the authorities and tell them of the situation."

"But Penny, the only real authorities here are the PLA. I just can't see any advantage in notifying the army."

Tara seemed to believe that the pair would not get far. "They have no interpreter. I don't know how much money they have but they shouldn't have much. They've never traveled alone in this region before. And they certainly can't have much of a concept of distance. To Lhasa? From here? On the ground? I don't know if we'd want to tackle it without a good bit of planning."

"Plus, Tara, we don't know anything about the so-called friends they're supposed to be traveling with. They could be con artists. Or worse. Somebody could have designs on Terry. My god, these little bastards! Those guys back home who dreamed up this program must be morons."

Walt didn't have any desire to drink more tea but the pot was empty and getting it refilled gave him something to do. He was just getting up to request a refill when the two PLA soldiers approached their table. The younger man halted a few paces away and the older man addressed Walt.

"You Professor Roberts, American from American university? Yes? Please, you to come with us? Request short interview with our commander. Mister Lo Wen-Tiao."

"I understand," Walt answered, his brain racing to determine how to respond. He looked at Tara and said in a low voice, "This is truly turning into the trip from hell."

"Well, Officer, these two people are my assistants, my translator, and my personal assistant. They will need to come with me."

"No need. Mister Lo have translators. You come with us, please. No problem for you. He need talk. Please." It was not really a request.

It was four hours later when the PLA vehicle and driver, accompanied by Mister Wu, the officer who had come to pick him up, returned Walt to his hotel. Tara and Penny were waiting for him in the lobby and they both looked shaken. During the time Walt had been gone, the sky had darkened toward the northwest and a brief sandstorm had spread a light coating of fine grit over everything. The sky was beginning to lighten as the storm moved to the east, but the gray sky had no doubt contributed to their gloomy mood. The air was electric with dust and ozone.

"What happened, Professor?" Tara blurted as he approached the two women. "Are we in some kind of trouble? Because of those kids?"

"The commander knows who we are—are supposed to be. And he knows that Warren and Terry have flown the coop. He also knows a lot of other stuff about us that tells me that we have been under surveillance for some time. He seems very angry about our two missing *students*. He says he thinks its highly unlikely that they will really make it to Lhasa. And he is skeptical that they are traveling with four Chinese youth."

"Who does he think they're with?"

"Doesn't know. Did you guys eat? What about the other grasshoppers? Where are they now? I'm starving, myself."

Penny wanted to know if the commander spoke English, or if he used a translator. Tara was concerned to know if Walt needed to get off his feet but she was reluctant to ask him in the presence of Penny. "How did you leave it with the Chinese commander?"

"I'm not really sure. Listen, when those two guys came in to pick me up, did you notice anything about their uniforms?"

"All I noticed was those funny blue tabs on their lapels," Tara said. "And the shiny badges on their caps. It looked like Greek pi with a line under it. Kinda like cloisonné."

"They're numbers," said Penny. "*Ba. Yi.* Eight, and one. They stand for August, first, 1939, which is honored as the birthday of the People's Liberation Army. Like our Fourth of July."

"That's right, Penny. But how about blue tabs? I don't know about those. I do know that blue is the color of the infantry in the US."

"Those blue tabs are for the PLAAF," Penny said. "The Chinese Air Force. We're probably somewhere near an airbase. You were just quizzed by China's Air Force. Probably a military security police officer. Why don't we go talk outside."

"Yeah. Because I have to go back to see him again. Early tomorrow morning."

"Early in the 1980s, Marshall began talking about "the Revolution in Military Affairs." The notion was that newly developed technologies in surveillance, communication, and missile accuracy had fundamentally changed the nature of warfare, making it possible to wage war around the world by remote control, striking at will at enemies far away who could be located, identified, and eliminated at the touch of a button, as in a—very expensive—video game."

Rumsfeld, His Rise, Fall, and Catastrophic Legacy
Andrew Cockburn

CHAPTER 40
A Visit with the PLAAF

The room smelled like something unpleasant that Walt was trying to identify. He usually thought his nose was pretty dependable, but for some reason he was having problems with his nasal calibration. *Dirty socks! That was it.* This place smelled as if it was full of dirty socks. Maybe it was.

The local Commander who had sent a vehicle to pick him up motioned to Walt to take a chair at the table. Walt was apprehensive while trying to remain cool. He was trying to think of resources that might be available to him in case of an emergency. There weren't many people he could call on.

Commander Lo Wen-Tiao, was seated behind a large table of dark wood with a finish that looked like maroon shading to black. He did not look like a happy man.

Commander Lo had apparently studied English at some time in the past, but he did not speak or comprehend sufficiently well to function without an interpreter. The young man who interpreted for the commander spoke with a British accent but Walt never had the opportunity to ask him where he went to school.

The interpreter addressed Walt first.

"Mister Lo says that you are American professor traveling in China."

"Of course. My visa is in order and I am traveling with a group of students studying the Silk Road. I am a professor in an American University. As I told him yesterday when we met."

"He says you are a former soldier. Do you deny this?"

"Of course not. I was once a soldier. Years ago. Now a civilian."

"He says you were wounded as a soldier. This is true? Yes?"

"That is no secret. I am an amputee. I was wounded. But now am back together."

"Mister Lo says 'Once a soldier, always a soldier.'"

"Mister Lo is a philosopher. Therefore he knows this is not true. I was once a soldier. Now I am an ordinary person, working in the field of education."

"He says that you are here to gather military intelligence."

"No, this is incorrect. If China is going to war with silk as her weapon, then he would be right. I am here with students who are studying the ancient Silk Routes across Asia. I study the entire route, and this is my first visit to China's southern route. It is most interesting."

"He says that few Americans come over the southern part of this desert.

"This is true. Because it is difficult, and because traffic flow may have once preferred the northern route much of the time. I visited the northern route last year. But the southern route, although more hazardous to early caravans, is very interesting. Especially Khotan, whose history is linked with the story of silk. My group is made up of young scholars."

"But some have disappeared into the interior."

"This is true. It is an embarrassment to me and to my university. But young people frequently do things that are unpredictable and difficult to understand. These youngsters wished to see Tibet.

"The commander says they wish to gain intelligence."

Walt laughed. "This pair wishes to seek intelligence because they have very little. It is doubtful that they are wise enough to make it to Tibet. Possibly, they may succeed, but—" he paused while the translation caught up—"it is unlikely they will make it. It is difficult for me to know how to respond to the Commander's questions. I am embarrassed on behalf of my country and my university, but I am fearful for two young people, alone in a difficult part of the world. Difficult for them. The idea that they seek intelligence is absurd."

"Mister Lo says you seem very certain."

"About some things. The two missing students are little more than foolish children."

"Mister Lo says he may keep you here until your two children are returned."

"The commander must know that we are in China with travel visas which have a limited duration. In approximately two weeks our visas will expire and we will be here, if we remain, illegally. If he wishes to detain all of us to recover two mischievous and unruly children, he must make us all criminals. I would hope he is not contemplating this response to our dilemma. We had planned to be out of China before the Olympics draw big crowds to Beijing."

"He says he is considering to do it."

Commander Lo was leaning forward, studying Walt intently. The Commander was a handsome man of around fifty with regular features, high cheekbones, and an extremely intelligent face. He did not look unfriendly but he looked like a man who was not to be trifled with.

Walt had not known what to expect when he had climbed into the military vehicle. But it was clear now that his group of grasshoppers had been under surveillance for some time. Probably beginning sometime after they reached the western end of the Taklamakan, possibly beginning as early as Urumchi. How else would they have learned about his leg? As far as he knew, the grasshoppers were unaware. His mind was racing as he tried to consider all the possible worst-case scenarios. Too many.

Commander Lo was tapping the tips of his fingers together, signifying impatience, and it looked as if he was trying to make a decision. Not good.

"Tell the commander that my students are expected back by their parents in less than two weeks. All of these young students still live at home and their failure to return on time are almost certain to trigger a government protest."

It took the translator about three times as long to explain as it had taken Walt to give the message, and during the translator's speech, Mister Lo sat back in his chair and turned to face the wall.

Walt had no idea what might be coming next. He decided to roll the dice.

"The commander should know that my students were enticed to go by Chinese friends who told them that they knew how to enter Tibet without travel visas. I hope this information will not reach the hands of the news media because it would be embarrassing for everyone. I hope the Chinese authorities will not decide to detain American university students—without reason—on the eve of the Olympic Games."

Walt was back at his hotel in time for dinner. No one had heard anything from the missing pair. After a long conference between the three adults, they agreed with the plan to press on and scheduled an early morning departure.

To ensure a prompt start in the morning, Walt asked the four remaining grasshoppers to load the bus before breakfast. Early next morning, the grasshoppers loaded their bags through the rear door at the back of the bus. Then the boys pulled them down the aisle and placed them in seats. There were no overhead racks in their vehicle, which resembled a short school bus. The bags on seats were kept away from the jerry cans of gasoline which were loaded last and secured with multiple bungee cords. Usually, the driver carried an additional twenty gallons in five-gallon cans. He preferred to keep cans filled to the top. Full cans tended to cut down vapor smell inside the bus.

Keith was curious to see how the driver would pour the cans, on which there were no spouts, into the tank, whose fill pipe was recessed in the vehicle's side. He watched with interest and amusement, as the driver appeared to be topping off his tank before refilling the jerry cans at the partially completed station next door to their hotel.

Keith didn't understand the process. The driver pulled out a hand powered lift pump that had a swing check valve at the bottom. This makeshift solution made Keith laugh. After the first stroke filled the pump's cylinder, every stroke transferred almost two pints of liquid. When the jerry can was empty, the driver yelled something Keith couldn't understand.

Fortunately Penny Liang had just arrived in the parking lot carrying her bags. "Get back, Keith!" she yelled. "He's telling you to move back out of the way. He wants to clear the pump."

Keith backed up and the driver tilted the pump cylinder as he gave a final two or three strokes. The remaining gasoline shot out of the nozzle into the sandy waste between the hotel and the station. The driver was still talking away in Chinese.

"He's telling you that he can't put the pump back in the bus until it's completely empty," Penny explained. "As it is, we'll probably drive with the windows open all day. That may be why we sometimes have headaches at the end of the day."

"Chinese forces have for years been battling a low-intensity separatist movement among Xinjiang's Uighurs, a Turkic Muslim people culturally and ethnically distinct from China's Han majority. Chinese rule has largely suppressed the violence, however, and no major bombing or shooting incidents have been reported in almost a decade.

Wang said the group had been trained by and was following the orders of a Uighur separatist group based in Pakistan and Afghanistan called the East Turkistan Islamic Movement or ETIM. The group has been labeled a terrorist organization by both the United Nations and the United States. East Turkistan is another name for Xinjiang."

"China says it halted terror plot at Games."
The Associated Press.
In USA Today, 3/1%8

CHAPTER 41
Early Warning

The bus was rattling along—eastbound on the southern route. Walt was racking his brain for workable solutions to their dilemma and Penny was contemplating the consequences of reassignment to Minot, North Dakota.

Today's stretch of road along the south-eastern edge of the Taklamakan was, without question, the longest and most remote stretch they would face without towns or amenities. For over 250 kilometers, there were no significant villages along this stretch. For this reason, Walt had confirmed that they had several jerry cans filled with gasoline aboard and they also had an extra couple of day's supply of drinking water in large plastic carboys.

This was the stretch about which Walt had the greatest misgivings. Despite periodic maintenance, drifting sand sometimes delayed progress. His driver assured him that he had made the trip of this road several times in the past, and that was encouraging. But there was one appealing factor which the professor would have been reluctant to admit. On his travel map of the region designated Sand Mountain Desert, a vast tract was bordered in red and labeled Wild Camel Protection Area. Walt was hoping that they might see wild camels.

Penny Liang had told him that somewhere near this region, located to the west of Dunhuang, a vacationing Air Force officer had once observed Chinese drone aircraft performing aerobatic maneuvers.

Walt was sitting at the window with a map of the region on his knees. Next to him, Tara, her legs drawn up on the seat back in front, was reading a book, *Foreign Devils on the Silk Road* by Peter Hopkirk. They had been on the road for nearly two hours. Four grasshoppers were sprawled over several seats. Some of them were asleep. Outside, the only views were desert and occasional patches of scrub.

"Can I get you to swap seats with me for a few minutes, Tara? I need to talk to Walt."

"No problem, Penny," the girl replied as she closed her book.

"What's up?" Walt said.

"Well...I know that you were encouraged—maybe bulldozed—to take this route rather than the one you took in the past. Looking at the map it just seemed like a good spot for the Chinese to build their Area 51."

"So what do your satellites tell you?" Walt said with a laugh. "This is a helluva big haystack."

"Yeah, I know. But on the night before we left Khotan... Do you remember the Chinese colonel from our little run-in at Kuqa? Wherever."

Uh oh! Here comes something I probably don't want to hear. "Sure, I remember him. He seemed like a very reasonable man. All things considered."

"Well, I haven't told you this, so you might not know. Unless maybe Tara mentioned it. I discussed it with her. The colonel has been following us—following me actually, that's what I think—since he met us."

Walt folded up his map and placed it in the pocket on the seat back. "Why would he follow us? We answered all his questions, and he said he was satisfied."

"Well—I know this will sound like I'm crazy—but I think he followed *me*. Please don't laugh. This never happened to me before."

"I'm not laughing, Penny."

"If it's true. Which maybe it isn't."

"But he never tried to get in touch with me? Or did he?"

"No. He just wanted to talk with me."

"I'm failing to see this as a problem, Penny."

"Yes, well... on the night before we left Kuqa, I was out with him for several hours. This was after I had talked to Tara. And until the small hours."

"You don't need to tell me this stuff Penny. *Major.* Please!"

"Just listen to me Walt, and let me get all this out. OK?" She waited for a nod before continuing.

"Colonel Huang says that he is concerned that a group of Americans traveling with only a driver and a Chinese guide might be very vulnerable to Islamic militants who are beginning to make their presence felt. As we get closer to the start of the Olympics, he feels that extremists may be encouraged to act up. Hostage taking, or even murders are distinct options for garnering world attention."

"This is certainly a possibility that has occurred to me. But I considered it to have a low probability. Otherwise..."

"Colonel Huang says that the upcoming Olympics are prompting terrorists to become more visible."

"But we're not even close to Beijing, or any Olympic venue. And we have no athletes."

"Huang says that the Chinese security forces have intelligence that groups in Xinjiang have been feeling pressure to take some actions to put them in the news."

"So why didn't the colonel pass this news on to me?"

"He wanted to talk to *me*."

"So you are relaying important news from the Chinese authorities...?"

"Come on, Walt. Don't make this difficult for me. Huang doesn't have any concrete intel on specific threats. But there are a lot of signs. And the grasshoppers made a stink in our last big stop. Huang knows all about that, and so, according to him, do the extremists."

"So why, if you knew this before we left, did you wait until now to tell me?"

"'Oh god, this is really hard for me."

"OK. OK. Relax, Penny. Really. I am on your side in this whatever it is, unnamable pickle."

"I probably should have told you earlier, but..."

"It wouldn't have mattered. Actually, I'm satisfied with this road."

"There's more."

"Yes?"

"Colonel Huang knows I'm Air Force. Don't ask me how. And he knows that I outrank you. He knows all about me."

"Aaah. Bad news. And about our *mission*?"

"If he does, he didn't say so. I'm inclined to think not. Otherwise..."

"Yes?"

"Otherwise he wouldn't have bugged our bus."

"Good grief."

"And is following us a couple of miles back. Just in case."

"Just in case? Holy mackerel. C'mon, Penny. This is water torture. Tell me what's happening."

"Colonel Huang thinks we could be an ideal target for a group of separatists representing the East Turkistan Islamic Movement. ETIM. They've been training and recruiting in this province and across the borders. He put a tracking device in this bus and he is following with a group of soldiers in case we hit trouble. Also..." Penny reached into the day pack between her feet and pulled out a small electronic device. "The tracking device in the bus will allow him to follow us anywhere and this gadget will allow me to signal him in case of an emergency. In which case he could be here with a security unit within minutes. How the heck could I lay all this on you while you were trying to get the grasshoppers loaded? And trying to deal with the news about Terry and Warren? And would it have made any difference?"

"OK. Don't talk for a minute. I need to think." He closed his eyes and leaned his head back against the seat. He ran through as many down-side scenarios as he could imagine. Then he considered the up-side possibilities. Up-sides won.

"OK, Penny. I got it. Message received. Thank you. Steady as she goes."

"Thank you, Walt," she said, obviously distressed. "Don't stop talking to me." She stood up, preparing to leave and relinquish her seat to Tara.

"Don't get up, Penny. Stay here. Tara is OK." He leaned over to get the girl's attention. "You OK, Silky? Penny is gonna stay here with me for a few miles. OK?"

"That's cool." She was deep in her book.

"Just stay here for a bit, Penny. We've got a long day ahead. And in case you haven't noticed, we've only passed two vehicles westbound since we left that little place marked Xorkol."

"I haven't been counting, but this stretch looks pretty empty." Walt took out the map and unfolded it to show Penny the barren stretch they were facing. "This is the region that used to be known as Chinese Turkistan. Today called the Xinjiang Uighur Autonomous Region."

This, of course, the major already knew.

Penny took a notebook from her pocket and began drawing a Chinese character. "Xinjiang," she said. "Here is *Xin*. It means "new." *Jiang* is a little trickier. Nineteen strokes. But still, very easy to remember. It means territories. New Territories."

"Was character writing easy to learn, Penny?" Walt needed to change the subject while brain was still trying to process the information he had just received.

"No. To tell the truth, it was hell. But my parents were insistent that I kept with it. Now I suppose I should thank them." She leaned back. "You wouldn't mind if I took a short nap? I've been going crazy."

"Go ahead. But I'd like to keep you nearby with that Aladdin's Lamp in your daypack. Just in case we need a genie."

Penny closed her eyes and tried to nap. This conversation had been stressful and she wasn't sure if she had made the right decisions. In this instance, her feelings were involved and this was new for her. Walt looked out the window, scanning the horizon for a glimpse of the wild camels that were supposed to inhabit the region. But sand dunes and scrubby grass was the only thing visible for miles. In places there were tufts of uprooted grass, buried in clusters to mark the presence of underground cables. Despite the macadam surface of the road, the ride was bumpy due to occasional ridges of drifted sand. In places the view of the desert was obscured except for the nearest dunes. It was clear that periodic visits from maintenance crews were needed to keep the road from disappearing in places. No sooner had Walt realized this than the bus rolled past a portable bunkhouse—about the size of a train's caboose—that sometimes housed small teams of road workers.

After a while the view grew monotonous and Walt closed his eyes. He may have dozed off when he was brought out of his catnap by the excited voice of the driver as the bus slowed abruptly.

Up ahead Walt could see that the road was blocked by three vehicles and several armed men, all hooded. Armed men were standing on both sides of the road and in the split second that he tried to assess their options, Walt concluded that resistance was likely to get them all killed. Maybe they would be contented with him. Possibly with him and Penny. It seemed like the only option open. Stop. See what they wanted, or if some deal could be made.

"OK, Penny," he said, giving her a nudge, but she had already taken in everything. "Time to push that button and hope that your genie is fast out of the bottle. Meanwhile, get a count on these guys. How many. I don't plan on going down easily." But while it was true that he did not intend to submit, he had no idea how he could resist, unarmed and unable to communicate. His brain was racing. Meanwhile the driver had slowed, then stopped. But now it was clear that a fourth vehicle had come up from behind them. When had they passed it? Now his brain was racing and he knew that every second counted.

"Tara! Look alive. We've got a problem. Grasshoppers! Wake up. Everyone pay attention. No talking. We have a problem. Keep your eyes on me and on Penny. And keep your mouths shut. We may be in for a rough time."

His mind was racing. *Fuck! Does this have anything to do with the departure of Terry and Warren?*

The grasshoppers were up, and looking at the armed roadblock ahead with a mixture of fear and curiosity.

Walt was focused on trying to get a count of the enemy they were facing. He and Penny were standing and the driver was still talking rapidly. "He's asking us what we want him to do," she explained.

"Well Penny, it looks like your colonel knew what he was talking about. We've gotta hope he's part of the solution and not part of our problem. I can't see where we have a lot of options right now. Job one would seem to be to stay alive for a while. Or at least 'til help arrives."

Tara moved to the empty seat behind Walt and placed both hands on his shoulders.

From the wire:

"Hostages freed: Police shot and killed a man armed with explosives who took ten Australians hostage on a tourist bus Wednesday in northern China, a state news agency said. Australian Foreign Minister Steven Smith said today that the hijacker's motives were not known. China is usually safe for tourists, but more problems have arisen recently."

The Associated Press
March 6, 2008

CHAPTER 42

Terrorists? Or hostage-takers?

The bus rolled to a stop about thirty or forty yards in front of the road block. Five masked men were standing across the road. There appeared to be at least three more behind the vehicles. Walt couldn't be certain of the number. At least eight. Not counting those in the vehicle behind the bus. At least two more. They probably had at a dozen men. *Maybe more.* All of the weapons Walt could see appeared to be old AK-47's. *Nope! There's an RPG. Oops! Another one.*

One of the armed terrorists waved the bus to come closer. Walt was wondering if the Chinese colonel was actually following them as Penny had explained. How far behind? Had he gotten the signal from her device? How long would it take him to catch up to them? They probably didn't have very long before they were either dead or on the way to someplace else.

The driver was talking frantically. "Tell him to edge up as slow as possible," Walt told Penny. "I'll go out first, but I can't communicate without you."

"That's why I'm here, Professor. I'll be right behind you."

"Tara, you stay inside and take charge of the grasshoppers. Nobody gets out until they're forced out by these goons."

"Got it. Be careful, Walt."

The bus had stopped and one of the masked men was banging on the door and brandishing his weapon. So far no one had started shooting and that was a good sign. If the goal had been to kill them, they would all have been dead by now. Maybe this group just wanted hostages for some type of political negotiation. That way, they would have some chance of survival.

"OK, Penny. We're on." The two stepped down into the doorway and Penny motioned for the driver to open the door. Their Chinese guide seated behind the driver, a man of at least fifty, appeared terror stricken and was cowering in his seat. Walt glanced back at the grasshoppers, most of whom were standing. "Do what Tara tells you," he commanded. "Don't follow me. That's an order!"

The door opened and he stepped out. The masked man hit him in the chest with the butt of his AK, and Walt knew at once that it wasn't intended to be lethal. It was just for intimidation. He might have a broken rib but in a way it was a good sign. He was on his knees hoping that Penny would not be struck; she had begun to speak in Mandarin—Putonghua—without receiving a blow. Half a dozen masked men had spread out along the side of the bus and were motioning for everyone to come out.

In the back of the bus, Keith had been looking out the window and day-dreaming as the bus jolted along. When the driver first began to slow, he looked ahead and saw the roadblock. As they neared the vehicles he could see that the men were wearing masks and carrying weapons. He recognized the familiar profiles of the ubiquitous AK-47s.

Keith's father was a model builder whose work frequently appeared in Hollywood productions, so the youth grew up around a wide variety of tools and mechanical devices. He was furious at the thought of being slaughtered like a lamb on a remote road in western China. His immediate reaction was to think how he could improvise some type of weapon. The back of the bus contained four or five jerry cans of gasoline, more than enough for an impressive fireball if managed correctly. He had been a visitor on a couple of sets where vehicles—*and hell, yeah, I forgot—even a school bus once*— had been detonated. But how to use the gasoline? The bus had slowed, the professor had stepped out, and he had been struck.

Walt rose slowly to his feet and was hit a second time. The blow took his breath away. This time he was pretty sure that ribs were broken. But still there had been no shots. There was a lot of talking going on but the terror-ists seemed to be unsure how to proceed and none of their group seemed anxious to enter the bus. Perhaps they thought there were weapons aboard the bus.

The driver and their Chinese guide had left the bus but—so far, as best Walt could determine—no one had been shot or even been struck. Other than him. They had obviously recognized him as an American and the group leader, so he was probably being used as an example to the others.

On the floor in the back of the bus Keith—experienced model builder and improviser—was considering his options. The driver had put gasoline in his fuel tank from the jerry cans using a manual lift pump. There had been a check valve at the pump's intake and he had seen that a single lift stroke could shoot liquid for at least ten yards. Maybe a bit more.

Shit, it's better than nothing. Better than being empty handed. He fumbled under the back seat where he had seen the driver stow the pump and pulled it out. He slid one of the five-gallon jerry cans over to his window which was down about four inches at the top. *Do I need another can? Maybe not. Not much time. Gotta get on with it. Stay calm. Don't screw up.*

He was on the floor between the seats as he unscrewed the cap from the can. He could see the head of one of the masked men outside, going down the length of the bus, trying to make sure that everyone was getting off. With Tara leading, the other grasshoppers had moved out of their seats, but they still hadn't stepped out.

Outside, the terrorists had pushed the driver and the Chinese guide around to the front of the bus and were examining identification cards. Penny was still few feet behind Walt and was being quizzed and tenderized by two of their captors. He had an armed man in front and behind. The man in front had already struck him twice and had threatened blows a couple more times, making Walt flinch. Even behind the mask, Walt could tell that the man was glowering. He was continuing to repeat the same couple of phrases.

"What the heck is he saying, Penny?" Walt called out. It hurt to yell.

"He's asking why infidel dogs are supporting China in their suppression of Uighur independence and religious freedom."

Walt recognized he was dealing with fanatics and that everyone's life was in danger. If the guy had been a Tibetan, it might have made sense. But Uighur muslims were still secure in their religion and, for the most part, in their property. True, China had resettled a lot of Han people in Xinjiang.

"Tell him to go fuck himself and kiss the million dollar ransom goodbye," Walt said. But Penny never had the chance. Walt's assailant got the drift and apparently he had heard the "f" word before. He apparently wanted to punish Walt without killing him. His fingers closed on the trigger of his weapon and the AK—its selector switch on semi-automatic—withheld its characteristic stutter. He fired three rounds into Walt's right foot, ankle and shin.

It took but a second for it to sink in. And in a flash he knew that he had to react enough to convince the shooter but not so much that he terrified his companions. He let out a slow, controlled groan and slumped to the ground over the perforated shoe. *I hope this SOB doesn't notice that I'm not bleeding. Or shoot me in the head while I'm down.*

In the back of the bus, Keith had the manual gasoline pump ready to go and he was thinking about the criticality of timing. The grasshoppers were leaving the bus and four masked guys were aligned along his side of the bus.

Two terrorists had begun tying the grasshopper's hands behind them with plastic cable ties. It would be nice if I could get six at a time, he thought. But that's asking for a lot. At that moment a fifth man came over an began prodding a couple of his colleagues to enter the bus. When the AK barked at Walt's foot that was all it took to trigger Keith. Inserting the pump nozzle through the partially opened window, he gave the pump a strong upward stroke.

The first spurt of gasoline soaked the two nearest terrorists pretty well and the next two reached the most distant man. Five quick strokes were completed before anyone knew what was happening and five men were instantly soaked in gasoline before they could react.

Keith angled the nozzle downward and let a dribble of gasoline trail from the nearest man to the side of the bus, and up the side to his window.

Moving quickly, he pushed the jerry can to the far side of the bus and shoved the pump under the seat. The boy's Russian cigarette lighter was in his pocket. He knew that it worked well, but to reach the gasoline trail he had to stick his arm out the window. As he lowered the window to reach wet liquid, the nearest terrorist came to grab his arm, or possibly to strike at him with the weapon. But the nearest man was also the wettest. At the first spark, the masked man was a human torch and with a swooshing sound the flame leaped for almost the length of the bus. Immediately, a handful of terrorists were ablaze in a manner they would not survive.

A few seconds later, the sounds of automatic weapons and semi-automatics seemed to be coming from several directions at once. The screams of burning men were mingled with shots from several different weapons. Walt, still kneeling over what he hoped looked like an injured foot, was hit for the third time with the butt of the AK and this time it knocked him unconscious. Tara, whose hands had been secured behind her back, yelled to her grasshoppers to hit the ground. Penny had called to their two Chinese hired hands who were still not bound, and told them to get under the bus. She hit the ground within a few feet of Tara.

Amazingly, the terrorists did not kill any of their prisoners, perhaps because they suddenly realized that they were under fire.

In the noise and confusion, it took Penny several seconds to realize that the Chinese colonel had arrived with half a dozen uniformed security police. If half the terrorists had not been set afire by Keith's impromptu flame thrower, the police would have been outnumbered two to one without a quantifiable advantage in weaponry. But the colonel and his team came on strong. None of these kidnappers were going to hear their Miranda-rights in Chinese.

The colonel's posse was making short work of the rustlers and from the looks of things they were not interested in going back home with prisoners. The new arrivals were carrying some type of Chinese-manufactured automatic weapon.

Despite having spent her adult life in an Air Force uniform, Penny Liang had never experienced anyone being killed in front of her. Now, in an instant, several men were being burned to death a few feet away as she hugged the ground. The masked man in front of her exploded gruesomely as a burst of automatic fire shredded his chest. Now, when she tried to see what was happening, she could feel something wet hitting her face.

The burning men were making terrible sounds. Gunfire seemed to be coming from behind the truck where she believed the guide and driver had been taken. Penny had lost sight of Tara and the grasshoppers, but Walt was lying prone a few yards away. He seemed to have his head up, taking in what was happening. His arms were drawn up under his chest giving the appearance that he might be trying to get up. But he was unconscious. The shallow wound on his head was already beginning to clot.

A few seconds later, the gunfire stopped and the only sounds were coming from the burning men. Then the colonel of the Security Police was helping her to her feet.

"*Ni teng ma?*" he was saying. "*Sheeng,*" she answered. Her own voice sounded shaky. "I'm OK."

The scene along the barren stretch of road between Minfeng and Andirlangar was one of chaos and pandemonium. Several terrorists from the original batch who had tied up the grasshoppers were human torches and their screams were terrifying. Tara and Penny Liang had been bound and hooded, as were the four grasshoppers. The driver and the native guide hired for the trip were unbound but cowering in front of the bus that, somehow, had avoided the flames. Later, after the smoke cleared, Walt would wonder if they had been tipped off in advance and were part of the proposed attempt to extort ransom. The Chinese Security force consisting of men under temporary command of the colonel who had followed the Americans, were milling around the scene, helpless to aid the burning men, one of whom was already partially carbonized and another who was no longer alive. The other three were still capable of sounds, but they would not live.

As the rescue force swept around the scene assessing their next step, several of the attackers had scrambled into two vehicles and taken off cross-country in a northerly direction, perpendicular to the highway.

In his after-action analysis, Walt later concluded that the escaping terrorists might have been attempting to cut across to the Cross Desert Road in an
attempt to evade capture. He would also conclude that the attack had occurred a few miles before the tiny village of Andirlangar, not far from the site
of ancient ruins identified with that settlement. But that would come later.

Moments after the security force arrived Penny Liang and Tara were un-
tied along with the grasshoppers, all of whom were badly shaken.

At first the colonel seemed to be unaware—possibly indifferent—that
several of the terrorists had escaped. Except for the men who had been set
aflame by Keith's prompt and imaginative response, the encounter might
have favored the hostage-takers. Now, the surviving men had escaped in
two of the four vehicles that had formed the original road block.

Tara went to Walt immediately while Penny stayed close to the colonel.
Her unplanned involvement in his actions quite possibly enabled the entire
group to survive this encounter with a group whose motives probably had
been hostage-taking. If this was the case, it was probably just dumb luck
that had saved them.

The colonel gave no command to follow the escaping vehicles that could
be seen in the distance. He did not seem concerned when occasionally they
dropped out of sight behind a dune, only to reappear on the next rise.

As he watched the vehicles grow smaller, Penny observed carefully as he
took a small lensatic compass from his jacket pocket and make an estimate
of their bearing from the site of the burning bus. Then he made a call on
what Penny took to be a satellite phone. He walked a few paces away from
Penny and she was reluctant to follow, but a few words came through clearly
and it seemed to her that he was providing information on the direction in
which the vehicles were heading across the desert.

The conversation went on for several more sentences that Penny missed
completely. Then he snapped the phone shut and went to look at Walt, still
unconscious on the ground. Tara had opened his shirt, elevated his head
and taken his pulse. He did not seem to be bleeding externally and when
she raised his eyelids to check his pupils they seemed to be normal. Neither
pinpoints, nor dilated. Her own pulse was beginning to return to normal.

In the intervening minutes as the screams of the dying men subsided and
the four grasshoppers huddled together like frightened children, Tara failed
to notice the passage of some type of aircraft overhead. But Penny was paying attention. She noted that the small helicopter was unmanned—with an
opaque canopy. It was a model she could not recognize, squat and ungainly,
with pods for some type of weapon. It passed nearby, not directly overhead,

less than a hundred yards or so to the north and after passing near the site of the attack, it appeared to be headed in the direction of the fleeing vehicles.

After seeing the helicopter Penny kept her eye on the colonel to see if he would make another call, but all that happened was that he looked as his watch and appeared to be adjusting the bezel.

While all this was taking place some of the colonel's men were shouting at the Chinese driver and guide who they suspected of complicity in the attack, while others were watching passively as the remaining men who had been set afire writhed in agony.

The grasshoppers, knotted together where they had been tied and hooded, had watched in shock and terror as the first man died horribly and the others appeared to be headed in the same direction but were taking their time about it.

None of them had ever seen anyone die before their eyes and death by incineration was a particularly gruesome introduction to a human's last moments.   Keith, who had been the cause of all these deaths, was weeping openly. Lisa was attempting to console him even though she was, herself, in need of consolation. None of the grasshoppers had any notion of what would happen next and the sight of several armed Chinese security personnel milling about, coupled with the smell of burning gasoline and flesh added to their sense of disorientation and shock. Frozen to one spot, they could not tell if Walt was alive or dead, but they had heard the shots that intentionally hit his leg below the knee and several minutes later with their hoods removed they had seen him on the ground. They were inclined to suspect the worst.

Penny, trained to professionalism, was attempting to see and comprehend as much as possible and to try to remember the sequence in which events were unrolling. When Tara called, Penny's attention shifted from the Chinese colonel to the pair on the ground a few yards away. Walt was regaining consciousness and attempting to sit up. Tara wanted to get some help in propping him up but there was nothing he could lean against.

He was still groggy from the blow. Tara convinced him to put his head on her thighs as she knelt behind him. It was an uncomfortable position for both of them, and in a few minutes she had to shift.

At least, Walt thought as his senses cleared, they were still alive. For now.

"...arms racing, rather than granting a significant military advantage, often simply raised the level of violence. Of course, the paradoxical nature of these mechanisms was hardly apparent at the time, and to this day, particularly among totalitarian regimes, weapons development programs are treated with obsessive secrecy. Yet it is not only advances in communications and observation which continually erode military secrets; they are by their nature self-defeating."

"Of Arms and Men"
(A History of War, Weapons and Aggression)
Robert L. O'Connell

CHAPTER 43
Cleaning Up The Mess

Minutes after Walt came to, he was resting on a canvas tarp that had been spread in a spot of shade cast by the truck. Tara was kneeling beside him and she was the first thing he saw when he opened his eyes. That was fortunate, because she was the first thing he wanted to see. His first words were, "Penny? The grasshoppers? Is anyone hurt?"

"Welcome back, sweetheart," Tara said. "Yeah. Everyone's OK. Driver and Mr. Wu, all unhurt."

Penny Liang came into clear focus, standing near his feet. She was grotesquely splattered with blood and tissue. "The bad guys came off much worse, Walt. Four shot and killed. Three dead from burns and two more who probably won't make it. It's gonna be pretty ugly for them. The others are all headed out—across the desert. There were thirteen in all. We think."

Walt started to sit up, but his head was throbbing, and Tara pushed him back gently. "Don't try to get up for a bit," she said. "You got whacked pretty hard. You're probably concussed. Take it easy."

"Who did the shooting?"

"The colonel, and six policemen who came with him. These guys came in like gangbusters. They weren't looking to take prisoners. They came in shooting."

"Then they must have been fairly close behind us," Walt said.

Penny kneeled beside him. "They were about a mile or two behind us. They heard my signal immediately and understood everything."

"But why woul..."

"There's more," Penny said. "They had bugged our bus. So they were listening to everything that we said. They knew about the terrorists as soon as we did."

"I still don't get it, Penny. Why, if they didn't think we were any kind of threat, would they go to the trouble of bugging our bus?"

"Part of their concern is related to the upcoming Summer Olympic Games in Beijing. They were anticipating that some of the more radical separatist groups would pull some stunt: Either a suicide bomber or a hostage situation or some other form of mischief to get their agenda into the international news. Our capture would have given the Uighur Separatist movement a volume of media coverage that would have cost a fortune."

"So where is everybody right now? I can't see too well and it hurts to move my head."

"The colonel and his men have the driver and Mr. Wu over on the dunes just past the bus," Tara said. "I think he's slapping the piss out of them."

"You said some of these guys got burned. How did he burn them? What happened?"

Tara and Penny explained how Keith had improvised a gasoline gun and taken matters into his own hands just before the colonel arrived with reinforcements. "If Keith hadn't created a diversion, there's no telling what might have happened."

"So will the colonel bring any charges against Keith? What kind of trouble are we in?"

Tara looked to Penny to answer this one. "We talked," she said. *Yes, I'll bet you did*, Walt thought. "And he wants us to pack up as soon as you're feeling better. And move on down the road. He'll take care of everything. Law and justice is a bit different in China than it is at home. By the way, the guys who are dead are already going in the ground on the other side of that dune and by the time the winds shift that sand, those guys will be bones. Their wives and sweethearts won't be getting back any heroes to mourn. They have simply vanished. Forever."

"Yeah, but the surviving prisoners will be certain to carry this story back to their main group."

Penny looked away and her eyes were focussed at infinity. "You're kinda naive for a college professor, aren't you? The odds of those four getting back home alive are slim to none. Once we're five miles down the road, those guys are toast. They'll be under this sand before the sun sets. By the way, our bus is still bugged, I've still got my gadget and he intends to follow us with his policemen all the way to Dunhuang." She hesitated. "I, for one, feel pretty good about that."

"How long have I been out?" he asked.

"About fifteen or twenty minutes. Maybe a little less," Tara said.

"Is my head cut? It's throbbing like it's cut."

"It's a gash. About three inches. It's not too deep. Bled a bit at first but it stopped pretty quick. You're gonna have a heckuva of a bruise."

"So are we waiting for me to get on the road?"

"Well— actually—yes. But you don't have to push it. We'll roll when you feel up to it. We've still got a long way to go before we hit anything that looks like a doctor or a clinic."

He really did not feel like moving. "Will it be OK if I take a short nap? And then we can leave?"

"Of course. You're still in charge. You can do anything you want."

Penny turned to walk over for a word to the bus driver—now bleeding from the nose—who appeared to be as shaken as any of them. Walt called to stop her.

"Penny. The colonel? Does he think this is the last of it? Or can we expect more trouble?"

"He has no way to know if we'll be targeted again. But is this the end of it? No. Of course not. We may not live to see the end of this separatist movement."

She had turned again to walk away when the group heard the dull rumble of two explosions several miles to the northeast. First, one. A slow growl, like thunder. Then another. The fireballs and columns of smoke were hidden from view by the nearest dunes, and they didn't see the two fires until later; after their bus had gone several miles down the road.

With the approval and encouragement of Colonel Huang, Walt, Tara, Penny and four grasshoppers boarded their bus with the driver and continued eastbound on the southern route. The colonel insisted on sending Walt's guide back for interrogation. He was suspected of some complicity in the attack on the American group and the colonel probably figured it could be squeezed out of him. He told Penny of his intention to continue to follow them, at least as far as Dunhuang.

The grasshopper group boarded their intact bus, performed a bit of housekeeping and then continued eastbound. They were still several rugged travel days away from Dunhuang. Walt—in considerable discomfort from the blows to head and ribs—put his head on Tara's shoulder and tried to sleep. The driver was told to keep moving until it got dark.

PART 6.
HOMEWARD BOUND

"When our enemies refuse to meet us eye-to-eye, surveillance is everything. Our state-of-the-art surveillance aircraft expose terrorist hiding places and feed critical information to our men and women on the ground. The U. S. Air Force is constantly developing new ways to address the changing needs of national defense. We are America's "eye-in-the-sky," watching over today and looking ahead to tomorrow. We stand ready as the decisive force for the 21st century."

NEVER LET THEM OUT OF YOUR SIGHT
From an advertisement by the U. S. Air Force
Time Magazine, March 24, 2008

CHAPTER 44
Grasshopper Tales

The group was back in Dunhuang for a full day and Walt was glad they were on the way home. He was definitely cataloging this adventure as "the trip from hell," and beginning to think about what he might want to say to his sponsors back in Washington. There was still no word concerning the whereabouts of Warren and Terry.

After much urging from his colleagues, Walt had seen a Chinese doctor about his ribs. Not much can be done for ribs, bruised or broken, but the doctor recommended acupuncture and Walt declined. His prosthetic leg was an ugly mess with three ragged holes in metal and plastic; but it still functioned. He borrowed some pliers at the hotel where they were staying and made some hasty modifications to keep from cutting his hands on sharp edges. It would get him home and he would let the Air Force get him a newer model.

Changes in the behavior of the four remaining grasshoppers was markedly different during this second visit to this city.

Much had changed in just a few days. Their two close friends had gone missing, they had been attacked by hijackers—or kidnappers or terrorists; nobody seemed clear—and they had seen nine or ten people killed before their eyes. They had been tied up, hooded, pushed and threatened, and they had seen their leader struck repeatedly and knocked unconscious. Keith had incinerated several men and Chinese soldiers had finished the rest. Keith was hollow-eyed. By almost any measure, this group of young people—edging into adulthood—had been traumatized. And for the next several days that's how they behaved.

Colonel Huang was now out in the open. He made no attempt to conceal his presence and no day went by when he didn't stop to check up on Penny and to inquire about the grasshoppers. Despite his contacts with the Chinese military, he had no knowledge of the missing couple. Walt hardly knew how to respond when Penny departed with the Colonel each evening after dinner.

"Are they screwing?" he asked Tara.

"How would I know?" she laughed. "I sure hope so. Otherwise, he wasted a lot of gasoline. And time. I would guess so. They're both adults."

"Well, I hope for the sake of...."

Tara was—perhaps for the first time in their relationship—unhappy with where she thought Walt might be headed. Had the blow to his head scrambled his wits? "For god's sake, Walt," she snapped. "Give it a rest. Those two are mature grown ups, and god knows they've been through a lot. We all have. Quit being judgmental. I know you're smart. And well intentioned. But leave the stuff alone that you don't understand." As usual, she was on the mark and he was chastened.

"You're right, Missy. I'm wrong, Thank You. On this topic its 'Don't ask! Don't tell!'"

The laceration on Walt's head appeared to be closing nicely without stitches and there was a big scab; the surrounding area was starting to turn an indescribable color somewhere between green and purple.

Now, with Terry gone, Lisa asked if it would be possible to stay in the room with Major Liang, and Penny agreed without hesitation. All three of the boys seemed shaken as well. Two rooms were still booked for the three boys but Walt saw that they were all sleeping in the same room.

Keith, who had been responsible for several deaths, still looked shaken and subdued. All of the boys were quieter and for the nights they were in Dunhuang they no longer went looking for Internet cafés or karaoke bars. They even expressed interest in visiting the Great Wall Museum near Jiayuguan. Privately Keith asked Walt and Penny if he was likely to get in any trouble back in the states and they both tried to reassure him in different ways. Penny shared what she had learned from Colonel Huang. "The colonel says that the incident will be reported as a road accident with no survivors. Bodies burned beyond recognition. Buried at the site. He says, not to worry."

At a food stand near the museum, the three boys, who now traveled in a pack, made a point to manage a private conversation with Walt. Lisa was sticking close to the major, who didn't seem to object to the girl's company. Tara read the tea leaves and left the four males to themselves.

"Professor, we want to tell you about a concern we have," Keith began.

"We've all been though a hard time," Walt said, trying to make it clear that he was sympathetic to what they might be feeling.

"Nothing to do with the bus raid," Keith said, and the others muttered agreement.

"It has to do with Warren and Terry," the boy continued. "We don't believe they are headed for Lhasa. We don't believe that was ever their intent."

"Then why did they leave?"

'We aren't sure. But we do know that they had four weeks more training than the AF gave us. We suspect that they are on some kind of intelligence mission that we don't know about. We think that possibly they were given some kind of training for a special activity."

"Yeah," Amory chimed in. "Like fuckin' Manchurian candidates."

"Wait a minute. Wait a minute." Walt said. "They were trained to leave the group? This was all planned? Is that what you're telling me?"

"I don't know what we're telling you," Keith said. "We aren't sure. This is mostly conjecture on our part. But we are dead sure that they aren't headed for Lhasa. Warren never talked about Lhasa. It's true that he wanted to get in Terry's pants. But that started—for both of them—right after they met for the first time. The AF was responsible for making them a team. That happened when they held them back in that first summer. Just before they enrolled us in your program at JBU."

Walt struggled to keep his emotions under control. What was he feeling? Anger? At whom? At the USAF who had orchestrated much of this fiasco? Paul Chapman, the likeable old intel bastard who engineered his share? Paul was almost too long in the tooth back in Afghanistan. His university, who understood little, but acquiesced in everything? What was their complicity? He was pissed! But he stood up and walked around the table where his charges were seated before speaking.

"So...get me to the bottom line, guys. What does all this stuff mean? What am I to understand out of this?"

"Professor, don't be mad at us. We're trying to help. We know less than you do. But you do know that this has to do with China's UAV program. And that the AF believes they are doing work in the southern regions of the Taklamakan. Because of its isolation. But more than that, they want to know more about the capability of Chinese kids who fly on computer simulators.

"That part we can probably help them with. Chinese kids are pretty damn good and they appear to be getting better at a fast clip. As more and more Chinese families can afford computers, more and more kids will be developing proficiency. It's inevitable. That's the message we can probably take home. But we think Warren and Terry may be after something else."

"OK. But what?"

"We're not sure. But something to do with the south road of this freakin' desert where we just nearly bought it. Those two bailed before we got hit."

Kevin interrupted. "If it hadn't been for Keith here, we all might be under a sand dune somewhere back there with those burnt Chinks."

"Duly noted," Walt said stiffly, attempting to redirect the conversation.

Keith continued. "We don't know what they were asked to do, or to find out, or to sniff at, but we do believe that the AF pushed them together to make a team out of them, so they would act together and reinforce one another."

"Pussy," Amory interjected softly.

Walt felt his anger intensifying. Had the USAF involved him in some complex psychological experiment that he had no interest in understanding? And, if so, what was the appropriate way to respond? It was interesting in a bizarre and maddening way. But in another way, it was ironic. He had begun life as an Air Force brat. Because of the USAF, he had been exposed to the world at an early age and had enjoyed experiences that had shaped and enriched his life. He looked back on the teen years he had spent in Turkey as some of the most magical of his entire life. *Excepting, of course, Tara.*

He knew that "only children" sometimes grew up lonely and deprived by the lack of siblings. But this had not happened to him. He grew up close to his Turkish friend, Ekrem, and he had never been lonely. Even during his darkest days of military hardship—in Afghanistan—he had never felt lonely. Scared shitless sometimes, but never lonely.

And with Tara—holy mackerel—the screen had shifted from black and white to technicolor, a transition he remembered from childhood days watching television.

"Look, guys," he said. "What are you telling me? What's going down? Quit bullshitting me."

"Sir," Keith said. "Did Penny fill you on that freakin' heli that came over to take out our kidnappers?"

"No, she did not."

"Didn't she mention the helis that took out the gang that escaped?"

"Not explicitly."

"Nothing?"

"Nothing in detail."

"Look. I don't know how you adults communicate. But here's what the three of us agree on."

"Bring it on," Walt said.

"The ship that came over? We all saw it. Confusing configuration. Our best guess? It was a rejiggered version of an old Kamov *Hormone*. Maybe reverse engineered by the Chinese."

Walt was completely in the dark.

"Enlighten me. *Hormone?*"

"The Kamov 25 was a Russian helicopter. Three-bladed. Counter-rotating. Well suited for air-to surface missiles."

"Hormone is the NATO code name," Kevin added.

Walt was thinking to himself, *They didn't give me enough information about these guys before we left the states.*

"So what's your take on what happened?" he asked.

"That 'copter had some type of weapons pods. We couldn't have any notion of what they might be carrying, but it was almost certain that they were weapons pods. Then later, when we heard the explosions and passed those two burning vehicles, we were certain that the 'copters were carrying some type of missiles. Heat seeking. Infra-red. We can't guess."

"So where do you think the 'copters came from?"

"We spoke to Penny. We think they were called in by the big Chinese guy. The one who came to help us."

"What makes you think he could call in anyone?"

"Shit, professor, he was obviously PLAAF. Plus, we already suspected something. He's was back there shadowing us for over a week."

"You guys knew this? And nobody told me?"

"We thought you must know. That Penny must have told you. You were still dozing when we went past the burning vehicles."

"Yeah," said Amory. "Talk to the major."

"You guys are just torturing me. You know I want to know what you're looking for—what you're expecting to find, or what you've been taught you might encounter. But I *only* want to know so that I can get you home safe and sound. That's what I was hired on to do."

"Professor, we all saw the same thing. All but you. Only thing is, it was just me and Keith and Amory knew what we were lookin' at. Those vehicles were destroyed by the helicopter."

"How can you be sure there were the same vehicles that stopped us? There are oil crews prospecting out in the desert."

"Professor, we may still be kids, but we're not stupid. It was our kidnappers. All dead."

"But how could you know they would all be dead."

"You really don't get it, do you Professor? We don't know what hit the trucks, or who might have survived. But the controllers piloting that little chopper could see everything from the air. And you can be sure nothing was likely to be moving when it finally flew off."

Kevin leaned forward, anxious to be part of the exchange. "We figured we had to be close to some kind of test facility. Possibly it was to the south of us, at the base of those mountains. But more likely it's in the desert. That's probably why this colonel dude is shadowing us. To keep us from getting too close."

This was getting to be too much for Walt to handle with equanimity. His head was throbbing and he was starting to get hungry. *What is it? Hunger, headache, or just plain anger?*

"OK. OK, guys. This has been a good session. Thanks for educating me. And we'll continue this again later. But right now, I'm going in search of some aspirin. Meanwhile, this place stays open for three more hours. See what you can pick up, and we'll continue this later."

"After months of hiatus, U.S.-Israel tension over China has returned. This time the dispute is over Israel's desire to upgrade the Harpy assault drone that it had sold to China in the mid-1990's. The drones are capable of destroying radar stations and anti-aircraft batteries; the U.S. fears that they could upset the delicate strategic balance between China and Taiwan as well as upset its interests in the Asia-Pacific region."

"Return of the Red Card: Israel-China-U.S Triangle"
www.pinr.com/report.php
May 23, 2005

CHAPTER 45
Out of the Blue

While they rested in Dunhuang before the push for home, Walt learned from the three boys what might have singled out his group as a target for attackers. They described—belatedly—some of the events that took place in Kashgar that had not come to his notice earlier. The incidents took place before Warren and Terry had peeled off and left their note behind. Gradually, the whole sequence of events became a bit easier to understand.

On their second night in that city, he and Tara had allowed themselves to slip into the honeymoon mode and they had neglected to brief the grasshoppers on behavioral ground rules. At the time he had probably deceived himself into believing that Penny—Major Liang—would step into the role of absentee parent.

In any case, he—the leader—had taken his eye off the ball and someone had kicked it out of bounds. On that first free evening in Kashgar the grasshoppers, traveling as a group, homed in on the local university and made friends with a group of Chinese youth. By this time Penny had taught them a few words of Chinese, not that they were actually needed for communication. A lot of Chinese students can communicate in English and a foreigner can go a long way with just *Ni hao—Ni hao ma?*

The evening was still young when the six grasshoppers and seven or eight Chinese youth had encamped in a local establishment with music, video games, alcohol, and an array of unidentified edibles, most of which were tasty.

The music was good, the room was smoky, and the ambience was conducive to reckless behavior. A bad moon was on the rise. Even before a new day had begun, the grasshoppers and their new found friends were all in varying stages of intoxication, as, in fact, was most of the crowd in the room.

At the crowded table seating the group of new friends, several conversations were going on simultaneously. The Chinese kids were curious to know whether the good times they were experiencing were, in any way, similar to the evening experiences of American university students. Warren waved for silence so he could answer the question.

"This is a great place and you guys are great friends, but to be perfectly candid, most of this group seems a bit repressed."

The English-speakers got about half of what he was saying. The part about *great* and *great friends* was clear enough and they understood that "but" was an important qualifier. The part about being *candid* and *repressed* wasn't clear. Maybe it sounded too much like *candied*. They had asked what was lacking, and Warren, slightly impaired, had been eager for an opportunity to clarify.

"OK. OK. Hold on. OK. What about your wet tee-shirt contests? Do you guys ever have wet-tee shirt contests? In a party this size we would usually have a contest with at least a dozen girls."

This was a concept that was not fully understood by most of the kids at the table; but those who were familiar with this American practice informed the uninitiated. The Chinese girls, of whom there were three at the table, appeared to be shocked but they laughed and giggled as they tucked in their blouses.

Based on what Walt later teased out of the grasshoppers, it might have ended there if Lisa, the most outrageous of the flock, hadn't been drunk. And if whoever was putting music into the sound system hadn't chosen that moment to play a CD by ABBA.

Using a practiced move she undoubtedly learned from watching Jennifer Beals in *Flash Dance*, Lisa slipped out of her bra under her sweatshirt and tee, and then peeled off the sweat and begin to gyrate on the table top in just the tee.

"C'mon guys. Let's show them what we mean. Somebody...wet me down." She beckoned to the closest Chinese girl. "C'mon Ping Ping. Get up here. Let's show 'em what we've got."

Even then, the disaster might have been avoided, had it not been for the fact that Warren, honestly enamored of Lisa's perky tits—*despite the fact that he was sleeping with Terry*—hadn't grabbed two full bottles of Chinese beer and given her as good a soaking as can be achieved with little more than two liters of fluid. It was, in fact, adequate to do the job.

Everyone at the table was in convulsions, and Lisa's performance did not go unnoticed in the room. None of the local girls, all Han Chinese, still giggling and talking rapidly among themselves, seemed anxious to duplicate Lisa's performance. Or challenge Lisa's for supremacy. It wasn't her first performance and she had previously won contests in three states. *And these*

were real contests. With a lot of other girls. Some of them pretty damn cute!
For Lisa, who was actually very attractive without being beautiful, it was a
big deal to be a contest winner.

Walt didn't learn of this party until days later, after they were on the road
out of Khotan, well to the east. He didn't learn about the tee shirt contest
until they were in Dunhuang. The party had broken up soon after Lisa's
performance, and Chinese friends had indicated that the management of
the establishment had been unhappy and had suggested that it was time for
them to leave.

There had been no unpleasantness at the venue, or afterward, so the grasshoppers had brushed it off without a second thought. But later, trying to
figure things out, Walt had speculated about the reactions from observers in
a region that had been conquered by Islam in the 9th century.

After their riotous evening in Kashgar, the grasshoppers returned to their
hotel the following day. The next full day had been uneventful and they
departed eastbound without any problems.

Looking back, Walt could only assume that the problems which occurred
later must have had their origin in some offense to the Islamic community.
The only major thing of which he was aware was the wet tee shirt "contest"—
that turned out not to be a contest at all, but rather a solo performance.

After this incident came to his attention, Walt was feeling disgusted with
the whole trip. He had learned that the kids as individuals were smart and
likeable, but in a group they were prone to behave badly. A couple of day's
rest in Dunhuang had been good for him and it was now less painful to
breathe or to bend. He had a conference with Penny and Tara.

"I don't know about you two," he said, "but I've had enough of the desert
for a while. What do you say we burn out of here at the fastest possible
speed? Starting tomorrow with first available flight out headed for Beijing?"
The two women were in full agreement.

Beijing was a zoo. The city was less than two weeks away from the start
of the 2008 Olympics, and the best accommodations were booked. The
shaken grasshoppers could have cared less. Seventy-two hours later the
group, still down by two, were back in Washington.

Walt never learned the full details—that Lisa eventually came completely out of the tee shirt—until his grasshopper flight was over the Pacific.
Progressive revelation!

"Chinese forces have for years been battling a low-intensity separatist movement among Xinjiang's Uighurs, a Turkic Muslim people culturally and ethnically distinct from China's Han majority. Chinese rule has largely suppressed the violence, however, and no major bombing or shooting incidents have been reported in almost a decade.

Wang said the group had been trained by and was following the orders of a Uighur separatist group based in Pakistan and Afghanistan called the East Turkistan Islamic Movement, or ETIM."

China says it halted terror plot at Games
The Associated Press
In USA Today, 3/1%8

CHAPTER 46
Big, Big Surprise!

As soon as he could, Walt cornered Paul Chapman. "Help me out here, Paul. A lot of people were killed and some of them from the actions of our kid. What are the Chinese saying about it?"

"Look Walt, as far as your gang is concerned, this is over and done with. I don't want to tell you more than you want to know, but you can forget it. We've been in contact with the Chinese through back channels. Nothing is going to happen. They scored this as an interrupted kidnapping attempt in which the kidnappers were thwarted and escaped. The attempt was aimed at embarrassing their government on the eve of the Olympics. Later—from their perspective—the would-be kidnappers had an accident. Apparently while they were attempting to refuel their vehicles. This has been disclosed and publicized in China, and now it can be forgotten."

"But what about the kid who…"

"To the Chinese, this never happened. We'll give him some special attention. Not to worry. He'll be fine. Trust me."

"Oh, fuck you, Paul. What are my options? Anyway, thanks for the run down. I'm forgetting everything you've said. I hope I'll never be sorry."

"All will be well, my friend. Once again, you delivered the goods. And all your group's regrettable unpleasantness is to be forgotten as if it never happened. Someone will be working with the boy."

"I plan to check up on him."

On the second day of the Washington debriefing for Walt and his flight of grasshoppers, the Air Force pulled a little surprise. (He and Tara had decided that a group of grasshoppers could reasonably be called a flight. She convinced him that "plague of grasshoppers" was unnecessarily harsh. Under the circumstances he agreed that "plague" would have been ill advised,)

The meeting had been scheduled into one of many featureless, unmarked sites outside Washington. *Guards at the gates and security everywhere, but where the hell are we?* Clearly, this one was shared by several agencies and branches because several types of uniforms were mingled with civilian dress.

A limo carried Walt, Tara and Penny though guarded gates to the doors where their escort, a marine captain, was waiting.

The four surviving grasshoppers had been put up at a different location and they showed up about ten minutes later.

There were several uniformed officers in the conference room. Mostly Air Force, but there were two naval uniforms and at least one Marine Corps officer. The total number fluctuated during the morning and Walt made no effort to keep track of who was present. He was trying to practice what little he thought he might understand of Chinese philosophy. *Heaven and earth are indifferent. They see the ten thousand things as straw dogs.*

The same Air Force General was in the room. Walt didn't even want to try to remember his name. This was rude, and also impolitic. He knew that. But damn. They had twisted his arm to make this trip. Offered no help along the way. And, evidently, they had done a poor job of screening the kids they assigned to him. There it was on his nametag. Bloodsworth.

Walt was thinking so hard about the headaches and perceived injustices that had plagued him as he crossed the bottom half of the Taklamakan, that he barely listened to the speech from the podium. In a word, he was behaving like a grasshopper. Tara could almost hear his wheels spinning.

But neither Walt nor Tara, nor Penny Liang, nor any of the four grasshoppers present were prepared for what their high-ranking speaker was just starting to explain.

"We know that all of you have been concerned about the unusual circumstances surrounding the departure of two of your party members during your recent excursion.

"We are aware that you have been worried regarding their welfare and even, perhaps, for their lives. So this morning we have prepared a surprise for you, one that hopefully you will accept in the spirit in which it is offered. So..." He gestured to his right and a door was opened by a uniform to admit Warren and Terry.

Walt realized that he had not been listening closely. He had long ago dismissed General Bloodsworth as something of a pompous windbag, but no matter what might have been said, it could hardly have prepared him to see his two missing grasshoppers bound into the room.

The four teens were out of their seats and a brief orgy of hugs and squeals ensued. Walt, Tara and Penny followed behind to hug their two runaways.

For the next several minutes things were noisy and disorganized but the general quickly sent everyone back to their seats and the meeting was brought under control.

"Some explanations are in order," General Bloodsworth said. "First of all, the excursion by Warren and Terry was not a random act of youthful indiscretion. Nor did they ever have Tibet as a destination. Immediately after a brief explanation you will all have a chance to meet with and talk with them. They can fill you in on all the details. But here are the key elements you need to know.

"For some time we have believed that China is developing and testing UAVs at numerous locations, including several deep in the Taklamakan desert. As this group is no doubt aware, there is a cross-desert road that transects the Taklamakan from north to south. It leaves the southern route in the vicinity of Minfeng, which you may remember passing. It heads north across the desert to intersect the northern route at Luntai, which is just east of Kuqa. In the center of this wasteland, existing maps and surveillance shows a tiny settlement, Tazhong, where there are several oil wells. But the volume of traffic observed by satellite makes this desert camp suspicious. To date, however, that region has not been made off limits to travelers. Probably for the reason that few travelers would want to go there.

"Back when this program was being conceived, we concluded that a couple of American adventure travelers might make it across this region and bring us back a better picture of what was happening there."

Walt was biting his tongue. And Tara knew that he was biting hard. He was succeeding, and she wondered if some of the Chinese philosophy he had been reading during the trip had been sinking in.

He turned to her and whispered. "Take notes." Then, as unobtrusively as possible, he slipped out of the conference room for the men's room where he splashed cold water on his face.

Before reentering the room, he waited for an interval that, hopefully, would get Bloodsworth off the podium. But he hadn't waited long enough. The general was still pontificating.

"This excursion by your companions was all part of a test to make an estimate of the facilities in the center of the desert and to see whether or not the settlement was primarily a military establishment. Plus, we wanted to do it in a manner that could not be interpreted as hostile. What better way that to send a romantically attached pair of young adventurers?" The general noticed that Walt had returned.

"These are the types of questions every intelligence community must consider. Your trip, Professor, gave us an opportunity to examine these questions and to form some preliminary conclusions. We consider your experiment a big success."

Walt was sitting back in his seat, and Tara was squeezing his hand.

"Once across—a trip they were able to make with the help of several Chinese youth in a private vehicle—they were able to make contact with Chinese youth in several cities on the northern route. These contacts enabled them to return easily to places they had already visited earlier and where they had some knowledge. Youth and inexperience could do easily what age and experience could not. The local Chinese youth have access to routes and techniques that able them to cross with relative freedom. The desert is, of course, always dangerous.

"While this is hardly counterintuitive to anyone who has ever lived near a major international border, or difficult terrain features such as deserts or mountain ranges, the specific details and techniques demand local knowledge that is difficult to obtain by non-natives.

"Our young team was able to establish connections with Chinese youth whose interests were compatible with their own. As a consequence, we now have several bits of data that were previously lacking. This courageous young man and woman were able to cross one of the world's most dangerous deserts. Without detection or challenge. Moreover—and this is most remarkable and valuable—they succeeded in carrying their cameras and they have returned with numerous photos of considerable interest.

"But now, I've been talking for a while and I see that some refreshments have been brought in. So why don't we take a break for fifteen minutes or so and you can talk to our young Marco Polos."

Don't get carried away,General.

Walt was confused by the Air Force response. It was difficult for him to understand what his group had accomplished. Even harder to understand the significance of the contribution from Warren and Terry. Penny and Keith had been taken aside by a couple of Air Force legal guys who apparently had a lot of questions about Keith's role with the gasoline at the "accident" site. Over two days the pair were interrogated and deposed. Apparently Keith was in the clear.

Walt failed to understand how the activities of his group could be of any possible use to the Air Force; but the evidence was undeniable. The people who had twisted his arm were satisfied with the results. It was a puzzle.

Feeling frustrated, he nudged Tara. "Why is everything so hard?" he whispered.

"I can help—when things get hard," she whispered back.

Little Ukrainian witch! She turns everything to sex, he thought.

"Coz that's how it really is." she whispered, reading his mind.

Damn girl! It's like she's inside my head. Already his exasperation with the missing teens had changed to relief that they had returned safely, and he was even—*just possibly*—taking some pride in the new knowledge that two of his "students" had been tagged by the Air Force for a special mission.

How could he be anything but happy that the pair had returned, safe and sound, and that some of their intelligence-gathering sponsors were pleased with some of the information they had brought back. It had ended well and that was what really mattered. Maybe they would all look back and it would seem like an adventure.

The fruit platter on the table included kiwis, star fruit and even pieces of pomegranate. *At the Pentagon?* He stood up and stretched his legs and noticed that his ribs weren't hurting.

During the lunch break Paul Chapman took Walt aside. "I could feel you getting pissed off when you learned what had happened. You did a good job of anger management."

"Learned over the past couple of weeks."

"You really did do a good job," Chapman said.

"If you say so..."

"I know that you probably left a lot of unfinished jobs back in Pennsylvania to take this assignment. I just wish there was some way I could help you out."

It just sounded like perfunctory politeness and no response seemed necessary. But after several seconds, something clicked in Walt's brain.

"Y'know, Paul, I do have a slight legal problem that has been dragging on for some time. I couldn't take care of it before we left Mercersburg."

"What kind of legal problem, Walt? We have some heavy duty guys in our legal department that can work miracles."

Suddenly, Walt thought, the trip from hell might not be so bad after all.

"And then, on page forty five, the *piece de resistance*, a whole puppy, roasted crisp, splayed out on a plate after having been attacked with a cleaver, so its skull is split in half, an eye and a nostril on each side, served with an elegant garnish of coriander, and flowers made from pink radish. Could any racist cartoon have created a better stereotype of the disgustingly omnivorous Chinese?"

Shark's Fin and Sichuan Pepper
(A Sweet-sour Memoir of Eating in China)
Fuschia Dunlop

CHAPTER 47
Back Home in the USA

Walt had wanted to meet with Paul Chapman privately before he confronted his Air Force employers. By any criteria he could imagine, his trip had been a failure. Depending on your point of view it was either disappointing with respect to results, or a total disaster in concept, planning and execution. At either end of the spectrum, Walt had anticipated a few rough days in D.C. Plus...he was tired. They had done a lot of walking. He had experienced the usual touches of diarrhea as had all of the grasshoppers. Most of all, he was angry at himself for allowing himself and his silky traveling companion to be bulldozed into an exercise that was a waste of time.

Well, maybe not exactly a waste of time. He had traveled the southern route of the Silk Road along the dreaded Taklamakan Desert, a trip he might never have chosen to make, without a nudge. It *had* been a bit tough. But no tougher than they had expected and factored into their plans. Now— under the right circumstances—with the right group of students, he might consider the southern route. *So maybe this trip wasn't a total waste.*

His advance meeting with Chapman hadn't been possible but they had talked at the AF debriefing and, later, Paul had offered to help him get things moving with Florence.

"Don't tell me any details," Paul had told him following the offer. "I'll get a couple of landsharks working on it. But if things don't work out with you and Tara, put in a good word for me." Paul's wife had died two years earlier of leukemia.

In a comfortable Georgetown hotel Walt catalogued the many weird co-incidences on this trip. A terrorist kidnapping attack? Tara's heat wave in the desert? How could he have expected to see Florence and her father in Beijing? How could anyone make up this stuff he had experienced?

How should he have responded on finding out that an Air Force offi-cer had been conducting a....well...better not even think about that one.

Thankfully, it didn't come up. And what about a teen age boy who had a meltdown on learning he had eaten dog meat?

Although Walt had known that the Chinese ate dogs, he had never given it much thought. He had seen hanging carcasses on occasion, they had never been in front of places where he was eating. So he hadn't given it a great deal of attention. In any event, dog meat was less popular in northern provinces than in the south. So when the kid who had nicknamed himself Red Baron had his hissy fit and freaked out, Walt had been unprepared. That may have trumped everything for weirdness.

Nothing in life, had prepared Amory Archambault, a.k.a. Red Baron, for the experience of eating a dish called hotpot, made from dog. That had been a traumatic experience for the red-haired youth. Much more unpleasant than merely being bound and hooded by would-be kidnappers or killers. Then, later, as they traveled east on the way home, the sight of skinned dog carcasses, hanging from meat hooks, finished the job. Red Baron had seen a familiar face. He had melted down a second time.

Thinking back over some of these details, Walt was truly happy to be back. He yearned to be back in his Pennsylvania farmhouse, alone with Tara.

The debriefing sessions stretched over two and a half days. The incident with the suspected terrorists from ETIM was discussed in detail, and a couple of officers from the Adjutant General's office took Keith and Penny away for one final time. The role of Colonel Huang Wang-Ming conversations with Penny was a matter of considerable concern. Major Liang was deposed separately. Although many of the relevant details of the Colonel's involvement came to light, no one suggested there might have been any emotional connection between the Colonel and the Major.

By noon of the third day, it was all over and the Air Force gave them a big lunch. Walt, Tara, Major Liang and all six grasshoppers had a final, private evening meal together in Georgetown. Naturally they chose a Chinese restaurant. Going in the front entrance, Amory called for attention. "Heads up, gang. I don't care how much maotai you give me, I ain't eating another freakin' chicken foot." That got a big hoot.

At their gathering, each person had to state where they expected to be going and what they would be doing. They had agreed to maintain contact in the future.

Major Liang was being assigned to a teaching job at the Air Force Academy.

Walt and Tara were headed back for JBU.

Lisa? Probably going to LSU in Baton Rouge.

Terry and Warren announced—big surprise!—they had plans to marry in coming weeks and after that, they might go back to school with their AF scholarships.

Keith was considering Air Force blue.

Kevin was contemplating aeronautical engineering. Possibly at Penn State.

Amory alone seemed vague about the future. "My folks want me to come home for a while. Maybe just hang out. I dunno. Still undecided, I guess."

On the way out of the restaurant, Walt had made a comment on Amory's lack of a firm plan to Tara and Warren had overheard. "Go figure," Warren said. "He's funny. For a while I thought he might be a freakin' fudgepacker."

Terry had laughed but Tara just looked puzzled.

Weeks later, Walt was surprised and disappointed to learn from Paul Chapman that Amory had been arrested on drug charges. Walt didn't press for details.

"In my prime, beneath my flag were ten thousand warriors.
My horsemen, in brocaded uniforms, burst across the river.
At night the northern soldiers held fast to their silver quivers.
At dawn our archers let fly their golden arrows.

Thinking back on those events,
I sigh over my present circumstances.
The spring wind will not darken my graying beard.
I've traded my ten-thousand word treatise on military strategy
For my neighbor's book on planting trees."

Xin Qiji (1140-1207)
In Chinese Civilization—A Sourcebook
Edited by Patricia Buckley Ebrey

CHAPTER 48
Parting Shots

"How do you like the new leg?" Paul asked. Walt nodded approval. This wasn't a topic that he wanted to discuss with Chapman, Once again the old intelligence pro had invited Walt and Tara out to dinner.

"Tell him about the rasta dude we saw in Xi'an," Tara said.

The three acquaintances had met at a small restaurant in Alexandria selected by the host.

Paul Chapman raised his eyebrows.

"You think I should?" Walt asked.

"Why not? You're usually right about things."

"You're not holding anything back from me?" Chapman said, curious now.

"It's probably nothing," Walt began. "But we saw a guy in Xi'an in circumstances that made us think about a trip with your herd of drug-sniffing cats. I guess we just got conditioned to be suspicious about unusual looking people and circumstances."

"So? And? Suspicious how?" Now Paul's ears were starting to perk up.

"We saw a big rasta-looking guy, about the size of a pro basketballer, in an eye catching suit, in the lobby of a big hotel in Xi'an. A Hyatt. Then, later the same day, we saw the same dude in a factory making terracotta statues, many of which were being shipped to the U.S."

"So? What's suspicious about that?"

"Nothing. Like I said, we may just have been paranoid. But this guy wasn't in the museum, or factory, or in the showroom. He was in the office. With two other black guys. And briefcases."

Paul Chapman chuckled. "Maybe you have gotten a bit paranoid from your association with us. After all, in this line of work, we're supposed to be paranoid. The worst flaw is inadequate paranoia."

"Tell him about the languages," Tara said.

"What about what languages?"

"'Oh yeah! It just seemed a bit odd. If he was a legitimate businessman it would be only natural for him to be fluent in Putonghua—Mandarin."

"The rasta spoke Chinese?"

"Mandarin."

"He could really speak it?"

"According to Penny. She said he was fluent."

"In Mandarin? That's the most common? Yes?"

"Also Cantonese. Yes, Mandarin is the national standard."

"He spoke Cantonese?"

"Well, I sure don't, Paul. So if you're looking for confirmation, you'll have to check with Penny."

"So listen Walt, this might be something worth looking into a little deeper. What made you suspect drugs?" Tara was grinning like a Cheshire cat.

"Those terracotta figures are crated and shipped to the U.S. In containers. Aboard Chinese container ships. And as we all know, the name of the game today is to find something clever to ship the stuff in."

"And?"

"And they're hollow. Dammit, Paul. Enough of the quizzing. You've got your heads up. It's a legitimate product that could be used to ship drugs and we saw a couple of stereotypes in the office. Not the showroom. It appeared to be some kind of business transaction. Not a purchase. Which is made in the showroom. Unless of course...."

"OK, I want you to describe these characters again. Especially the one you called the rasta-guy."

Three weeks later the DEA made a raid inside Oakland's vast container terminal and apprehended a large quantity of heroin concealed inside terracotta replicas of the world famed terra cotta army uncovered at Xi'an. Several containers were involved and they had been discharged from a COSCO container ship that was already westbound when Walt had spoken with Chapman. The haul was estimated to have a street value in excess of seventeen million dollars.

Paul called to let Walt and Tara in on the news. "I want you two to come back for..."

"Ixnay on the iptray," Walt said.

"To come back and get your just rewards. We have some discretionary funds that we want to share with you. Actually, we think we know the identity of the rasta man, and your description was a big help. This guy is big in Jamaica, but he grew up with a Chinese couple for parents and, besides teaching him Chinese, they led him down the paths of darkness. Anyway...."

"Look, Paul. I appreciate the information. But right now I'm teaching three classes and trying to get ready for my next trip. Plus, Tara and I are trying to figure our how everything went so sour on the grasshopper trip."

"Seriously, Walt. You guys are amazing. It has to be beginner's luck. But whatever it is, I'd like to recommend putting the two of you sleuths on retainer."

"Forget it, Paul. We've been though this before."

"Don't decide now. I'm not asking you to give me an answer right now. Talk to Tara. Call me back. You've got my home number. Call me at home. Better yet, get Tara to call me. I'd rather talk to her anyway. You're getting too grouchy."

Later that evening, Walt shared the news with Tara.

"I think we oughta go," she said. "You deserve the money. We can get this place painted when the weather is nice. Plus, you can take me to dinner at some place romantic in Georgetown. Let those guys pick up the tab for our orgy in a comfortable suite. Can you handle that? Take me out somewhere? Someplace Chinese. Or Mongolian. Someplace Asian. Have you ever heard of scorpion kebabs? They're supposed to be like oysters. I heard that from Penny."

He wiggled his finger for her to come.

"With you," he whispered, "anywhere is romantic. Even the Magic Wok. OK?"

"Um!"

"The golden crow sinks in the west; the jade rabbit rises in the east."

Proverbs and Common Sayings from the
Chinese
Arthur H. Smith
American Presbyterian Mission Press, 1914.

EPILOGUE

The Silk Road continues to loom large in the world's imagination. Every year someone comes up with a new slant to maintain interest; books, movies, CDs, music. Japanese composer Kitaro has taken the Silk Road as a theme for a major piece. World famous cellist YoYo Ma has written and performed using this route as a motif. The Chinese group *Twelve Girls Band* perform compositions inspired by the route.

Each year, new travel books describe the history and lore of the fabled cities of the remote regions once known as Chinese Turkistan.

Just as the American west is a magnet to visitors from Europe, the Chinese west draws tourists and travelers from around the world. But the world is changing. Nothing remains static and while travel becomes easier and accommodations improve, other factors—such as safety and security and barriers to access—change constantly. In years and months to come, Walt will go back with his students but things may be different.

The Chinese Olympics of 2008 focused world attention on Beijing and on China in general, and this increased focus was certain to attract terrorists seeking media attention. In addition, better access to China's west resulting from improvements in road, rail and air transportation will, increasingly, continue to open this, once isolated, heavily Islamic region of the world to culture and commerce from the west. And vice versa. This has, in the past, frequently resulted in friction—and violence.

Overarching all these factors is the steady rise of China as a world power, based on many elements; its rapid industrial expansion, vast quantities of human and natural resources and the productivity and intelligence of its population. The steady growth of China as a military power is a factor that America's leaders must consider.

The future of warfare is likely to be altered by the role of unmanned machines of war maneuvered from remote locations. The contents of this Pandora's box of grief is only too apparent to planners and military men; in all countries. We might well be thankful that they have not been used more extensively in the past. In the next big confrontation between major powers, look for robotic weapons to be employed on land and sea and in the air.

Walt's mismatched group of amateur intelligence gatherers added a tiny fragment to the accumulating evidence of Chinese capabilities. His experience barely touches on this field which, increasingly, is in the daily news. But why say more?

The grasshopper Walt and Tara had known as Keith surprised everyone by returning to JBU and pursuing a degree in political science. His experience in China may not have taught him a great deal about the Silk Road, but it gave him an active interest in Chinese girls and he made an solid effort to hook up with several of the Chinese students on JBU's campus.

Keith's interest in radio-controlled flying continues undiminished. During a brief visit to California he attempted to resume the relationship he had enjoyed with his model-building father. Unfortunately, dad has linked up with a new lady who is not particularly interested in sharing her new hubby—her third, with a demanding collegian. The youth managed to compete in a few air shows but he had to do all the work himself and he could tell he was now, in the presence of the new wife, merely excess baggage. Somehow, it didn't bother him as much as one might have expected.

Before completing his first full semester with lackluster grades pending, he peered into the future and was not particularly happy with what he could discern. The U. S. Air Force had three recruiters on campus and Keith stopped in for a chat sometime during the middle of exam week. He had been admonished about revealing his prior involvement with the USAF and it was easy for him to honor this obligation. Questioning by the recruiters quickly revealed his interests in radio-controlled flying and his experience as a competitor. Actually, Keith knew more about aerobatics and aerial maneuvers than any of the men—two sergeants and a captain—who interviewed him. The Air Force wanted him and they had a program that would be compatible with his interests and skills.

A couple of phone calls back home revealed that dad had no objections. In fact, dad had been planning to call to tell him that he and Darlene were planning a two week trip to Branson to get back to their country roots. Dad was going to suggest that Keith try to get a summer job at the college and they could get together at the end of summer; before the start of the new school year.

Five days later, Keith was wearing Air Force blue and learning how to march, salute and stand in line. Adaptable and intelligent, things went smoothly for him. Don't be offended if you're an AF vet, but AF training isn't exactly like the Marine Corps. Our grasshopper breezed through basic training without a scratch and was immediately cut out for further training. It doesn't always work out this way, of course, and sometimes guys who were bakers as civilians get sent to carpenter school. But the services are getting better and in Keith's case he went straight to special training as a controller for UAVs.

His first overseas assignment will probably be with a unit supporting the UN in Afghanistan where he will fly observation drones.

Terry and Warren are married now and she's expecting.

Lisa is still dancing on tabletops—in Baton Rouge where she attends LSU. Amory—a sad story—is in drug rehab.

Kevin is attending Penn State where he intends to pursue a master's degree in aeronautical engineering. He still flies in competitions when he has time.

Back in their old farmhouse outside of Mercersburg, Walt and Tara were having coffee in the kitchen. Tara was barefoot and she was wearing a shortie gown of silk, the color of tangerines. Walt was biting his tongue to keep from telling her how good she looked. She was making his chest ache, but it was a good ache.

"You're glad to be home, aren't you Professor?"

"Aren't you?"

"Sure. But I had a good time. Even with all the bullshit. I'm ready to do it again when you are. I know this wasn't your favorite trip.'

"It was fun being with you, though. But damn those kids...they made me worry."

" A lot of the blame should fall on those Air Force guys. That was dirty trick they played on us."

From the other room they could hear music from the CD player, and Walt had just turned it on without paying attention to what was playing. He had just wanted some music in the house. Elton John had just finished and Linda Ronstadt's *Lush Life* was next in the stack.

"I like Linda," Tara said. "But would you care if I put those Chinese girls on? The Twelve Girl Band? I'm feeling kinda Chinese still."

"Go ahead. Anyway, looking at you in that silk makes me think I'll have to give you a Chinese name."

Tara laughed from the other room. "You're speaking Chinese now?"

"Don't be mean, Silky Pants. I know a couple of words."

"Sure, sure. You know how to say *Shi-eh, Shi-eh*. Who am I gonna be? *Please? Or Thank you?*"

"You're such a brat. And you think you're so smart. Do you know the Mandarin words for America? Smarty pants?

"*Mei guo*. I think. Yeah. Penny taught me. But I can't remember what it means."

"*Guo* is kingdom. *Mei* means beautiful. America is Beautiful Kingdom to the Chinese. I'm naming you Mei Mei."

Tara swanked up out of her chair and did a brief dance around the kitchen floor.

"I like it," she said. "I like all the names you call me."

"Good."

"I never know who I'm gonna be."

"Nor do I."

"I still like it, though. Keeps me thinking. I want to live up to all your expectations."

She walked over and tousled his hair and he pulled her down to kiss her.

"The child that is loved has many names."

"Who said that?"

"Dunno. I think it's Polish. But I'm not really certain." *Maybe it's Ukrainian.*

Outside, it was starting to rain. Softly. "Let's go out on our patio in the rain," she said, taking his cup. "When this silk gets wet against me, I think you're gonna freak. I'm hoping." She hadn't yet started to show. *Maybe just a little?*

"Tara, Tara, I've been freaked by you for quite a while. What am I going to do with..."

"Maybe do me outside. In the rain." She was already getting wet—in the orange silk.

Actually—she was thinking—*this is more like persimmon. Oh, yeah*! Walt was looking at her the way she had hoped he would when she made that first trip with him.

"Oh, Mei Mei!..."

When they are married, she will stop biting him so hard. Well...maybe on occasion.

In thirty years from now, Walt will come to understand things in a way that he only dimly comprehends today. He will realize—and it will come a shock—that Tara loves him in the fashion that normal women love normal men, but that he loves Tara in the manner that normal men love magical women.

PREVIEW OF COMING ATTRACTIONS

"Today, smaller and lighter models are being introduced, new 'bugs,' as they are known, that can fly into village compounds and look around at human eye level. Dragon Eye is being phased out; only about 100 remain in action. 'There are unmanned aerial vehicles in development that fly like insects,' says Colbow. 'We'll see these systems doing more and more.'"

Under the Radar
(The five-pound RQ-14A takes high-tech reconnaissance to new heights)
Owen Edwards
Smithsonian, March 2009